PRAISE FOR
THEN SHE VANISHED

"T. Jefferson Parker's fourth Roland Ford mystery lodges the detective firmly in the crosshairs once again."
—*BookPage* (starred review)

"Parker's incisive character portraits and smooth, confident prose make his latest thriller taut and engaging."
—*Kirkus Reviews*

"The atmospheric SoCal setting provides a brilliant contrast to what Ford calls a 'republic of violence,' rife with grievances and a gun in every hand to address them."
—*Booklist*

PRAISE FOR
THE LAST GOOD GUY

"[An] adrenaline-charged adventure."
—*New York Times Book Review*

"A twisty cautionary tale that will leave readers pondering the damage done in the name of misguided religious fervor and patriotism and yearning for more good guys like Ford to bring justice to our world." —*Los Angeles Times*

"Parker tells the tale in tight, vivid prose that at times borders on the lyrical." —Associated Press

"All the good gals and guys in Mr. Parker's winning story have the reader rooting for them."
—*The Wall Street Journal*

"T. Jefferson Parker is one of our great novelists as well as thriller writers, the reasons for which are all keenly on display in *The Last Good Guy* . . . [The novel] may share ground tonally with the works of the genre's masters, but Parker has wondrously carved out his own territory as well in crafting an extraordinary, pitch-perfect tale that just might be the best crime thriller of 2019."

—*Providence Journal*

"[T. Jefferson Parker] does a masterly job of ratcheting up the tension, and the often lyrical prose is a pleasure to read. This entry could well earn three-time Edgar Award winner Parker a fourth Edgar."

—*Publishers Weekly* (starred review)

"In this powerful thriller, Parker leaves us aching for the damaged souls left behind by false prophets and hate-mongers, and hoping that there still really are some good guys."   —*Booklist* (starred review)

"In the third case for his franchise hero, the prolific Parker summons the memory of retro hard-boiled crime yarns."

—*Kirkus Reviews*

"As is typical for Parker's novels, the stage upon which the story unfolds is a microcosm of today's America, with racism and intolerance, the escalating struggle between conservatives and liberals, and the pervasive intelligence of megachurches and the politics espoused therein. As is also typical of Parker's novels, it is a mighty fine read."

—*BookPage*

"T. Jefferson Parker draws the classical hard-boiled detective story out of its mythic past and into our contemporary landscape, much like the last great exemplar of the form, Ross Macdonald—and like Macdonald, Parker goes deeper with each book. The payoff for his readers is serious thrills."   —Jonathan Lethem

"*The Last Good Guy*, the third outing for smart, tough, insightful, sympathetic Private Investigator Roland Ford, is nothing short of brilliant as it morphs from a simple missing persons case into a complex and nuanced exploration of the dark side of American culture."

—John Lescroart

"T. Jefferson Parker's *The Last Good Guy* is a riveting crime drama with an engaging hero up against insurmountable odds as he tries to track down a woman's missing sister. With intelligence, action, and humor, the pages turn themselves to a thrilling climax." —Mark Greaney

"Fabulously atmospheric. Parker writes with a cinematic eye and a thrillingly dark heart." —Peter James

PRAISE FOR
SWIFT VENGEANCE

"Non-stop action. [T. Jefferson Parker's] new series succeeds not only in entertaining but also in challenging readers to ponder the circle of vengeance unleashed by the Iraq War and America's seemingly endless war on terror."

—Associated Press

"Roland Ford is a compelling hero: financially comfortable but not emotionally complacent, empathetic and equipped with the training and inclination to vanquish wickedness." —*Wall Street Journal*

"Parker remains one of our finest novelists as well as mystery-thriller writers. He has fashioned a powerful tale rich in both character and story." —*Providence Journal*

"Parker keeps quite a few balls in the air, skillfully steering us toward and away from a batch of possible killers while maintaining a twisty, relentless pace. As a result, his "Vengeance" is swift, indeed." —Minneapolis *Star Tribune*

"Terrific . . . The hunt for Caliphornia is suspenseful, the backstory behind the threats is disturbingly horrible, and the denouement is scary and satisfying. Parker deepens the narrative with musings on Ford's life, the horrors and ambiguities of the war on terror, and the fine line between justice and vengeance."

—*Publishers Weekly* (starred review)

"Three-time Edgar Award winner Parker delivers another superb, fast-paced noir thriller. Readers of C. J. Box will enjoy the strong character development, while T. C. Boyle fans will appreciate the story line and the atmospheric California setting." —*Library Journal* (starred review)

"[Roland Ford] is a kick-ass warrior with a heart of gold. . . . Parker's writing is sharp, and each character in the extended cast is unique and finely nuanced despite the super-fast-paced narrative . . . This is quintessential California noir." —*Booklist*

"Prolific Parker's impressive prose and skill in sketching concise character portraits makes his complex follow-up to *The Room of White Fire* an all-too-believable page-turner."
—*Kirkus Reviews*

PRAISE FOR
THE ROOM OF WHITE FIRE

"A fast-paced, beautifully written thriller."
—*The Washington Post*

"Ford's assignment, as he redefines it, becomes much more complex than tracking down a missing person. His noble goal is not only to find Hickman but to heal him."
—*Wall Street Journal*

THEN SHE VANISHED

T. JEFFERSON PARKER

G. P. PUTNAM'S SONS
NEW YORK

PUTNAM
— EST. 1838 —
G. P. PUTNAM'S SONS
Publishers Since 1838
An imprint of Penguin Random House LLC
penguinrandomhouse.com

The Library of Congress has catalogued the
G. P. Putnam's Sons hardcover edition as follows:

Names: Parker, T. Jefferson, author.
Title: Then she vanished / T. Jefferson Parker.
Description: New York : G. P. Putnam's Sons, [2020]
Identifiers: LCCN 2020013625 (print) | LCCN 2020013626 (ebook) |
ISBN 9780525537670 (hardcover) | ISBN 9780525537694 (ebook)
Subjects: GSAFD: Suspense fiction. | Mystery fiction.
Classification: LCC PS3566.A6863 T48 2020 (print) |
LCC PS3566.A6863 (ebook) | DDC 813/.54—dc23
LC record available at https://lccn.loc.gov/2020013625
LC ebook record available at https://lccn.loc.gov/2020013626

First G. P. Putnam's Sons hardcover edition / August 2020
First G. P. Putnam's Sons premium edition / August 2021
G. P. Putnam's Sons premium edition ISBN: 9780525537687

Printed in the United States of America
1   3   5   7   9   10   8   6   4   2

Book design by Kristin del Rosario
Interior art: Concrete wall by Guenter Albers / Shutterstock.com

THEN SHE VANISHED

ONE

Lately I've been turning over some advice my mother gave me when I was eleven. Roland, she said, you need three things to be happy: something to do, something to look forward to, and someone to love. My mother isn't a sentimental person and I believed her. Still do. Once, I had all three of those things going in my life. Then, my someone to love was swallowed by the dark Pacific, taking with her my something to look forward to, and most of my something to do. This was some years ago. We don't heal stronger in the broken places, but we do heal. I'm a private investigator. You need certain qualities for my kind of work, such as being mostly sober, alert, and mission driven. Durability helps, too: I was once a marine and once a deputy and am forever a Ford. I can take care of myself and I am not above revenge.

Most private investigators you've heard of were born of simpler times, when the world was noir and the streets were mean. But as you know, more than the streets are mean. Schools and churches, synagogues and mosques, casinos and nightclubs. Our republic of violence. A gun in every hand and a million camps of grievance. Fresh menace in the air. We PIs have changed with the times. We're a tougher crew these days because we have to be.

Even without our afternoon appointment, I would have recognized Dalton Strait when he came through the door of my office.

We had both fought in the First Battle of Fallujah, Iraq. April 2004. Some of the darkest days of that long and wasteful war. But we never met over there. Different battalions. I knew of his decoration for valor in combat, and later learned that he'd lost half his leg to an IED, but that also wasn't why I knew his face.

Now Dalton Strait (R), 82nd California State Assembly District, limped across the wooden floor with his wry, TV-tested smile, his wing-tipped prosthetic foot clomping heavily on the worn hardwood floor. A wrinkled navy suit and a worn brown briefcase in one hand. He looked like a salesman on his last call of the day.

We shook hands and he sat across the desk from me, setting the briefcase on the floor. Full face, blue eyes, thick brown hair. The suit looked expensive and fit well. White shirt, a red-striped tie.

"Nice office," he said.

"Not really."

"No. But we have a lot in common."

I told him I'd followed his political career.

"I should have hit you up for campaign money. November's just six months away."

"I hear it's going to be a close election," I said.

Strait shrugged, gave me a blue-eyed inspection. "Then I'll put you down for a grand. That'll get out three thousand more mailers. They're nice, three-color and glossy. You're right, the election is going to be close. My opponent is cuter than I am, and she's outspending me four to one. I love representing the North San Diego County. I love this little Fallbrook."

He nodded at the window toward Fallbrook's Main Avenue, a quaint street in a small town in the most populous state in the union. Part of his 82nd district. Fallbrook is old-fashioned, but evolving with the times. Norman Rockwell with occasional shadows. Rich and poor live together here. We try to be race tolerant. Conservative territory sprinkled with liberal outposts. And plenty of characters. Originally founded dry, there are still many more churches than bars. Classic cars sail the winding roads, grand as yachts. We grow the best avocados on earth, and bill Fallbrook as the avocado capital of the world. Don't you forget it.

In fact I'd known of the Strait family since the year I moved here after Fallujah and became a deputy. The Straits were long and well-known to the sheriffs—a plainly visible line of scofflaws and small-bore criminals fired into California by the Depression and the Dust Bowl. They'd settled in an East County of few people, sparse law enforcement, rugged mountains, rock-heaped hills, and low desert. Pulled themselves up from poverty, made their runs at the American Dream. Their present-day patriarch was Dalton's grandfather Virgil, a retired personal injury lawyer turned judge who'd been convicted decades ago for taking bribes. Dalton's father, who'd founded the local Better Burger fast-food chain, had been wounded during an armed robbery of his flagship store in El Centro twenty-one years ago, and remained bedridden ever since. Last I'd heard, Dalton's younger sister, Tola, was running a string of almost legal marijuana dispensaries in and around San Diego, while his older brother, Kirby, had just finished prison time on fraud and tax evasion charges.

Dalton turned from the window to me, used his hands to lift and cross his plastic leg over the flesh-and-bone one. A silent flinch.

"I was brought up to believe that a good PI always has a bottle in his office somewhere," he said.

"You were brought up well."

Bottle in the drawer, old-fashioned glasses by the coffeemaker. "RF" etched into them, set of four, a birthday gift to a happy husband from a happy wife. Once upon a time. Bourbon neat with a small splash of water. We tapped glasses and I sat back down.

We talked about the Padres, the drought, the fires, and—briefly—the battle we'd shared. U.S. forces in Fallujah numbered just over two thousand but we managed to come up with a few names in common. Dalton had seen the burned Blackwater employees hanging from the bridge over the Euphrates and the anger was still in his voice. I had arrived a week later, and done a lot of door-to-door clearing of homes, looking for insurgents hiding among the friendlies. A buddy had bled out on me in a Fallujah doorway. His name was Ernie Avalos. Dalton had spent his tour on Humvee patrols, which, I remembered, was how he'd earned his Silver Star. And later the Purple Heart, when the IED took his leg.

Then came the long moment of silence between combat vets, as our memories tailed back into their holes.

"The reason I'm here," he said, "is that Natalie is missing. My wife. As of Tuesday, two days ago. The only things I know for sure are gone are her and her car. Maybe some clothes and personal things. She has lots of stuff so it's hard to tell. She hasn't come home or returned my calls. No action on her credit cards. No one I've contacted has seen or heard from her."

The last time Dalton had talked to Natalie was Monday night, in bed. He had flown to Sacramento early Tuesday morning; Natalie was due at work at eleven a.m. but didn't show and didn't call in. She sold BMWs at the Escondido dealership.

Dalton had already talked to the San Diego County Sheriff's Department, whose jurisdiction covered the Straits' semi-rural residence southeast of here. Due to his status, Dalton had been immediately introduced to the Special Enforcement Detail. He had not filed a report yet because he didn't want negative publicity and didn't believe that the sheriffs would aggressively investigate so soon after her disappearance. The Special Enforcement Detail said that if Natalie had not been heard from in the next forty-eight hours, she would become a high-profile priority. They gave Dalton the usual assurances that missing spouses almost always return within a week. This had pissed Dalton off but he'd held his temper.

"So I came to you," he said. "I want you to find her and bring her home. Now. Not two days from now. Not a week from now. She could be in danger. Abducted. Her car could be in a ditch. I know you're good at this. You've been mixed up in some heavy stuff lately and you always come out on top."

I'd come out of some heavy stuff but I wasn't sure about on top. My ribs and legs still hurt, though less.

"Has she done anything like this before?"

Dalton sipped the bourbon and looked away from me, out toward Main Avenue again.

"Fourteen months ago she took off in her car and went incommunicado for three days," he said. "Called me from Las Vegas, disoriented and afraid and something north of forty thousand dollars down. She'd been gambling and shopping. I hired a Vegas PI to keep her safe until I could get there. A well-known and very expensive La Jolla shrink examined her. Said she'd suffered a psychotic break. After tests and some long interviews with each of us, he pronounced Natalie bipolar. Something had likely triggered the manic phase flameout in Vegas. Family helped us out with the money, but that diagnosis changed our lives. Nothing has been the same. Her condition hovers over everything we do. Hovers over the reelection campaign. We've kept it quiet. Natalie is great about taking her meds. Flattens her out a little, but no dramatic relapses, until now. If, in fact, this is another break."

Dalton tilted his empty glass and set it on the desk. I poured us each another drink. Liquid gold, settling in the late-afternoon sunlight through the blinds.

"Did you see something like that coming?" I asked.

"Nats has always been a real up-and-down person. She'd get down, spend money on things we didn't really need. On the up weeks, pure positive energy and no stopping her. Gradually more intense, over the years. That Las Vegas episode was like an explosion, though."

He looked down at his prosthetic with dislike, then hiked the cuff, unwound a couple of feet of medical tape, popped two latches simultaneously, and wrenched off his calf.

Tossed it to me, shoe and all, high, like a free throw. I caught it, held it in both hands, arched it back to him. Dalton caught it with one hand. Slammed it down on the desk, raised his glass. We toasted silently. Then he reached into his pant leg and kneaded the stump hidden by his trousers.

"Has she talked of suicide?" I asked.

Dalton pursed his lips and shook his head. "Never."

"Does she believe someone is out to get her?"

"Yeah, *me*. Very critical of me. She also claims there's a stalker she almost sold a car to. There's no evidence that he's actually stalked her. Possibly, he drove by the house once. And she talked about a volunteer on my campaign committee who looks at her the wrong way. Somebody Weld, I think."

"Do you put any credence in them? As threats?"

"Little."

Dalton rolled the empty cuff, guided the prosthetic calf in and latched it back into place. I felt some admiration for him. And a sliver of gratitude that it hadn't happened to me. And of course the weighty guilt over having such a thought.

I had seen Natalie Strait on local TV news, and featured in BMW of Escondido ads. A head-turning woman, bright personality, and something of the diva about her. Abundant black hair led by a widow's peak. Dimples. If I remembered right, she and Dalton had been together since high school. They married young, had children. Then military service for Dalton, right after 9/11. Followed by college, family life. And a hero's election to the state assembly in his hometown district, the 82nd, in spite of an extended family well-known to law enforcement in rural San Diego County.

"I'm not after the marine-brothers military discount," said Dalton. "I expect to pay you full retail, although it won't be until late next week. An assemblyman's hundred grand and change, and a part-time car salesperson come up a little short sometimes here in California. We've got two boys in college. And I'll tell you, this is a bitch of a campaign. I've spent more of my own money this time around than any time before. This is my fourth run. The Dems are funding my opponent with a vengeance. She's Muslim and has terrorist links in her family past, and I intend to go public with that very soon. The Dems are trying to run the last Republicans out of the state assembly, me being one of them." He took a breath. "More to the point, I miss Natalie and I'm worried. Very worried."

I considered Dalton Strait's open, almost boyish face, his wintry eyes, his heft and implied strength. I considered my current active caseload: a young wife had hired me to determine whether her husband was having an affair, and I already had the unhappy news ready to give her. That, and a grouchy old local had hired me to talk to one of his neighbors about her barking dog. He didn't want to call the police because he hated the police. Didn't want to talk to the woman because he hated confrontation. So, a slow week in May. The hillsides in bloom and the birds at play and Roland Ford waiting for something more meaningful to do than sadden a young woman and fight a curmudgeon's battles.

"What do you know about the bomb at city hall?" asked Dalton.

"Only what I've read," I lied.

The pipe bomb had arrived Monday, via United States mail in a flat-rate box, addressed to San Diego's mayor. It had exploded in the mail room, injuring a young city hall intern, not seriously. There was swift reporting that the bomb had been more sophisticated than the crude pipe bombs sent to notable Democrats a couple of years back. And that our mayor had been targeted for different reasons. He is a Republican.

Yesterday, Wednesday, a letter signed "The Chaos Committee" had been published online and by *The San Diego Union-Tribune,* claiming responsibility for the bomb, and promising more bombs for "government thugs and conspirators throughout our once great state."

An FBI friend of mine had told me just a few hours ago that the city hall bomb was well made but not intended to be deadly. A warning, maybe. He—Special Agent Mike Lark of San Diego FBI—had also told me that the flat-rate package had been mailed at the Fallbrook post office and he would have some post office security video of the mailer for me to look at. Lark's theory was that Fallbrook is a small town and I've lived here several years and must know a good many of the people in it. Our population is roughly 37,000. So my theory was that the FBI was desperate for a lead.

"Do your old sheriff friends have anything noteworthy?" asked Dalton. "About the bomb?"

"Not that I know."

"You probably don't have any sheriff friends."

"No," I said. Not after I officially questioned my partner in the fatal shooting of an unarmed man who shouldn't have been shot. I betrayed the blue religion. I will be forgiven gradually if at all, but more likely never. I understood this when it was happening and would do nothing different if that shooting happened tomorrow.

Dalton considered me again. The assemblyman was renowned for his battlefield valor and the oorah marine spirit he brought into public office. He was a tireless supporter of veterans' programs for California and a stronger defense for the nation. He was the dictionary definition of *team player*. Me, on the other hand, I'm wired for noncompliance. Which lowers me in the eyes of some and raises me in the eyes of others. In the eyes of some, it suits me to stand alone, resistant to bureaucracy and conformity. But in Dalton's eyes I suspected I stood lower. In my own eyes I mostly break even.

"I'll find Natalie."

"Semper Fi, man."

"Sometimes fi, anyway."

"Maybe it's just a marine saying to you," said Strait. "But it's my faith. I believe we're brothers. I believe we were heroes for what we did and lost over there. We can be heroes again."

I thought about that for a short moment. "I'll settle for finding your wife and a check that doesn't bounce."

"You're not much fun but I'm told you're good."

"I'm plenty fun and all good."

I got what I needed from Dalton Strait—names and numbers for Natalie and their sons, extended family, friends, doctors, and coworkers; credit card numbers, PINs, passwords, and security codes; vehicle information; pictures to my phone; favorite local hangouts; favorite Las Vegas hotels and restaurants; the names of the maybe stalker and the man on the reelection committee who looked at her wrong, etc. I got a promise of future payment.

"Who was the last person you know to see her?" I asked.

"Her younger sister, Ash. They're close. She raises gundogs."

He downed the bourbon, reached into his briefcase, and came up with a thick handful of campaign posters.

Handed me one—a close-up of his youthful-looking face, both innocent and worried at the same time. Bold red and blue text:

Dalton Strait

Assembly

Straight for California

He stood, and set the rest on my desk.

"Self-adhesive," he said. "Easily removable, so don't be shy with them. And take them down after I've won. I'll look bad if you don't."

His parting handshake was powerful so I powered back. Men. I listened to him going down the old wooden stairs, good leg softer and bad leg louder.

TWO

The road to Ash Galland's Wirehaired Pointing Griffons wound through Pauma Valley then into the Palomar Mountains northeast of San Diego. Poppies and lupine swayed on the road shoulders in the late-morning sun while hawks wheeled high in the blue.

She came from a ramshackle ranch house, down the porch steps, the dogs parting around her. A pink ball cap over dark hair, a red flannel shirt, jeans and black rubber boots with bright pink soles.

"I hope you don't mind dogs," she said.

The dogs wiggled and wagged and sniffed but didn't touch me with anything but their snouts. Wirehaired Pointing Griffons have bushy mustaches, and soulful brows over deep-set, intelligent eyes.

She nodded toward a barn and stayed a half step ahead of me. We crossed a barnyard with a big central oak tree and grass still green from April showers, the dogs a squadron of energy around us.

Inside were facing rows of chain-link kennels, clean and neat and identically furnished: water buckets in like corners, food bowls elevated on stout terra-cotta flower-pots, sleeping pads mid-floor, and wooden doghouses parked along the back ends.

The gate on the first kennel squeaked open and two of the Griffons entered with an air of disappointment. The gate squeaked shut. Ash Galland dropped the fork latch with a clank and looked at me.

"I met Natalie for breakfast at Deke's Tuesday morning in Valley Center," she said. "It's a halfway point for us. We said goodbye around nine. No one I know, or Dalton knows, has seen her since."

"How was she?"

She nodded but didn't answer. Opened the next gate and two more Griffs slumped in, one looking back at her. *Squeak, clank.*

"Natalie rarely burdens others with what she's thinking or feeling or going through. Sometimes I get her energy. Her smile. I get her attention, full and empathetic and helpful. Other times, her exhaustion and her faraway eyes. But either high or low, I don't get much of *her.*"

"Was she anxious or worried? Expecting something bad to happen?"

Into the third kennel went two more Griffons, their free ranks now cut in half. A half-dozen Jack Russell terriers nipped and bounced around us like popcorn.

"No. She was happy and animated."

"Leaning toward the manic," I said.

"You do understand. Like a flower toward the sun. That's the heart of this problem. Two poles. All her brightness and energy can . . . spill out. Overflow. Overwhelm.

"She was dressed for work in a trim black suit, a light blue satin blouse the color of her eyes. Black heels. Freshwater pearl earrings and choker. She was beautiful."

I pictured Natalie Strait from the TV commercials. She and a crew of other salespeople surrounding the latest swanky BMW. I own a Ford F-150 king cab, a battered 1955 Chevrolet Task Force pickup, and a red Porsche Boxster once loved and driven hard by my wife, Justine. I keep the Boxster—clean and covered and ready to run—in a barn not unlike Ash Galland's.

"Did she have any errands or appointments before or after work?"

"Lunch with Virgil Strait. Dalton's granddad."

I let that sink in. The former Honorable Virgil Strait, taker of bribes. Wondered why Dalton hadn't known of this lunch, or hadn't bothered to tell me about it.

Ash had an expectant expression but said nothing.

"What did she have for breakfast?" I asked.

"*Why?*" An exasperated look. Blue eyes, too, like Natalie's. And her big sister's thick dark hair, ponytailing from the ball cap.

"Because sometimes one thing leads to another you don't expect," I said.

"Fruit, dry toast, and cottage cheese," she said sharply.

She threw open another kennel gate, then another. The dutiful Griffs went in. I'd never seen a pack of such well-behaved dogs. The terriers slowed and studied her, keen to her change of tone.

She sighed and looked down at them. "Sorry. I've never been able to put on the happy face like Natalie does. I'm worried about her. I know she's capable of going off her rails. That men are drawn to her and not all men are trained well. Or even close. She had coffee, too. Black."

I accepted her apology and asked about the stalker who almost bought a car from her.

Ash said the stalker had driven by her sister's house several times. Dalton had offered to set up on the front porch and shoot him. Shortly after that, Natalie filed a complaint with the sheriffs, who interviewed him and the drive-bys stopped.

I asked about the Strait reelection campaign volunteer with the roving eyes.

"Brock Weld. She's mentioned him more than once. Natalie said he's polite but . . . bold."

"Does Natalie alarm easily?"

"No. And she's a good judge of character."

I made a note to have my associate, Burt, get Brock Weld's whereabouts the morning that Natalie vanished.

She kenneled the last of the Griffons then started down the opposite row and herded a Jack Russell into each. They feigned defiance and confusion, then obeyed the hardening edge in Ash Galland's voice.

Back at the first kennel she cracked the gate and let a slender young Griffon wriggle through.

"This is Wendy. Still shy with strangers."

Ash grabbed a walking stick propped near the door, then led us back into the May sunshine on the barnyard.

While on the topic of animals, it seemed like the time to mention the eight-hundred-pound gorilla always looming in the background when a wife goes missing.

"How is Natalie's relationship with Dalton?"

"She only talks about him in glowing terms. Pure Natalie."

"Do you suspect anything un-glowing between them?"

"Well."

We left the barnyard and the shade of the big oak tree and started down a good dirt road. Ash said, "Hunt 'em up," and Wendy quartered out ahead of us, nose to the ground. She looked back to Ash often, her body trembling with energy. I'd noted on the Ash Galland's Wire-haired Pointing Griffons web page that a new litter would be ready for homes in June. All but one male had been sold at $2,000 a copy.

"It's very stressful being married to a public figure," said Ash. "Natalie is Dalton's support system. She's also a mother of two boys and she works hard part-time, selling the cars. There are good money months and not-so-good. She spends lots of time and energy on Dalton's campaigns. A California assembly term is only two years, so they're constantly campaigning. This next election will be for Dalton's fourth. He can have six. Then, on to the state senate, maybe."

"Do they owe money?"

"I wouldn't be surprised. Of course, no complaints

from Natalie. But they have nice things and live in a pricey part of California. One son in a high-dollar college and another at state. The Straits don't take home mountains of money."

"Did they pay off Natalie's gambling and shopping jag in Las Vegas?"

"The families stepped up. Mom and Dad. Me. The extended Straits, of course. The dire Straits. In all their tainted glory."

Ash gave me a half smile, acknowledging the reputation of her East County in-laws. In this moment her face seemed like a psychological negative of her sister's—the same shape and shades of hair and skin and eyes, but opposite spirits. TV Natalie was big-smiling and exuberant. Kennel Ash was tight faced and controlled.

"These may help you understand Natalie better," she said, un-pocketing her phone. The picture gallery was mostly selfies of Natalie and Ash, with an assortment of others thrown in. Natalie and Ash and Dalton, of course; Natalie and Ash with Natalie's BMW cohorts; Natalie and Ash with a skinny old man I recognized as Virgil Strait; Natalie and Ash and a pale, red-haired hombre with a killer's grin.

"That's Dalton's older brother, Kirby," she said.

I flipped through the rest of the images in that folder and handed back the phone, catching Ash in a focused study of my face.

"Would you send me those?"

"Of course. You're not the first one to come snooping

around my sister lately. There were state people, and the FBI."

Interesting.

We headed back up the road, Wendy at perfect heel. Ash told me that these aforementioned "leeches" were interested in Dalton and Natalie's personal finances. Which were complicated. Since part of Natalie's responsibility as head of the Strait Reelection Committee was tracking donations and thanking the voters for their generous support, she'd been deluged with questions from both state and feds.

"I'm not sure if what I just said helps you," said Ash. "But maybe it will lead to something you don't expect."

I heard a rustling in the grass and saw Wendy lock on point. Body down, left front paw up, tail out. Movement in the wild buckwheat ahead of her.

"Hold," said Ash, stretching out the "o."

Wendy held beautifully and shivered. The quail *chick-chi*cked like they do before bursting into the air.

"She's too young to hold that point very long," said Ash.

As if in agreement, Wendy bolted toward the birds. Two quail whirred into the air ahead of her, curving up and away, twin blurs, Wendy humping after them.

"We will walk you out."

Wendy maintained a perfect heel as we went back up the dirt road toward the barn.

When we got to my truck, she said, "I haven't slept well since Natalie disappeared. My nerves are shot and my patience is gone. The dogs all know something is wrong. So, sorry for my brevity."

I told her there was no need to apologize at a time like this, gave her a card and asked her to call if she had any contact with Natalie, or remembered anything that might help me locate her.

Headed back down the hill. I stopped in Valley Center and found a coffee shop. Incidentally, Valley Center is where the largest grizzly bear ever killed was killed. Two thousand something pounds. It was called Bear Valley then. A much smaller bear is on display in a small museum here. I've always been fascinated by the top of the food chain.

The coffee shop's windows were hung with campaign signs for Dalton Strait's opponent in November, whom Dalton was threatening to link to terrorists in the Middle East.

VOTE!

AMMNA SAFAR

This State Is Your State

82nd Assembly

THREE

Special Agent Mike Lark was in his late twenties, with a boyish face, a budget haircut, and raptor's eyes. We sat in a windowless conference room in the new FBI building off Vista Sorrento Parkway in San Diego. It was afternoon but you wouldn't know it.

Lark swiveled the monitor so we both could see it, then anxiously spun the cursor about the screen. Mike, all energy. We had a history, brief but intense.

"Not the best quality pictures," he said. "What is it about post office security cameras?"

"The cameras in the Fallbrook post office are old-school," I said. "I watch them as I stand in line."

Lark moved the cursor some more. "Bomb makers are rodent secretive," he said. "Kaczynski up in Montana. McVeigh at the lakeside compound. Or our very own terrorist Caliphornia in his Chula Vista storage unit. The city hall bomb came from the Fallbrook post office, Roland. We have two almost decent images of who dropped it off. So maybe you can help us. Maybe she's a neighbor of yours."

"She."

"Why not a she?"

"Well, the post office has the return addresses in their computer," I said. "So just knock on her door."

"Her alleged return address is a Fallbrook gift shop whose owner has never seen this woman."

The cursor finally stopped and Mike clicked the mouse.

In the macro shot, a young dark-haired woman wearing skinny jeans and a dark sweater. Thick shoulder-length hair parted in the middle, partially obscuring her face. Jackie O sunglasses. In the closer-up shot her expression looked pinched, as if she was in a hurry. Impatient. Again, the quality was poor. She could have been almost any dark-haired woman—Latina, Greek, Italian, Armenian, Semitic, or Arabian.

"I've never seen her," I said.

"Take your time."

"I don't need time."

"There were showers in Fallbrook that morning," said Lark.

"But she's got sunglasses," I noted.

Mike nodded. "Sure, spring showers—they come and go fast. Okay. Maybe she needed sunglasses. But if she knew what was in that box, maybe she was wearing them for curious people like us." I thought. "Maybe the mailer was running an errand for a friend or employer. Part of a job, or a favor. Had no idea what it contained."

"Of course. It happens."

Mike cued up three more pictures, none more helpful than the first. The longer I looked at the screen the more I was sure I hadn't seen the woman.

"What can you tell me about that bomb?" I asked.

"Smart, thrifty, and reliable. Commercial gunpowder, ground match-heads for ignition, and a rubber-band striker that went off when the package was opened. Common materials, hard to trace. This is interesting: there wasn't enough charge in it to do more than blow off a finger, maybe take an eye. Not even enough to destroy the return address on the box. The pipe was hardware store PVC, not metal—less pressure to build the blast. So we figure that's what they wanted to do. Frighten and maim, not kill. The restraint worries me as much as the anger behind it."

"They? Do you believe this committee stuff? Bombers like working alone."

"They almost always have help," said Lark. "I sense organization here, Roland. Planning. This isn't some moron living out of a van. This committee's the real deal—one guy or a hundred. The surest way to miss the possible is to close your mind to it."

I liked Lark's young, federal, not-afraid-to-state-the-obvious kind of thinking. He handed me an enlarged copy of the Chaos Committee letter that was published by the *Union-Tribune*. It was marked up with notes and questions in his condensed, fast-forward handwriting.

Dear California,

The bomb sent to the mayor of San Diego is the first that will be mailed to government thugs and conspirators throughout our once great state. We deem these acts to be necessary to stop the spiral of decay that is rotting our republic from the inside out, namely our broken non-government; a fraudulent one-party system, maintained by the rich on the backs of the poor; narcissism and moral decay through technology. We are post-political. We, the Committee, believe that only the People can overthrow this system, and that only chaos, fear, and terror can drive the power brokers, the moneylenders, and the godless technocrats from our collective temple. We will provide the protection of anarchy, fear, and terror. The People will rise and take back the levers of power and California will once again be of and by and for the people. People at one with the great land that we have inherited. Rise when you are ready.

The Chaos Committee

I'd read it before but I read it again. A little grandiose for a pipe bomber, but not unintelligent. Angry but reasoned. Nothing misspelled. A call for the end of the two-party system, the end of politics, the necessity of anarchy as a prelude to a new America. Familiar. The old Unabomber, eco-terror stuff. Death to technology. Back to nature and farming. Luddites with explosives.

"What about a signature in the device?" I asked. "Some kind of taunt or gamesmanship?"

"Good," said Lark. "And you can't know this but one of the end caps on the bomb wasn't plastic at all. It was threaded metal, like they used for irrigation before PVC. 'CC' was carved into the top."

Still on the screen: the indeterminate young woman apparently impatient to mail off a bomb to San Diego city hall.

I looked up to find Mike's sharp eyes on me.

"So, Natalie Strait has been missing since Tuesday," he said. "And it's not the first time she's gone missing like this."

"No. She's had some problems."

"You could say *they* have had some problems," said Lark. "You fought with him in Fallujah, didn't you?"

"Concurrently. Not beside. Why?"

Mike gloved the mouse again, did his annoying ritual with the cursor. Closed in and clicked: two images side by side. One well-focused picture of Dalton Strait going through the Main Avenue door to my office, and another of him coming back out.

"We're surveilling the politician, not you."

"Looking for what?"

"Irregularities," said Lark. "Sorry, but that's all I can say right now. I suspect he hired you to locate his wife."

I shrugged, countering his evasion with one of my own. The door opened and an older man in a gray suit leaned in. An outdoorsman's craggy face and a crown of hair that matched the suit. He looked surprised.

"Oh. Sorry," he said. "Ten minutes, Mike."

Lark nodded irritably and the man vanished with a soft close of the door.

"Anyway, we're taking a look at the Strait family businesses in East County," he said. "The formerly Honorable Virgil Strait's solar farms, crook Kirby's possible cartel connections, Tola Strait's stake in Indian reservation pot palaces. A wide net."

"What's Dalton got to do with any of that?"

"Damned little, he better hope." Lark smiled. "How is he taking the disappearance of his wife?"

"Unhappily."

"She's done this before," said Lark.

"That's kind of an open family secret."

"So you didn't know Dalton in Fallujah?"

I shook my head, studied the pictures of him on the monitor again.

"Silver Star and Purple Heart," said Lark. "I never served. I do have some regrets about not serving."

"You all say that."

"You're right. I don't have any regrets. I'm not so sure I could hobble around on one leg the rest of my life. Not sure I have the stamina for that."

I asked Mike to get the post office woman back on the screen. He scrolled through the pictures and we studied her again in silence.

I looked at him and shook my head.

"Thanks for coming in and trying," said Lark. "Old man Taucher asked about you. I told him you were fine."

Old man Taucher was Joan's father, and Joan was a woman who touched both Mike's and my lives, in deep but different ways. Mike's boss—and, as it turned out, his lover. But my responsibility. In my mind, at least. She'd died in the line of duty, in my arms, not quite a year and a half ago, a bloody and terrifying December for San Diego.

I glanced down at the just arrived message on my phone, a text from Dalton Strait.

> **Natalie's car found off Valley Center
> Road. Am stuck in Sacto.
> SD Sheriff Lt. Lew Hazzard will
> take your call.**
>
> **4:09 P.M.**

"Tell old man Taucher hello from me," I said.

Lark stared off as if through a window with an interesting view, but there were no windows in the room.

"I have to see a man about a horse," I said, standing.

He came back from his reverie with a sharp-eyed stare.

"What's going on?"

"Irregularities. Sorry, but that's all I can say right now."

FOUR

Natalie Strait's BMW X5 was discovered at 3:15 that afternoon at about the time I was leaving Lark. Four days had passed since her disappearance.

Dust choked and somehow forlorn, it sat not far from the Tourmaline Resort Casino on the Pala Reservation, behind a cluster of small, now derelict homes set off the road behind a windbreak of towering eucalyptus trees. The surrounding meadow looked to have once been a commercial nursery but was now grazed to the nub by a herd of plump Herefords. The workers' former homes stood naked of doors or window glass, some of them even without roofs, some of them only foundations.

A flotilla of San Diego sheriff vans, SUVs, and prowl cars was parked on one side of a yellow crime tape, and a *Union-Tribune* police reporter I recognized was quarantined on the other. The afternoon sun was high behind them, girders of sunlight through the empty window frames of the houses.

Sheriff Lieutenant Lew Hazzard of the Special Enforcement Detail led me through the dead little enclave to where Natalie's car had been found. He was tight within his uniform, ham faced and blue eyed. He had been a sergeant during my SDSD days, a brusque cop's cop who liked bodybuilding and flying model airplanes.

We walked past empty beer bottles and soft-drink containers, a fire ring, a plywood lean-to probably made by kids. Hazzard said that a ranch hand had seen the SUV parked here on Tuesday afternoon, and it was still here today, Friday, so he'd finally called it in. Which made Hazzard wonder what some people were thinking, if anything. He nodded toward a young man sitting on a eucalyptus stump. Nearby stood a small bay mare tied to a rusted transmission half-buried in the ground.

Natalie's X5 was last year's model, a striking cobalt blue, now dust covered. Brawny tires and complex wheels. All four doors were swung open, and the lift gate, too. A tan leather interior trimmed in shiny dark wood.

A team of blue-gloved crime scene investigators moved patiently within and without: a videographer, a photographer, a sketch artist, two techs lifting latent prints with clear tape, another combing through the driver's floor mat, wearing a hiker's headlight on her head and magnifiers over her eyeglasses. I noted no blood or damage or other signs of mischief, and that the driver's seat was much farther back than five-foot-four Natalie would need. An automatic exit convenience?

"Was it locked?" I asked.

"Un," said the lieutenant.

"How much gas was left in it?"

Hazzard looked at me as if even this was highly sensitive information. "Half."

"I appreciate this favor," I said.

"Not yours to appreciate," said Hazzard. "Dalton Strait's."

And walked away.

I loitered. Watched the tow truck rumble toward us on a dirt road. Soft, dry soil, I saw, poor for traction and retaining tire prints. I asked the hair-and-fiber collector if they'd checked the navigation unit for recent addresses.

She looked up and shook her head. "Talk to the lieutenant."

"He's mad at me."

"Is crime scene contaminator your job title?"

A young fingerprint tech looked at her. "Susan, he's just doing his job."

"So am I."

I waited for Susan to thaw but she didn't look up again so I wandered to the other side of the vehicle. A member decal for the Vista Valley Country Club was stuck low on the windshield. A small wooden cross on a string of leather dangled from the rearview mirror. The mirror, I noted, was tilted up for a driver much taller than five feet four, in keeping with the backed-up driver's seat.

Through the open rear door I could see the handicap parking plaque lying on the back seat. And an *LA Times*, wrapped in its traditional orange plastic bag, and a *Union-Tribune* in its blue plastic bag. I recognized Tuesday's front-page picture on the U-T.

And saw the word *HELP* written in crude red lipstick letters on the rear of the front seat, above the map pouch.

FIVE

My scalp crawled and the old boxing scar on my forehead tingled. I'd assumed that Natalie Strait's status as a VIP had promoted her abandoned car into a full crime scene. But with *HELP* lipsticked onto the seat, her husband's celebrity was now beside the point.

The photographer nudged in front of me, squatted to shoot straight-on, and patiently captured the lipstick letters. *Flash-click. Flash-click.* He leaned closer, camera pointed down, and studied the word. Repositioned himself and took another six shots. Stood and looked at me.

"I want this shot right," he said.

Around back I studied the cargo space: two large, heavy-looking cardboard boxes labeled CAMPAIGN POSTERS, a plastic box overfilled with bundles of new wooden stakes, a heavy-duty staple gun wedged in handle-up, a couple of colorful fabric grocery bags, one stuffed inside the other. On the bumper was a San Diego State University Lacrosse team sticker, a decal for the band The Garden, and a Trojan Mom oval in crimson and gold.

I approached the ranch hand, who stood. He looked under twenty years old and thin—worn jeans and a blue work shirt and a white straw Resistol cowboy hat. Took off the hat and eyed me. The horse shook away a fly and lowered her head to the grass.

"I'm not going to arrest or deport you," I said. "I'm a private investigator, not government." I showed him my enhanced PI photo ID card, required by California, and my pocket license, also required. Together, they're a combination that is impressive or at least puzzling to most people. I'm licensed to carry a sidearm, too. It's a Colt 1911 .45 that fits not quite inconspicuously against the small of my back in a leather paddle holster.

He gave the card and license a long look.

"Habla inglés?" I asked.

"A little."

"My name is Roland."

"Jesús."

"Thank you for calling the police about the vehicle."

He nodded.

"Did you look inside?"

"Sí. I tell the other police."

"Did you open a door?"

The mare came up from her graze, looked at Jesús as if she was particularly interested in his answer, then lowered her head again.

"No," said Jesús. "I look in the window."

"What did you see?"

"I tell the other police."

"Tell me, *también*."

In his sparse English, Jesús told me that the windows were very dark and the sun was low and he didn't see anything important when he looked in. He saw the cross hanging by the mirror and the newspapers and the handicap placard on the back seat and that was all. When I asked him about *HELP* written on the back of the front passenger seat, he said he didn't see it. He didn't remember looking at the backside of that seat at all. It was difficult because of the dark window glass and the sun.

When I asked Jesús why he hadn't called the police until today he said that he tried to stay away from other people's problems. He said there were casinos not far from here and he'd seen many cars speeding and swerving and going through stop signs. Once he had seen a new car smashed like a beer can against a telephone pole. Once he had seen a man chasing a woman along the side of the road and when he had tried to help her they both attacked him.

"So . . . I no call. I wait when the blue truck is very dusty and maybe forget."

Forgotten, I figured.

The mare whinnied softly and shook off another fly.

"Did you show it to anyone else?" I asked. "Or tell them it was here?"

"No."

"Did you see anyone around the car?"

"A woman is here, *miércoles*. Wednesday? She drive a

small white car. Go around the blue BMW and look. Go slow. Stop and open driving door. Go in. Sit. Then drive her car back to Valley Center Road."

"Describe her."

"Don't see good. Dark hair. Sunglass. *Grande*."

"The woman was *grande* or her sunglasses were *grande*?"

"Sunglass big. Woman no big."

Sunglass big, I thought, *twice in one day*. I don't believe in coincidences but I do believe in luck.

"What kind of car?"

He shook his head. "White. Much . . . how you say *arena*?"

"Sand."

"Much sand. And big *abolladura* on the driving door."

A dent.

Based on Jesús's description, I found Lark's possible Fallbrook bomb mailer on my phone, shading the picture with my hand so Jesús could see. Your basic one in a million.

"*Sí.*"

"Yes, but *absolutamente o quizá*?" I asked. Absolutely or maybe?

A troubled smile from the young man, sensing my urgency.

"Maybe. *Es difícil.*"

I turned back and looked at the BMW again. I imagined a tall man at the wheel, another man—or was it a woman?—beside him in the front passenger seat, and a distraught and disbelieving Natalie Strait sitting behind them. Maybe she's arguing. Or pleading. Maybe she's too frightened for that. After all, they've forced or tricked her off the road on her way from breakfast with her sister in Valley Center back to work in Escondido. Jacked her car with her in it. Maybe roughed her up some, too, or showed a weapon, to spoil her mood for conversation. I pictured her scrawling *HELP* onto the seat back, eyes up to avoid attracting attention, just going by feel with the lipstick and hoping she was leaving a clear, meaningful message. I wondered why they hadn't smelled it and rubbed it out. But they had their own levels of excitement to deal with. I pictured the getaway car, driven by associate number three—pulling up over there by the derelict little home, beside the SUV so the passengers could board.

This is what I saw. You learn to trust what you see, even when you doubt. And to doubt, even when you believe.

Jesús set his cowboy hat back on. I saw Hazzard and two of his uniforms heading our way. The mare gave me a glassy-eyed stare.

Hazzard waved me off like a picnic wasp. I retreated to the SUV. When I glanced back, the lieutenant was bearing down on the young cowboy, who again had his hat in his hand and a penitent expression on his face.

SIX

The once Honorable Virgil Strait lived atop a boulder-strewn mountain near the border of San Diego and Imperial counties. The East County badlands, hot and windblown. A pickup truck carrying two stone-faced gentlemen fell in behind me as I climbed that mountain. Rifles racked in the cab. I had passed a similar pair in a similar truck about halfway up.

If you squinted you could call his property a compound. Trailers and storage sheds and a rust-eaten metal building. A dilapidated wooden corral, the lumber blackened by the sun. Trails had been etched through the enormous boulders everywhere you looked, disappearing downhill toward Jacumba and its labyrinthine caves and tunnels used for smuggling drugs and humans from Mexico to California.

As I parked, the first truck pulled up well behind me,

turned broadside, and stopped. The second one curled away and disappeared.

Strait's home was an asymmetrical rock-and-concrete anomaly with a roof made of old license plates. Views of Jacumba, the border and beyond—deep into Mexico and Imperial Valley. It was early morning, the day after I'd talked to Ash Galland and seen Natalie Strait's resounding *HELP* written in the back seat of her luxury SUV.

Virgil Strait had the leathery neck and wrinkled face of a desert tortoise, and small, clear eyes. He wore a knit cap against the morning chill. Flames lapped in a cavernous fireplace at the far opposite end of the room. He sat in an old-fashioned wing chair with his back to the window, giving me the endless eastern view. The walls were made of irregular rock slabs, closely cut and precisely mortared. Hung with rifles and shotguns, vintage and modern, lightly strung with cobwebs. Revolvers heavy in their holsters. Posters of cowboys and Indians in combat, Civil War and World War I battle scenes. Some faded and some slipping off their mounts.

His granddaughter Tola, Dalton's younger sister, handed me a bloody Mary, smiled, then delivered one to Virgil. Tola owned a chain of legal marijuana emporiums in the rural county, and was often quoted and interviewed on the subject. She was a green-eyed redhead in skinny jeans and a long-tailed blue-striped business shirt that might have come from Brooks Brothers.

"Thanks, dearie," said Virgil.

"Enjoy your primitive booze, gentlemen," she said on

her way out. "But remember, good cannabis doesn't rot your liver or your brain."

"Kids these days," said Virgil. "I've tried that stuff. I wandered through the boulders singing the Sons of the Pioneers' 'Cool Water.' Saw a rabbit almost as tall as I was, then I saw a posse of county, state, and federal officers all in cannibal masks, heading up the road here to arrest me. Their guns were drawn. Five hours later I'd sobered up enough to realize I'd imagined it all. But I also knew the coming-to-get-me wasn't paranoia. Story of my life, Mr. Ford. People like you always ahold of my ankles, trying to drag me down."

"I'm a private investigator," I said. "As I'm sure Dalton told you."

He peered at me. "I admire that. I'm private, too. The only thing I believe in is family. I have two living ex-wives, three sons and three daughters, eighteen grandkids and a dozen or so great ones. And cousins, nieces, nephews, and bastards of all description running around this fine county. They're my confederacy, Mr. Ford. My partners and my protection. One snap of my fingers and they appear like a herd of banshees. I'm sure you took note on your way up my mountain."

"I did."

And the night before, in anticipation of this interview, I'd spent some time on IvarDuggans.com, searching the extensive Strait family entries for possible enemies of Natalie or Dalton. IvarDuggans.com is the best of the online investigator's services, and I pay good money for my membership. And it paid off, as it almost always does: nearly twenty-five years ago, Dalton's older brother Kirby had beaten Dalton bad enough to require hospitalization for a concussion and twelve stitches. Dalton was fifteen. The reason? An apparent problem with Dalton's new girlfriend, Natalie. A year later, Dalton had retaliated with a ball-bat beating of Kirby for which Dalton, still a juvenile, was never questioned or charged. Both incidents took place in the small border town of Buena Vista, in Imperial County, whose three-man police department included Chief Everett Strait, Virgil's brother. Thus, little press or media. Kirby had recovered in a small Buena Vista hospital owned by his grandfather, San Diego Superior Court judge, the Honorable Virgil Strait. Virgil had taken the hospital as payment for services rendered in his lawyering days.

The brutal brother-on-brother violence had gotten my attention. "Is there anyone in your family who would abduct Natalie?" I asked. "Maybe to get at Dalton?"

"Mr. Ford, the Straits may bicker a-twixt ourselves, but we prey on the world, not each other."

"Except maybe Kirby."

"Best leave Kirby out of this."

"You know what I think when I hear that."

"Think what you want. He's hardly six months out of prison. Give the boy the benefit of the doubt."

"Do Dalton and Natalie have other enemies?"

"Name me one consequential man or woman who does not."

"Then who are these enemies, Mr. Strait?"

"You would have made a good bailiff in my court," he said. "Beefy but polite."

I made a mental note of that evasion and sipped the bloody Mary. Looked past him to the clear spring day. Two vultures circled slowly in the eastern blue. A black SUV came slowly down a dirt road from Jacumba, dragging a cloud of dust behind. So far as current-day enemies went, I had Natalie's divided into two camps: sexual hunters and enemies of her husband. They both sought to use her, in different ways and for different reasons.

Tola strode back into the room now dressed in black and red motorcycle leathers and boots. Carried her helmet under one arm like a pilot. Her hair was pulled back and channeled through a long medieval leather-and-brass tube that rode to the middle of her back. She gave me a brisk smile. Reminded me loudly of Justine—the hair and eyes, the strength of presence. Quick and bright was the spark that flared up in me as I watched her.

Next came a white-clad orderly pushing a hospital bed, half-reclined, in which a sixtysomething man lay peacefully, his head bobbing slightly with the motion of the bed. Eyes closed. The orderly was a large, muscled Anglo with a jarhead's high and tight haircut.

With a glance my way, Tola bent down to whisper in Virgil's ear. The old man nodded and whispered something back, while beyond them the orderly steered the bed to a sunny window, got the angle right, and pressed the foot brake.

Tola kissed her grandfather's cheek, then came my way, extending a hand and a card. "Don't get up," she said.

I already was. I took the card.

"Nice to meet you, Mr. Ford. If you find yourself in need of peace or excitement, swing by one of my Nectar Barns and we'll fix you right up. We've got some incredible edibles if you're the type to be discreet about such things. You look like you may be."

Biker boots on tiles. The orderly followed her out. Then a small-toothed grin from Virgil and the distant slam of a door. "Beautiful, isn't she?"

"Yes."

"Thirty-five, but not married yet," he said. "Teamed up with the Indians and making money hand over fist but no bank will take it. Dangerous—all that cash in boxes. She's still looking for Mr. Right, Mr. Ford, but she's fussy, fussy, *fussy*."

I refrained from laughing at the prospect of joining the Strait family.

Through the big window I saw the candy-apple-red-and-black Harley Davidson come slowly down the drive, flatulent and loud, a customized Sportster with dazzling paint and sleek saddlebags streaming leather pendants. It rumbled past. The pickup truck driver waved at her and followed her down the mountain.

Virgil pointed a bent old finger. "Meet my firstborn son, Archibald. Archie, this is Roland. As you know, some years ago bandits shot up Archie for less than a thousand dollars in Better Burger money. Not one of them lives today. You may approach the bed."

I stood at a respectful distance. Archie Strait looked to be sixty or sixty-five, movie-star handsome, freshly shaven, with tanned skin and gray, razor-cut hair. He looked ready to throw back the sheets and get out, any second. Archie's younger face had smiled down on motorists from Better Burger billboards across the Southwest for over three decades. In the billboard shot, Archie Strait wore his killer smile and a red bandana around his neck in the style of John Wayne. These days the signs were sun faded but seemed somehow eternal.

Virgil silently appeared beside Archie, reaching out a hand toward his son. Trailed Archie's cheek with the backs of his fingers; touched his thick, up-brushed hair; spread open Archie's eyelids one at a time to reveal the clear gray eyes. The lids stayed parted, as if trained.

"Hmm," said Virgil. "They say brain damaged since that night. They say he doesn't feel, think, or know much anymore. Tola's got him doped up with that stuff of hers. Not the druggy version but the medicinal one. Seems to work. He's peaceful, and I think his mind is sometimes alert. Chews his food now. Hums, too. Not a tune, just a humming sound. Hard for me to believe, when I look into those eyes, that nobody's home. I think he's aware of a lot. Aren't you, son? I'm no fool, Mr. Ford. And I'm no crackpot. But I do believe in God and I think God is still inside this boy. Do you?"

"I don't know what to say to that."

He turned and looked at me as if I'd failed an important test. "If you stand in the middle of the road, you will be run over from both directions."

"Who's standing in the middle of a road?"

The old man's look was quick, sharp, and satisfied.

"Because of the lipstick on the back of Natalie's car, we know she's in serious trouble," he said.

"Narrow it down."

"This is about money. Not some rapist who's seen Natalie on TV."

"Maybe," I said.

"The abduction was not impulsive, Mr. Ford. It was done with planning. Daylight. In public. A fit, spirited young woman. They took the extra time and risk of being seen, to get her into another car. To go where? Perverts would have done their deeds and killed her out in Pala. It was perfect—a private place and her own car. If that's all they wanted, they'd have left her there. No. Dalton will get a ransom demand. They'll want some kind of cryptocurrency through the Internet and the FBI will have almost nothing to go on."

"I thought that at first, too. But it's been five days now."

Virgil frowned, lowered Archie's eyelids both at once, with thumb and index finger. Walked slowly away, his body following his straining, tortoise-like head to the window. I got my first full view of him—shorter than I'd expected, thin and leaning as if into some private wind. Thermal long johns, a canvas barn coat, and calf-high shearling boots.

He sat back down. Took off the knit cap, shook it once, and rearranged it over his sparse white hair. Then turned to the window, giving me his back.

"Your thoughts," he said.

"If it's not sex and it's not money, then another reason comes to mind," I said. "Revenge."

"For what?"

"I was hoping you may have some ideas, Mr. Strait. Now we're back to the enemies question you didn't answer."

He turned. "The Democrats of California hate him. They're financing that awful woman against him."

"I doubt that the California Democratic Party had Dalton's wife kidnapped," I said.

"Why not? How is my grandson to run a reelection campaign with this hanging over his head?"

"Not to mention hers."

"Why do you think he's hired you to find her, instead of trusting the police? Because soon as the media get into this, it will become a circus of fake news and speculation, and he'll be in the middle of it. His opponents will find a way to use it against him. Isn't that plain to you?"

The old man had a point but it wasn't sharp enough. "I mean vengeance for an action taken. Or perceived to have been taken."

Virgil locked his tiny, shiny eyes on mine. "Enemies. Vengeance. I like the way your mind works."

"Where were you set to meet Natalie for lunch on Tuesday?" I asked.

"Vintana. It's above the Lexus dealership near her work."

Strait told me he had waited there for forty minutes, made three calls to her but got no answer. Tried her boss, who said she still hadn't showed up for work and hadn't called. It wasn't like her. Strait had lunch, two martinis, and drove himself home. Said he met Natalie for lunch twice a year unless there was some special reason they needed to talk.

"Was there some special reason?"

Virgil considered, his eyes hard upon me again. "Yes, there was. Want to see my scorpion collection?"

"Of course."

SEVEN

We climbed down the stairs to the basement. Cold rock walls, poor light, and the smell of earth. Virgil pushed through a rusted iron door on squeaking hinges and into a dark room. He flipped a wall switch but no light came. He pulled me in and shut the door. Before us, luminescent blue-green creatures scuttled and stopped, scuttled and stopped.

"They're most active at night," said Virgil Strait. "So I keep it dark here during the day, hit them with the UV so I can see them frolicking."

As my eyes adjusted to the dark I saw the terraria built into the walls and the big desk in the middle of the room, stacked with books and papers, and a high-backed leather chair behind the desk and the two folding chairs opposite. The scorpions surrounded us in their glass cages, heavy armed and high tailed, all sizes, some small as a house key, some half a foot long at least.

"I liked them as a boy and never outgrew the fascination," said Virgil. "Carried them around in my lunch bucket at school. Used to keep a new specimen or two in my chambers, which had a distracting effect on squabbling lawyers. Scorpion venom is mostly overrated. Still, you don't want an Arizona bark scorpion or a spitting thick-tailed black to get you."

"That's a big one," I said, nodding to a crawdad-sized scorpion eyeing us from a top-row cage.

"Emperor scorpion from Africa."

"Why did Natalie want to see you?"

Virgil regarded me in the near dark, though I couldn't make out his face.

"She wanted to talk about moving her family here. In with me—Dalton, her, and the younger boy."

"Why?"

"Circle the wagons. Debt. Years of living beyond their means."

I thought of Dalton's comments about his assemblyman's salary of a hundred grand and change, coupled with that of a part-time car salesperson. They were not a money machine, but they made just enough to live a decent, frugal life. You had to factor in a son away at USC—one of the most expensive private colleges in the nation. You had to factor in a forty-grand gambling/shopping loss and the cost of Natalie Strait's medical care. Which, my research had discovered, was only partly covered by the Straits' State of California and Natalie's BMW health plans. You had to factor in Dalton spending more of his own money on reelection than he'd ever spent before. And maybe the fact that he couldn't even pay my up-front engagement fee.

I watched the blue-green scorpions moving about, determined but defeated by glass. "Have Dalton and Natalie borrowed money from you?"

"Those days are over."

"Were you going to let them move in?"

"Sure, but it's a crazy idea. Both boys in college. She works in Escondido and Dalton's in and out of Lindbergh Field every other week it seems. This place is hours from everywhere they need to be. And look at it. Who'd want to live in this rock pile of hell in the first place?"

"They must be desperate," I said.

"Yeah, well, you dig a hole, you fall in. That's what I used to tell the unfortunate souls who ended up in my court."

"Until you fell into your own."

"Who are you? Roland F. Christ?"

"I'm just a PI, locally sourced and hopefully sustainable."

"Life is surprise."

Virgil hit the lights and the glowing arachnids receded into the pebbled flooring of their cages. Up close and in good light his face looked like a wrinkled map, cross-hatching and contradictory lines in all directions.

"You want enemies of Dalton and Natalie?" asked Virgil. "You were right about Dalton's older brother. Kirby's

the one who took up with her first. He never got read-
justed quite right after she went with Dalton. Nobody
falls in love like a Strait."

———

I bumped down the mountain drive from Virgil Strait's
rock castle, followed by one of his watchdog trucks with
the rifles in its window. Howard Wilkin, my contact and
sometimes ally at the *Union-Tribune*, called, his voice
cutting over the radio speakers loud and clear.

"I'm working on a story about Natalie Strait," he said.
"But nobody knows how I can get in touch with her. Do
you?"

"I saw you out in Valley Center," I said.

"They're treating it as a crime scene," said Wilkin.
"And asking me to stand down for now. Asking as a reporter, Roland, what were you doing there?"

"I got a tip, Howard. Just like you probably did."

"From Dalton?"

"Maybe."

"It would make sense, with him being in Sacramento."

"What did the crime lab find in her car?" I asked.

"They won't say anything. They won't even confirm
that the vehicle belonged to Natalie Strait. My contact at
the DMV came in handy. Help me out here, Roland."

"They're telling me less than they've told you," I said.

"But you got a lot closer to the crime scene team than
I did. They must have shot two hundred pictures. What
did you see in there?"

"Nothing unusual that I could see. I can't comment for publication, Howard. You know that."

"Do you have a number for her? For Natalie Strait?"

"Talk to Dalton."

"He said talk to you."

I had expected more of Dalton. Maybe name, rank, and serial number. And some good old-fashioned political evasion.

"I'll ask her to call you when I find her, Howard. Let's let the cops handle this for now. Give the Straits their privacy."

"He's the assemblyman for the eighty-second district, Roland. People should know if his wife has been the victim of a crime."

"Nobody's saying that, Howard."

"That's what bothers me. I know something's wrong here. The Straits have been living pretty big for years now. I'm the only media on this story, and this could be big with the election six months out. I need more than an abandoned car. You owe me from last year."

"I haven't forgotten."

I ended the call, turned the radio back on, made a fist and tapped it on the steering wheel. I called Dalton to find out why he'd handed me over to Wilkin, and to find out what, if anything, Lew Hazzard of the Special Enforcement Detail had told him about Natalie's vehicle. The call went to message.

Next I called Dalton and Natalie Strait's three current credit card companies, gave Dalton's account numbers,

PINs, passwords, and security codes, and the last four digits of his social security number. Yes, I was calling from a new phone number. Asked for balances and recent activity. The balances for April—the most recent full month of activity—were $5,705, $4,013, and $7,922, and all of the monthly minimums were past due. None of the credit cards had been used in the last four days. Would I like to speak to an account representative?

I logged in to my mobile IvarDuggans account to pry into Dalton and Natalie Strait's credit history. The security site doesn't have access to current balances, but they do have a list of credit cards, both active and closed, that are "associated" with practically any individual who has ever used a charge card.

Dalton and Natalie Strait's information popped right up. I noted the card issuer and account numbers, logged off, and started calling.

By the time I hit Alpine, I'd come up with three more active credit cards not listed by Dalton but used by both Straits and discovered balances totaling $37,039.

I clicked off, wondering how Dalton's hundred grand and Natalie's up-and-down commissions in the fickle car market could cover mortgage, private college expenses, taxes, insurance, food, utilities, gambling, everyday expenses, and roughly $55,000 in credit card debt.

A few minutes later the phone went off again, this time with a San Diego County Emergency Alert:

An explosion has been reported at the San Diego County Administration Center downtown. Multiple injuries have occurred and first responders are on scene. Authorities are asking all citizens to stay away from the building, which is located at 1600 Pacific Highway . . .

Which is about two blocks from the city building where the bomb addressed to the mayor had gone off five days ago.

EIGHT

By the time I got to the city, the waterfront was barricaded and the traffic was inching through downtown. I pulled into an airport parking structure on Kettner, paid the attendant for a few minutes on the rooftop, and wound my way up four stories to the top. Plenty of spaces. I stood with the breeze in my face, looking out at the airport and the tuna fleet and the county center. Raised my binoculars and saw the stately old building surrounded by emergency and media vehicles, SDPD prowlers, and fed and state vehicles of all description. Fire companies and medics still deployed, crews standing outside their engines and trucks. A helicopter hovered low. Various personnel came and went through the cop-clotted entrance, with attitudes of purpose but not emergency. Just doing their jobs now.

I called Lark, not expecting him to answer.

"I'm in the county building," he said. "You have twenty seconds."

"Another mail bomb?"

"But stronger. Blew three fingers off the supervisor's aide who had gone in on a Saturday morning to take care of a few loose ends before a vacation. She's going to live."

"Who was it meant for?" I asked.

"Supervisor Holder. The package originated at a FedEx franchise in Ramona. Time's up, and mum's the word, Roland. Over and out."

I looked down on America's Finest City, at the emergency crews and law enforcers traipsing in and out of the county building. I glassed the cruise ship terminal and Tuna Harbor and Marina Parks and the *Midway*. The statue *Unconditional Surrender*. The convention center and the tall hotels. A sleek black helicopter angled down from the blue. My city, America's finest or not. My turf now. My beat.

I had met Justine in one of those hotels, at a tedious Christmas party that changed my life. That memory drifted across my mind's eye like a movie clip as I lowered the binoculars and looked at the hotel and I saw her face as it had once been before I'd spoken a word to her. The memory clip played for a moment, pleasantly, but was soon overtaken by another, in which a little pink plane fell into a dark ocean and was swallowed up. That plane will still be crashing on the day I die.

All we control is the volume knob. How much to remember? How much to forget?

I glassed the county building again. The sleek black

helo lifted back into the sky, its mission apparently complete. A white SUV rolled to a barricade gate and a cop looked inside and waved it through. I wondered at an America where people blew fingers off of other people they believed to be enemies because they held certain beliefs or opinions. An America where a thousand differing ends now justified the means. An America of open-carry hate.

Which led me from the buzzing of my phone to the latest words from The Chaos Committee, streamed live on my Emergency Alert app:

> *Dear California . . . only the People can overthrow this system . . . only the People, armed with chaos, fear, and terror can drive the power brokers, moneylenders, and the godless technocrats from our collective temple. THROW THEM FROM OUR TEMPLE! We will provide the protection of anarchy, fear, and terror for the restoration of God's one true nature.*

Which made me wonder: *Who's going to throw out you?*

=====

Dalton called. It was barely noon and he sounded drunk.

"She's chained to a wall. Real shackles, like in a dungeon," he slurred. "They sent me a self-destructing video. An *ephemeral* message. It only lasted maybe five seconds."

"When?"

"Just now. She had on a bathrobe like a prairie girl would wear. Buttoned up and long. Looked out of it,

Roland. Didn't say anything. Just looked at me. My heart's pounding out of my chest right now. Maybe somewhat a little drunk. I'm getting my gun and going out looking. All the places she might be."

"You stay put, friend. Where are you? I'm on my way."

I found him in a bar in Escondido, not far from Natalie's dealership.

Managed to get him home, where he poured vodka from the freezer into a large tumbler.

"Sit with me awhile," he said.

"Where's the gun?"

"Up in the nightstand. Don't worry. I'm in no shape to go hunting right now. You shoulda seen how sad she looked. So afraid. But the worst part was, she wasn't resisting. Like she'd given up. Like I feel."

"You don't give up until you talk to the cops. Hazzard's on his way," I said. "Your sheriff friend. I'll make some coffee."

NINE

In the Marine Corps I boxed and never lost a match. I was a tall, lanky heavyweight who could punch and get out of the way. No big talent, but good reach. I could keep cool and land punches unexpectedly. I had one professional fight after discharge from the corps, as the newly minted pro Roland "Rolling Thunder" Ford. Late in the fight and tiring, I was hit hard by a superior ring journeyman known as Darien "Demolition" Dixon. I saw my mouthpiece arching through the overhead lights. I saw the ref above me. I was helped to my stool, where I was able to look out at the mostly empty arena. And I could also see myself from above, sitting way down there on that stool, looking out. I was myself, then outside myself; me then not me. I'd seen the punch coming but didn't have the reflex left to slip it. It landed on my forehead and left a scar that still itches and heats up and annoys me from time to time. Usually at a time when something bad is about to happen. I never fought again. It wasn't that I'd been knocked out, or even that I'd lost. Nothing to do with shame or pain. I quit the ring because I didn't want things shifting around upstairs. More concisely: I never wanted to get hit that hard again. I understood that I'd lost this fight but I would find another.

But throwing punches is still a violent pleasure, something I'm good at, and I do it most days in my barn.

After talking to Lark that afternoon, I finished my sit-ups and the jump rope, breathing hard, stomach tight, and arms already heavy. I prowled around the drafty old space, shadowboxing with my back to the spring light that poured through the wide barn doors. Then I attacked the speed bag for three rounds of boxing action. Panted deeply on a barstool for a minute, listened to the pigeons cooing in the rafters before starting in on the heavy bag. I wear ankle weights and extra-heavy gloves.

When that was over I stripped off the weights and gloves and ran for it. Across the barnyard and around the big pond behind the main house, then along a narrow trail leading into the rocky hills of the rancho. This property is called Rancho de los Robles—Ranch of the Oaks—founded in 1894 by immigrants from Germany and later sold to the Timmerman family, originally from Boston. The Timmermans owned several properties in the West, and occupied the rancho only briefly before leasing it out to a thoroughbred breeding consortium that ran it for nearly fifty years. When they moved their operation north into less expensive country, the Timmerman family sold off the bulk of the acreage but kept twenty acres, the structures, and the spring-fed pond. The rancho had fallen into general disrepair by the time Justine Timmerman and I received it as a wedding gift. Our little fixer-upper. I offered Rancho de los Robles back to the Timmermans after her death, but they would hear nothing of that idea: family was family.

Leaving me suddenly rich, free to climb on the backs of the poor. I don't feel rich. I make a modest amount of money. My tax bite is low. Electricity, water, and propane are high. The property is still in general disrepair. I rent out the casitas down by the pond for income and company. I donate generously to the Food Pantry, the Animal Sanctuary, the Land Conservancy, and the Boys & Girls Clubs of North County. Sometimes I walk through my large adobe house, rich in personal history but also in histories larger than my own, looking into the theatrically draped rooms and out the old sagging-glass windows. Always, somehow, I'm a guest here.

I churned my way up a rise, braked on the steep decline, startled three coyotes way out in the meadow; they froze and watched me with sharp-eared caution. Looped around the far, unfenced perimeter of the property, down into an oak-shaded arroyo with a tiny creek winding through it. I thought of Dalton Strait clomping into my office, hiring me to find his wife. I pictured Natalie shackled to a wall. Thought of him telling me that Natalie's car had been found abandoned but he was stuck in Sacto. Could I deal with it? I thought of Natalie Strait writing her SOS in lipstick on the back of her BMW seat. Then of her sister, Ash, clobbered by worry for her sister. Thought of Virgil Strait's luminescent scorpions and his stubborn surrender of grandson Kirby as a person of interest in Natalie's disappearance. And his granddaughter Tola, so assured within herself, so blithe an echo of Justine.

I ran off-trail toward an outcropping of vertical sandstone boulders tall enough to make shade in the late afternoon. Here they stand in a loose ring, used for various purposes by the native Luiseños, Spanish explorers, Franciscan padres, rustlers, bandits, prospectors, drifters, bikers, hippies, and migrants. There are metates—grinding spots—up on the sunny surfaces, and the earth between the boulders once held arrowheads, pottery shards, and the remains of native woven baskets. I can still find them if I dig deep enough, and in the right places. I found a Spanish doubloon once, very deep. And pieces of ironware and a small wooden cross misplaced by a priest or perhaps discarded by one of the doubtful natives. The sheltered space within the boulders is pocked and scarred by decades of fire rings and open-pit cooking stations, benches and tables made of slate slabs rounded by the elements and blackened by fire. The walls are littered with five-plus centuries of drawings and messages and inscrutable designs left by rock, stick, knife, and paint. A deer jumping over the sun, far up and hard to see, is my favorite.

I picked my way through the boulders, around the fire pits and stone furnishings, then over the buried treasures to the other side. My ribs and legs ached from a spectacular beating I'd taken a few months earlier from some bad men in a bad place. I skidded down an embankment of loose rocks trying to be light on my feet—impossible—then strained up a sharp, short rise and picked up the trail that would lead me home.

Home, at a distance: a silver pond with its cattailed banks and wooden dock, my adobe house on a hillock just beyond, and six casitas below, small and neat, perched along the narrow beach. A big palapa shaded the patio, barbecue, the picnic benches, and the Ping-Pong table, ready for play. A scattering of mongrel chaise longues and outdoor chairs left where last needed for sun or shade. My beloved sagging old barn, from which I had recently emerged, and the flat green-dandelioned barnyard overhung with a tremendous coast live oak that a local padre had referred to in a diary from 1887.

════

That evening at sunset I sat under the palapa with my five current tenants, whom I refer to as the Irregulars. They are not named after Sherlock Holmes's Irregulars, who are of course only fictional. Cocktail hour is our social time, an informal commitment at best. We are not exactly friends, but we have more than the standard landlord-tenant relationship.

I began renting out the casitas not long after Justine died, which was five years ago last month. In those days I'd felt trapped by the old home in poor repair, numbed by the absence of my someone to love, and suddenly—for the first time in my life—unwilling to live alone. I was also open to the idea of collecting rent. My PI practice had begun to suffer from my own blank ineffectuality and I was casting about for dollars and distraction.

So I ran a for-rent ad in the local paper and online, sensing good conversation and easy money. I pondered ground rules. Anticipating my arrivals, I wrote a brief constitution, had it professionally printed and housed in a weatherproof acrylic frame, and hung it on one of the palapa uprights not far from where we now sat:

GOOD MANNERS AND PERSONAL HYGIENE
NO VIOLENCE REAL OR IMPLIED
NO DRUGS
NO STEALING
QUIET MIDNIGHT TO NOON
RENT DUE FIRST OF MONTH
NO EXCEPTIONS

Here is the current starting lineup of Irregulars, in order of seniority:

Burt Short, fiftysomething, indeterminate profession and background, a scratch golfer, casita five.

My grandpa Dick Ford, eighties, retired advertising executive, casita one.

My grandma Liz Ford, early seventies, retired teacher, casita six.

Francisco "Frank" Cuellar, nineteen, Salvadoran immigrant, and his dog, Triunfo, casita two.

Odile Sevigny, mid-twenties, psychic, casita four.

I keep casita three unoccupied in case of emergency.

Liz had just proudly poured a round of her "commercial grade" martinis, then set the glass pitcher back in its bowl of melting ice. Francisco's glass she filled with bubbly water because he's underage. Burt doesn't drink.

We lifted the glasses carefully.

"So, you didn't actually get in to see the blast scene," said Grandpa Dick.

"I didn't even get near the building," I said.

"You'd think a good PI would find a way in."

"No need for the likes of me," I said. "They have an entire federal bureau dedicated to things that blow up. And the FBI and local cops, and so on."

"How bad was the injury to the aide?" asked Liz.

I told them again what Lark had told me. It's funny how people like to hear grim details more than once.

At seven we watched the news, as usual, with the complete text of The Chaos Committee's second letter to the *Union-Tribune* writ large on the palapa-mounted big screen. Apparently the streamed diatribe I'd heard hours earlier had been an impromptu rant.

Dear California,

You have now seen a more powerful and directed sign. The collateral damage will decrease as we increase the payload to reach our intended targets more accurately. You must be asking if there is anything you can do to make us stop, and yes, there is: Join us. Assault your political leaders and all police on the job and in the streets.

Bear arms against all oppressors and let your anger be your conscience. Destroy government property no matter how innocent it may seem to you, specifically city halls, county seats, courts, public parks, and public schools. Set afire houses of worship. Drop your cell phones and computers into the nearest body of water. Load up. Lash out. Be heard.

The Chaos Committee

"Pompous horseshit," said Dick.

"But scary when you think about it," said Liz.

"Everything's scary when you think about it," said Dick. "Just ask our nation's military-security complex. Scary is what keeps them in business."

"This letter will make people feel empowered to commit violence," said Liz.

"There's a puppet for every string," said Burt.

"Many guns here, like Salvador," said Frank.

"I shudder," said Odile.

Odile has been here for only three months. Her most striking feature is her height—same as mine—six-three. We see perfectly eye to eye. Slender, a kindly face, big brown eyes, and short, corn-silk-yellow hair. Her Psychic Matters parlor/office/studio is a converted downtown Craftsman home next to Little C's Tattoo. As a psychic, a lot of Odile's conversation springs from the emotional, premonitory tuning fork inside her. Sometimes she'll carry on without a comma, halfway in—and halfway out—of what I think of as the real world.

But now silence fell upon her as the commentators tried to parse the communiqué while the text remained on-screen.

"You've been gone a lot lately, Roland," said Dick. "What are you working on?"

"You know the deal, Grandpa."

"Ah, come on. Just a clue."

I make it clear to all the Irregulars that prying into my work is forbidden. That doesn't matter; they never stop trying. I wish I'd posted this important rule along with the others. Thought of adding it but that's a lot of work. The Irregulars and I have other dustups as well: they uniformly point out that although I insist on collecting my rent on time (rule six), I don't keep up on repairs. I admit to this, but point out that no Irregular I've ever hosted, with the exception of Burt Short, has ever paid reliably on time (rules six and seven).

More important, the Irregulars—past and present— have stood behind me in some dire situations, personal and professional, and more than once. They have acted on my behalf. They have given sanctuary to the innocent, protected this property from armed invaders, helped to dispatch terrorists, and given me useful advice on certain love affairs. Collectively, they often reach a higher moral truth than I can manage alone.

Burt in particular has helped me in tough professional moments. I literally owe him my life. We are more than friends and more than partners. There's no good noun for us. We are a gang of two, bound by loyalty, made stronger than we are as individuals.

TEN

After the cocktail and a fine paella with scampi dinner, I lumbered off to my upstairs home office, poured a bourbon, and called retired colonel Jim Young. I'd served under him in First Fallujah. After his thirty years in service, Jim had settled in Tucson to pursue the pleasures of bird-watching and photography. These are logical pursuits of a retired military mind, if you think about it—all about pursuit, acquiring your target, and forms of capture. After some catching up, I came to the reason for my call.

"What can you tell me about Dalton Strait in Fallujah?"

"A good enough marine," said Jim. "But he carried himself more like an officer than an enlisted man, which he was. He served because his father served and his grandfather served, and of course nine-eleven. I think

Dalton was eager to get on to more important and less bloody things. Then he lost the leg and he was on his way home. He's your state assemblyman now, isn't he?"

"Yes. He's up for reelection in November."

"Are you looking for anything in particular, Mr. PI?"

"Just his general character, Jim. I never ran across him in Fallujah. Had my own beat."

"Jolan district, if I remember right," said Young.

The Jolan. My cradle. Twisting warrens and alleys, homes and shops all huddled close, resentment thick as the smoky air. Images rose to my mind's eye, rarely summoned but always ready. I thought of the Blackwater men. Bodies on the bridge. I thought of my Five.

"Dalton was out in East Manhattan. That's where he rescued the Humvee driver and got himself the Silver Star."

I redirected my memory to the goofy nomenclature we used to distinguish one part of crowded, hostile Fallujah from another. We used names that we Yanks could relate to: the Brooklyn Bridge, East Manhattan, Highway 10, Queens, the Pizza Slice.

"Did you talk to him after the rescue?"

"You bet. I wanted to thank and congratulate him. Offered to do the Silver Star nomination paperwork. Funny thing was, Dalton didn't seem to want it, the medal. The driver he rescued, Harris Broadman, got burned pretty badly. Dalton was really down about that. Broadman was his sergeant. Older than Dalton, and well respected. A few days later, Dalton was blown up himself. Now this was just gossip, but I heard that his behavior on patrol that day went beyond careless, all the way to risky. Really, all very sad for those two. Dalton was married, you know. Had two sons."

"Have you kept up with him?"

"Not really," he said. "I donate to his campaigns, send him an occasional email to his office. You, on the other hand, have had some pretty spectacular action out your way. Between the torturers, the terrorists, and the evangelicals. Makes Fallujah sound tame."

"I'm a lightning rod for calamity."

"You're just the man for the job. I restrict myself to birding and photography in hopes of peace and a long life."

"I might consider those activities."

"Two secrets as you consider: birds will help you laugh and photography will help you see."

"Thanks for the secrets, Jim."

"If you talk to Dalton, say hello."

I put some music on low and hit the computer to find Harris Broadman. Harder than I thought it would be. No web page, no social media, no Google or Whitepages hits for a former marine in his age range. None of the Marine Corps fraternal organizations had him listed. I finally found his name in a Marine Corps roster of personnel in the Battle of Fallujah in the appendix of a book by Bing West. And that was all. No cross-references or links.

I resorted to expensive IvarDuggans—they charge for membership and minutes in use, not hours.

And again, thirty seconds later, proof of why I happily

pay up: "H. Broadman, WM, entrepreneur/innkeeper, born in Kenton, Ohio, in 1976, grad Kenton High School 1994, enlisted U.S. Marine Corps 1/1/1997, attained rank of sergeant, Purple Heart, honorable discharge 11/12/2004, LKA 25 Bighorn Circle, Borrego Springs, CA."

An innkeeper. I did a Google search, got the Bighorn Motel on Bighorn Circle in Borrego Springs, then its website. Clean, low rates, air-conditioning, a pool, some rooms with kitchenettes and back patios. Weekly rates available. Close to nature's splendors in Anza-Borrego Desert State Park, and near downtown.

"Proprietor, H. Broadman welcomes you."

I was taking my Bighorn Motel virtual tour when Dalton Strait called. He sounded rattled.

"Natalie called me one minute ago. I think she was forced to call me. She said, 'Dalton, it's me.' Then the call ended. It was her. The calling number was unavailable."

I took a moment to process this, made a note of the time on my desktop legal pad. Asked him how sure he was that it was her.

"Absolutely positive," he said.

"She said only those three words? Nothing more?"

"Help me, Roland. Tell me what to do."

I told him to call Hazzard as soon as we were done, keep his phone close and tell me immediately if she—or anyone on her behalf—called again.

"On her behalf is right," he said. "Someone's got her. I knew it when I saw the pictures of the lipstick. Someone goddamned took her."

In the long pause that followed I heard Dalton's measured breathing, slow and even.

Then he surprised me.

"I'm introducing a new bill Monday morning, here in Sacramento," he said. "I want you to be here."

"Why?"

"As a friend."

"But I'm not a friend."

A pause. "Okay. Pretend. Just be here. Capitol building Assembly Chamber, eleven a.m. Easy. If you want to fly up tomorrow, give them my name at the Westin downtown. You fly your own plane, don't you?"

"We'll get her back, Dalton."

"I don't need a pep talk, man. Just be here for me on Monday. I'm paying you for every hour. I need you."

The strange end of a strange call.

＝＝＝

An hour later, Burt knocked on my office door, took a seat in one of the old, handsome, and uncomfortable horsehair-stuffed chairs that came with the hacienda. He had his something's-up expression on his face, a handful of papers in one hand.

Burt Short really is short. He sat forward so his feet would reach the floor. He's built like a bull, big headed, big shouldered, and small footed, and he's uncannily strong.

Burt remains something of a mystery. He's virtually unresearchable, even to IvarDuggans.com and Mike Lark's FBI, so all of his biography comes from him and only him. If he's being truthful, Burt Short is not his birth name. His personally suggested bio includes boyhood time in Italy and Japan, a college education and internship in nuclear risk management in Finland, an on-again, off-again relationship with American intelligence, membership in the PGA, some golf teaching, and time on Wall Street, where he claims to have done very well. He's conversant with firearms and self-defense, comfortable with and adept at violence. He's currently retired and plays golf every day. He's quiet but charming when he wants to be, with a full face, a weirdly disarming smile, and good manners. He becomes angry if anyone mentions his height. Animals love him.

"You asked about Natalie Strait's love of gambling and shopping," Burt said, reaching out to set the papers on my desk. I looked over the first sheet as he talked.

"Considerable, when you factor in their finances," he said. "Almost all the gambling was at local Indian casinos, except that banner Las Vegas run fourteen months ago."

"Where did you get these numbers?" I asked.

Burt shrugged. "They're solid."

Natalie Strait had run up a grand total of casino gambling losses of $357,285 in the last three years. She and Dalton had paid back $278,000 in four payments over the past year, leaving them roughly $79,000 in arrears, plus interest and penalties, mounting daily.

Figured loosely, the $357,285 was well over triple Dalton's annual salary. Dalton had told me that Natalie's average annual part-time earnings from the BMW of Escondido were $70,000. Again, figured loosely, Natalie Strait's gambling losses for the last three years were $177,000-plus dollars higher than their combined annual income.

Burt's second sheet of paper showed an itemized combination of the Straits' April charges, including overdue balances from months past. From my own talks with the Straits' six credit card companies I knew the rough totals, but seeing exactly where some of the money had gone put the Straits in a different light: the University of Southern California ($11,885); San Diego State University ($3,800); their home mortgage ($2,000); line of credit on said home ($820); the Maui Queen Hotel and Resort ($1,900); the Blue Marlin Restaurant of La Jolla ($1,400); Nordstrom ($650); Coach ($520); Cartier ($370); Island Golf ($340); Dick's Sporting Goods ($290); Men's Wearhouse ($275); Brooks Brothers ($220); BMW of America ($490); and a combined total of $2,200 for water, utilities, prescriptions, gasoline, and groceries.

Not to mention their $79,000 in arrears gambling debt and unpaid card balances of $55,000.

"Do they have assets?" I asked. "Real property, IRAs, cash, art, jewelry—anything?"

"Nothing," said Burt. "Their home is for sale."

"It hurts just looking at this," I said. "How are they coming up with enough money to live?"

"They aren't," said Burt. "They've buried themselves to the point where the basics aren't being covered."

"Then where are those payments coming from?"

"Exhibit three."

I leafed through pages from the State of California's campaign finance Political Reform Division website, a dizzying array of information on the Strait Reelection Committee. Clearly listed were contributions and expenditures.

The committee had taken in contributions of $317,855 year-to-date, and had expenditures of $280,514.

Which caught my eye. "That expenditure is very close to what they paid down on Natalie's gambling debts. And of course, campaign funds used for personal expenses is a felony."

"So is conspiracy," said Burt. "If it's a team effort they're looking at four to six years in federal lockup."

I pictured Dalton Strait sitting in my Main Avenue office, massaging the stump of his leg while his plastic calf lay on the desk in front of him. A burly young man with a smile on his face and an old-fashioned glass of bourbon in one hand.

"But there's no trail from the Strait Reelection Committee to their purchases and debts," I said. "No trail on the campaign finance forms. Expenditures are just expenditures. If they're covering gambling, restaurants, and USC tuition with campaign money, they've hidden it."

"Wouldn't you?"

I read through Burt's notes, seeing that wire fraud and falsification of records were two more crimes that Dalton and Natalie Strait might well also have committed en route to the misuse of campaign funds.

I straightened the papers on my desk, groaned and sat back. "I'd like to see the reelection committee books," I said quietly. "Natalie's real books—not the whitewash they're reporting to the state."

"Well," said Burt. "You could break in like a Watergate burglar."

"I wonder if Dalton might give me a look at his uncooked reelection committee books," I said.

"Ask him," said Burt. "Your war buddy isn't the sharpest pin in the cushion."

I nodded.

"I assume the state, the FBI, and possibly the sheriffs are onto this by now," said Burt. "And some of the progressive Dems and media go-getters."

"Howard Wilkin of the U-T is," I said.

I imagined the rough consequences for Dalton Strait's reelection, should discrepancies between contributions and expenditures prove criminal. Scrutiny and scandal. An immediate drop in donations and votes in November, just six months away. Enough time for an indictment, then later, a nasty, high-profile trial. All of this as the Democrats were pushing hard for young, bright Ammna Safar in the 82nd district.

"I'll see Dalton in the Assembly Chamber on Monday," I said. "He's introducing a bill and he wants me to be there. I'll fly *Hall Pass* up there, bright and early tomorrow."

"My regards to Dalton," said Burt. "We've met more than once on the fine San Diego links, as you know. He's powerful, but a terrible hook off the tee. Tough pivot with that leg of his, so he overcompensates. Good mid-game and surprisingly deft on the greens."

"A betting man," I said.

"Carries a wad just for that. By the way, Natalie Strait's campaign admirer, Brock Weld, told the campaign people that he missed work the day Natalie disappeared because he was home sick with the flu. None of his neighbors saw him that day. He's got a dog that barks when he's away. A yapper named King. King barked all day until evening, when Mr. Weld came home."

"Where's he work?"

"He works security at the Tourmaline Casino."

———

My flight over the local mountains and the eastern flank of L.A. was scenic and uneventful. Always gets me how the earth seems counterintuitively larger from the air, not smaller. The morning was clear and cool and there were still pockets of snow on Mount Baldy, often used as a snowy backdrop in photographs of greater Los Angeles.

I named my Cessna 182 *Hall Pass II*, after Justine's original pink *Hall Pass*, her pride and joy. I bought mine, well used, a few months after she crashed in the ocean near Point Loma. Painted mine classic Cessna yellow. *Hall Pass II* was intended to honor her memory, and the devout enthusiasm she brought to flight. I love it, too.

As was *Hall Pass*, my plane is powered by a venerable Lycoming engine, a grumbling powerhouse identifiable even from the ground when the plane is flying low enough. Sometimes when I fly *Hall Pass*, or hear a Lycoming-powered Cessna from the ground, I think of her and for a moment we touch hands across space and time.

As California's Central Valley came scrolling slowly under me, the vast horizon frowned over miles of amber grain and vegetable green, tomato red and spring corn yellow. Two-thirds of the fruits and nuts grown in the U.S. are raised right down there under the moving shadow of my wings. Land of fruits and nuts indeed. Fifty billion dollars a year of agricultural output, baby. They didn't name it California and croak out *Eureka!* for nothing.

ELEVEN

In contrast to California's enormous Central Valley, the state Assembly Chamber is patterned after the proper British House of Commons, a handsome blend of dark hardwoods, brass, and green carpet. Eighty-two seats for eighty-two legislators. You feel important just waddling in.

I sat in the Assembly gallery, with a nice view of the proceedings below. Only a few citizens in the gallery this late morning, each of us ushered in under the baleful eyes of the sergeant-at-arms. Security had been tight as I knew it would be. The Chaos Committee's influence had been swift. My weapons and phone were locked in a pistol case stashed in the trunk of my rental car.

Dalton Strait looked up and waved shortly after I sat down. He was seated on the right side of the chamber floor, on the Speaker's left, along with a few of the Republicans still left in the assembly. He wore a trim beige suit on this spring morning. Even from the gallery he looked to be intensely focused.

Today's session was a "third reading" on the floor. Which meant that bill AB-1987, authored by Dalton and narrowly having made it out of his own Committee on Veterans Affairs, now needed an assembly majority to send it to the California State Senate, where the process would repeat. Should AB-1987 pass both houses of the legislature, it would be sent to the governor to sign, veto, or allow to pass into law unsigned.

I'd read the bill in my hotel room the previous night: "Increased Funding for Veterans' Home Mortgage Programs, Counseling, and CalVet Scholarships." It carried a massive price tag.

Then I'd read the Sacramento, San Francisco, Los Angeles, and San Diego newspaper analyses of AB-1987, and downloaded a collection of TV and radio pieces—including one of our governor—opining on the bill. AB-1987 wasn't a front-page or top-of-the-hour story. But the consensus: "taxpayer dollars could be used in smarter ways. Health care industry and bankers may rejoice, but Vets deserve better." Only the *Union-Tribune*, Fox News outlets, and conservative talk-radio stations were in favor.

So it looked to be tough sledding today for Dalton and the rest of us needy warriors. Not only did Democrats outnumber Republicans sixty-two to twenty, they had a much cheaper bill coming up through another committee. And of course, Dalton Strait himself—one of the most conservative members of the assembly—was a thorn in the side of the legislature's supermajority. As such, he was clear in the sights of the California Democratic Party, as represented by Ammna Safar.

After the roll call, prayers, and previous day's journal was read, Dalton had the floor. He had taken off his coat and now stood with a microphone in his hand. His shirt was crisp but his hair looked shaped by the pillow.

"We are here today to decide the future of AB-1987. This bill will give much needed help to our veterans who have served bravely and selflessly around the world. The price of America's greatness is high and no one has paid a greater share of it than our men and women in combat. It is dangerous, bloody, and sometimes lethal work. Life and friends are lost. I know."

Strait's voice was deep and I heard a slur far back in it. Exhaustion? Or something to fight off exhaustion? He seemed oddly detached from this proceeding, as if he was talking mainly to himself.

"It is clear to me that my fellow armed services veterans are in great need of help. I see them almost every day. Our suicide rates are up. Our instances of untreated PTSD are unacceptable. Our dependence on opioid painkillers has skyrocketed to the point where none are available at our VA hospitals for men and women who sorely need them. *Sorely*." He shook his head. "That's an understatement. Our limbs are missing and our minds find no rest and our families are damaged—sometimes beyond repair. Some have no homes. That is shameful. There can be no partisan divide on this issue.

"The great State of California has been generous with our military, but not generous enough. My bill will bring additional millions to the table. For housing, better medical care, and education. These veterans want out of the past. They want to heal their wounds and create new lives from the destruction that they have nobly endured. They want to wake up and see the day as new. Far from the past. The very least we can do is help to make them whole again. Put your fingers on those Yes buttons, people. Do the right thing this time."

A collective groan and shuffle of the members on the floor, then the Speaker rose and the sergeant-at-arms called for order.

"Thank you, Mr. Strait," said the Speaker. "But not so fast. As is our custom, we'll no doubt have some questions and comments on this bold attempt at lawmaking."

For the next hour, Dalton Strait's bipartisans railed against, defended, and questioned his bill. The attack was heavy: "We'd be remiss to pass along this extravagant bill . . . It is tantamount to throwing away taxpayer money for programs that are already working well . . . double-dipping . . . reasonable adjustments . . . smarter ways to address these problems of our veterans, Mr. Strait . . . can't vote for this as written . . . Mr. Strait, can you trim down the excessive dollars here?"

Unless there were forty-two silent aye voters amid the negative vocal majority, it looked like AB-1987 was nearing the end of its run.

I watched Dalton as he listened. For a while he sat still, resting on his elbow, his big frame draped over his desk. Then he sat back, slid down in his seat a little, and crossed his arms. Maybe bored. Maybe disgusted.

The vote went along party lines—twenty Republicans in favor and sixty-two Democrats against—not quite the end of the story. It was now Dalton's option to seek reconsideration and another vote.

He stood again, took a deep breath, and gave a rambling recap. Talked about the vets sleeping on the sidewalks in our cities, hungry and cold and hopeless. Said how fast even the lucky ones could spiral down. Talked about how easy it was to just give up, especially when you looked around and saw not one person who knew what you'd been through and what it was like to come home to nothing. Said if anything, the bill wasn't big enough. Money, money, money, he said. That's what it's all about.

There was a long silence in the chamber when Dalton was finished. Seemed like the assembly members didn't want to move. But the vote was the same, sixty-two against and twenty in favor of AB-1987, six months authored and steered through committee by Dalton Strait, now burning in lopsided flames on the assembly floor.

=====

Dalton and I sat deep in the Butcher's Block, far from the windows and the May sunshine. A late lunch on the way, bottles of Drake's 1500 Pale Ale and one-ounce pours of WhistlePig twelve-year-old rye whiskey on the table before us. Shortly after sitting down, we had gotten onto sports, the usual for us San Diego guys: odds of the

Chargers coming back to town, Padres, Phil Mickelson, Aztec basketball.

Now he tapped his half-empty whiskey glass on the table and caught the waitress's eye.

"I knew they'd shoot it down," he said. "It's pro forma at this point. But I like watching them stumble over their own feet, trying to find ways to make sense. Now you watch, the Dems' version of the same thing will come along, watered down and budget minded, and it will stand a good chance."

"Riding your wake," I said.

He shrugged, opening his hands in helplessness. "Off with their heads."

"Now, Dalton," said the waitress, setting forth fresh whiskeys. "You be nice and play fair."

"And what will that get me in this town?"

"A smile from your server."

"Oh, Betsy, I shall be nice and play fair."

"Happy hour menus?"

"But of course!"

Time flies when you're in good company, have drinks courtesy of your state assemblyman, and he has invited you to dinner at his favorite Capitol-close restaurant. Hailing the cab with a hearty wave, Dalton didn't look like a man who was in debt more money than he made in a year. And would have been much deeper had he and his wife not apparently been spending campaign dollars given to him by the People.

I wasn't exactly sure what he looked like.

TWELVE

Two pharma lobbyists—McKenzie and Augusta—joined us for dinner at Frank Fat's. Dalton ordered Leopold's Navy Strength martinis all around. I sipped mine as Dalton performed highlights from his reading of AB-1987, mostly impressions of the bill's detractors. One round of martinis became two, then we ordered and braced ourselves for a Chinese feast.

McKenzie Doyle was an elegant Newport Beach blonde, bare shouldered and athletic. She'd played tennis at UCLA until tearing an ACL in a tournament final. Went on to an economics degree and an internship with the pharmaceutical company that made the painkillers that got her through the knee blowout. Augusta Bennett was actually from Augusta, a curvy brunette in a business suit, and a smile that could set off a fire alarm. She was a scuba diver and a recreational pilot like myself, and we quickly got into all that. I noted no engagement or wedding rings, and an easy banter between them that suggested friendship.

Their tone with Dalton was both earnest and light; they refused to let him denigrate himself for the futility of trying to ram AB-1987 past an assembly packed with foes. Their own company certainly had a stake in funding hikes for veterans' medical care, but they never referred to anything of the kind. I knew that Asclepia Pharmaceutical of Irvine, California, had taken one of their recent cancer treatments off the market and suffered a drubbing on Wall Street. And had just come to market with a third-generation opioid painkiller. I also knew that Asclepia was lobbying lawmakers to defeat a "pay for delay" bill, which would prevent pharmaceutical giants from paying competitors not to make cheaper generics, thus keeping their prices higher.

After dinner we walked down to Pelleriti's, an assembly hangout for decades. Brick, black leather, and tasseled lampshades, the old West meets Chicago speakeasy. A dining room up front and a softly lit bar in back. Surprisingly busy for a Monday night. Dalton weaved to one table with his awkward gait, high-fived one of the Republican assemblymen I recognized from the reading and another Republican I recognized as the minority leader. Passed a table of apparent Democrats, then suddenly spun and gave them a cross of his index fingers, as if they were vampires.

I opted out of a round of Jagermeisters, sensing practical limits and more alcohol to come. The women seemed light and unaffected, but Dalton's slur was back and his eyelids had gained a little weight. But the distilled spirits had lifted his animal spirits, and he told us war stories with frank, self-deprecating minimalism. He presented them considerately for the noncombatants, too, with just enough suggested brutality to keep them uncomfortable. By now I'd noted that there was something extra between Dalton and McKenzie, a subtle tuning to each other. And that I had a small majority of Augusta's attention.

The conversation naturally arrived at the moment's biggest political story: the two mail bombs directed to two Southern California elected officials in less than a week. With more and more powerful bombs promised soon.

"The Chaos Committee is the most dangerous terrorist organization in the United States," said Dalton.

"Unless the committee is one crazy loner like the guy in Florida," said McKenzie.

"Either way," said Augusta, "innocent people are being maimed, and the fear is growing. What do you think, Roland?"

"A loner will be harder to catch but a group can do damage faster," I said.

"Do you think Sacramento may be next?" asked Augusta. "It follows."

"I don't think he's done down south," I said. "It's a gut feeling, nothing else."

"Well hunched," said Dalton. "And I could use another drink."

Thus, Delord Bas Armagnac 25 Year from France and

decaf. Followed by sherry for the women and for Dalton a pint of Guinness Stout and a double Glenfarclas 21 Year Old single malt. And another whopping bill for Asclepia Pharmaceutical.

Of course, a pit stop before departure. I joined Dalton at the sinks and mirrors, saw him tapping a small brown bottle into his hand. Palmed a couple of white round pills and slurped them down with faucet water. A slight sway as he recapped the bottle and put it in a coat pocket, and a not fully focused stare at me in the mirror.

"Stump still aches like a motherfucker."

"I'll bet."

"My pecker took a hit, too. Still functional but blemished. I'm a tad shy about that sometimes."

I nodded.

"This political shit is a lot less fun than it looks, Roland."

"I couldn't do it."

His not-quite-right eyes lingered on me from the mirror. "You'd be good at it. You know when to say no. Me? I feel like I'm falling down a black tunnel. I think of Natalie being abducted and the spiral starts up and tries to suck me down. So I kill all pain and make it worse."

We taxied to the Capitol building and the three of us walked Dalton to his office.

He swung open the door and turned on a light and we crowded in. It was small, nicely furnished, with a large desk overcrowded with a computer and peripherals and another, more elaborate, noisy fan-cooled computer and a twinkling red LED keyboard I recognized as a gamer's machine. Counter, sink, microwave. A washcloth folded neatly over the bend of the faucet and two face towels over the counter edge. A foldout couch had sheets, an unzipped sleeping bag, and two pillows on it.

We said our good nights to Dalton, who hugged each of us a little clumsily, and I watched for a telltale moment between him and McKenzie but saw none. He had already gone to his gaming station when I closed the door. Back outside we found Augusta's car waiting.

"I'm going to walk the city," I said. "You're both invited."

McKenzie demurred and got into the car; Augusta handed me a business card. "In case you'd like to investigate me sometime," she said.

"I'd like that very much."

I watched the car roll away toward Governor's Drive, then went back inside the building behind a political-looking man who eyed me hard, planting my face in memory.

"You were with Strait tonight," he said.

"He represents me."

He nodded knowingly but I wasn't sure what he thought he knew.

Past Dalton's office I found a good hallway corner where I could skulk and view the comings and goings. I wasn't expecting Dalton to answer the bell and come bouncing out for round ten, but maybe. I wasn't expecting McKenzie to come back but I thought it certainly possible. Less so Augusta, whose card I idly fingered in the pocket of my suit coat. Life is waiting.

Ten minutes later came Dalton's sister, Tola, hogging the middle of the hallway, red hair dangling under a Zorro hat, and a calf-length chartreuse satin duster swaying. Swiped herself into her brother's office with a key card and let the door slam shut.

I did a cost/benefit analysis of waiting. Decided on an hour. If she left soon, that was one thing. If she stayed inside with him much longer, or all night, well, maybe that was another.

Twenty minutes later they came out, Dalton snugging down his necktie, his hair damp and freshly brushed, talking energetically about something, limping hurriedly, his sister half a step ahead of him heading back toward the exit.

I tailed them through the unfamiliar old building as best I could, navigating mostly by the sounds of their steps and voices, hoping not to run into them in some quirky roundabout or dead-end elevator bank. They took the stairs, easy pickings for me. I followed them outside undetected and used a stately sycamore tree for cover as I watched them hail a taxi. I did, too, and all three of us landed at the Shady Lady, R Street at Fourteenth, at roughly the same time.

I dawdled with my cash, counting it three times but mainly watching the Strait siblings as they went inside. Finally paid up, got out and took up a position across R. Got my Canon out of my coat pocket just in case, and fired it up. The G9, my miniature friend, about the size of a pack of smokes, with a 28-84mm lens.

An hour later, just before two a.m., Dalton, Tola, and

two older gentlemen came out and headed north on Fourteenth toward the Capitol. I gave them a lead before crossing R. Fourteenth is a classic tree-lined Sacramento street; the night was breezeless and still. Even at this distance I could see that the foursome's mood was subdued, their voices soft and their words lost. Tola's dramatic hat hung on its strap over her back. They stopped under a streetlamp and one of the older men lit up a cigar. I took cover behind a grand old elm tree and shot away.

Through the zoom lens I got better looks at the Straits' after-hours company. I didn't recognize Cigar Man. He looked to be mid-sixties, with a shaven head and enough of a belly to hold in. I knew the other by his craggy face and silver crown of hair and his accidental interruption of Lark and me in the FBI conference room. Tola hung an arm over his shoulder in a gesture of easy affection.

An hour later in my hotel room I tapped into the IvarDuggans facial recognition feature, using Cigar Man's nicely captured mug from my Canon. The program can be used on one image at a time, for a small fortune, payable up front. It's less than reliable but more than a long shot. So I paid up.

I doubt that the program would have identified a common criminal or innocent citizen, but it had no trouble with this guy: "Heath Overdale, 68, chief operating officer for Kimmel, Overdale & Schmitz, a consulting firm specializing in freight and direct-delivery companies." They listed two big national accounts and a roster of smaller shippers and start-ups as clients. Kimmel, Overdale & Schmitz specialized in "targeted" public relations, and "result-directed lobbying" at the federal, state, and all local levels.

I sat for a while looking out at the dark, uneasy with the facts as I knew them in the disappearance of Natalie Strait, wife and mom and car seller and reelection campaign manager. Gambler, shopper, and a sufferer of bipolar disorder.

But it wasn't Natalie who was making me uneasy. It was Dalton. The way all roads were leading me to him. The way her life seemed to be less a storm of her own making than a portion of Dalton's. No wonder she wanted to move the family to Virgil Strait's compound near Jacumba. It seemed like a matter of moments until their finances caught up with them. Not just the gambling debt and credit card charges. How about the $280,514 in campaign donations they had apparently conspired to use against gaming debts? *These are felonies, Your Honor, and easy to document.* I supposed Dalton's real goal was to get himself reelected first, then deal with all that later.

What kind of man was I really dealing with?

In the grainy first light of morning I drove to the airport and got *Hall Pass II* ready for flight. Made arrangements by phone to fly into the Borrego Valley Airport, planning to drop in on Harris Broadman, innkeeper, and the man whom Dalton pulled from the burning Humvee in Fallujah, 2004.

THIRTEEN

Borrego Valley Airport is a small flat patch of ground surrounded by desert. A few low buildings, one of them a restaurant, one a fueling station, and some hangars for rent. I taxied off the rough asphalt runway, *Hall Pass II*'s engine grumbling as if disappointed to be back on earth again so soon after leaving Sacramento.

For a moment I stood in the shade of the restaurant. It was already 91 degrees, and not quite noon. The airport and the town of Borrego Springs are surrounded by Anza-Borrego Desert State Park, the largest in the state and one of California's wildest places—mountain lions, bighorn sheep, abundant reptiles, birds, eye-popping wildflowers, and desert-dwelling arachnids, including scorpions. Virgil Strait probably spent his vacations here. From my shade I looked out at the wide horizon, pale mountains rising west and east, a green splash of distant palms against them, a wash of orange wildflowers on white sand.

My rental car was waiting and the Bighorn Motel was easy to find. It was old enough to qualify as old-fashioned but not quite old enough to be desirably retro. Which meant a three-sided horseshoe of separate bungalows built around a central swimming pool and the parking spots. The sun-faded sign was pocked by rust.

The hillside behind the motel was scarred by mounds of mine tailings and open pits blockaded by rusty chain link, and dotted with homes built into the boulders. Homes of rock and wood, recessed against the elements. If it wasn't for the sun on the window glass I might not have known what I was looking at, so well did the buildings match the hills.

The hum of air conditioners greeted me when I got out of the car. It was near the end of the wildflower season, but the motel looked busy. Kids and young parents in the pool. Desert all around. Isolated homes in the shimmering distance.

The office was a squat stucco block with a canvas awning over a recessed entryway. There were blinds behind the glass front door and the windows, and an intercom built into the alcove wall. A small camera was recessed into the upper left corner of the entryway. The office door was locked.

A young man stood in the entryway, curtly talking to the box. He was having trouble with his A/C and wanted some help, like now. A woman's voice asked for his room number, and said that maintenance would be there soon.

"Great day for the A/C to fail," he said on his way past me.

I pushed the Talk button, gave my name, and asked to see Mr. Broadman.

"I'm sorry, he's not available at this time."

"May I come in?"

"Why?"

"I have something important to discuss with him."

"He's not available. At this time."

"I was in the war with him. I'd like to leave him my name and numbers."

"Just put a business card in the mail slot. It's the way we do it."

"No, it's not the way I do it. I told you this was important. Please open the door."

I held my PI license up toward the little camera. Legally, of course, it gives me no powers whatsoever, but not everybody knows this. It looks intimidating to some.

I heard another voice from inside, a man's voice, but I couldn't make out the words.

"I suppose that is okay," she said.

The power dead bolt clanged open and I went in. The lobby was cool but poorly lit. Small, nowhere to sit, just a high counter on which a variety of desert-activities brochures stood tilted up in a box. A small calendar in a stand and a dish of plastic-wrapped mints. Behind the counter was a door, closed, and a large windowed cabinet featuring desert animals preserved by taxidermy and arranged with care: a tiny owl, a small fox, a bobcat, a covey of Gambel's quail—mom, dad, young.

The desk clerk was a young woman in her mid-twenties, with tired brown eyes and thinning white hair. Her dress was tan, cut loosely like a smock. She wore a mini-mic clipped to one shoulder strap. Her name plate said Cassy. She looked like people I'd known who were undergoing chemotherapy. Pale, braced, and accepting. She said that Mr. Broadman wasn't in, and there were no rooms available.

She stepped back into an inner shadow and the man's voice I'd heard a moment ago came through a speaker over the closed door behind Cassy. Above the speaker was another camera, aimed right at me.

"How can I help you, Mr. Ford?" His voice was soft and unhurried.

"I'm a PI working with Assemblyman Dalton Strait. I'd appreciate just a few minutes of your time."

"Are you affiliated with any media or news organization, traditional or online?"

"I am not."

"Please give me a few minutes to prepare. Make yourself comfortable, Mr. Ford. Cassy, you may offer him a cold water."

She bent to a mini-refrigerator and set a plastic bottle on the counter.

"Thanks, Cassy. Exactly how does someone get comfortable here?"

"It's just an expression."

"I see the motel is full, or almost."

"Wildflowers. They're mostly gone by now, but . . . excuse me."

She turned and went through the door behind her, closing it firmly. But not before I glimpsed the room beyond: a slant of sunlight through cracked blinds, a plaid stuffed chair with a coffee table in front of it, and an IV drip station waiting in a corner behind them.

I shot an annoyed look to the camera over the closed door. Sipped the water and riffled the tops of the Anza-Borrego brochures. I'd hiked in the park but never seen a bighorn sheep in the wild. A long few minutes went by. Strange being watched but maybe not watched. Better when you know.

"Mr. Ford, I'm sorry for the wait. Please exit the lobby and go right to bungalow six, at the end of the first row. The door is open."

I took another look at Cassy's closed door, then pushed outside, blinds banging on the glass. Took my time to room six. A maintenance man with a big red toolbox waited outside room twelve. Gave me a nod.

Six was cracked open and I knocked.

The same soft, patient voice: "Come in."

FOURTEEN

Inside was dark at first, even with the rush of sunlight following through the open door behind me. I closed it on a living room, indeterminately furnished, and a man sitting at one end of a short-legged, turquoise mid-century modern sofa.

"Please take the chair in front of me," he said.

"Thank you." I pulled the folding chair away from a wide, low coffee table and sat.

In the growing light I looked directly at Harris Broadman. Face shaded by a plain white ball cap, bill tugged down low. Aviator sunglasses. A crisp white dress shirt buttoned at the collar and cuffs. White pants, white canvas slip-ons, white socks. White tufts of hair below the cap.

"I'm sorry I have nothing to offer you," he said.

"You've already been generous," I said.

"Delete all pity."

The room materialized around me: one wall of bookshelves neatly stocked, a TV in one corner facing a recliner, identically adjusted blinds on windows looking over the parking lot and pool, framed photographs on the walls.

"How is Dalton?" he asked. As through the intercom, his voice was calm and soft, as if coming from a longer distance than this.

"He's running for reelection against some big money. More than he's got to spend, anyway. He's working hard, anxious."

"He was a worrier," said Harris.

"He tries not to let it show," I said.

Harris seemed to think about this. His expression was impossible to read behind the dark sunglasses and the steep bill of the ball cap. In the shuttered half-light the flesh coiled and rose on his cheeks, records of fire and surgeries. Incomplete nose and lips, like features that had never matured.

I had no idea.

"I haven't talked with Dalton since the war," said Harris. "But how exactly can I help?"

I told him about Natalie Strait's disappearance, the sheriffs recovering her car.

"He's hired you to find her?"

"That's correct."

"And you are a licensed private investigator?"

I nodded.

"Do you suspect Dalton is responsible?"

"Should I?"

"I'm not qualified to say. I know little of Dalton except what happened sixteen years ago in Iraq. I know nothing of his wife except what you've told me. I can't help but think you've wasted your time coming all the way out here."

"I want to know how he behaved that day. When your Humvee hit the IED. That may tell me more about Dalton Strait than he's told me himself. More than his campaign flyers and billboards on I-15."

A long, air-conditioned pause. I could tell that Broadman was considering my request.

"I was in Fallujah, too, when that happened," I said. "On foot patrol in the Jolan. House-to-house three-stacks. I think you were just east, in East Manhattan."

"Do you think about it a lot?" he asked.

"Sure. But now, sometimes, a few days will go by . . ."

Broadman issued a soft grunt that I interpreted as a very dry chuckle.

"I think about it a lot, too," he said. "Every day. I admire people like you, who can forget. Or almost forget. Do you use alcohol or drugs?"

"I drink. Only occasionally to excess."

"I drank rivers of vodka and ate pills by the handful. Then one night an overdose, touch-and-go in the hospital for a few days. But the skies cleared. A terrific doctor. She got me through. I haven't touched any kind of painkiller in five years. Except aspirin when my face heats up."

"I admire that."

"Delete the pity, Mr. Ford," said Harris in his soft, slow voice. "I asked you once."

I could have explained I meant no pity at all in my admiration but that would have been a small truth within a larger lie: I did pity him and the world pitied him. No way to avoid it. But why should Harris endure it? Why shouldn't he live in a remote desert motel, unavailable and hidden?

"We had a run to make to Volturno," he said. "Uday's and Qusay's old palace."

"I remember it."

"We were actually on a humanitarian mission that day," said Harris. I heard the calm in his voice, its controlled emotion. "We had a transport truck full of food and medical supplies for the citizens we thought were friendlies. We were ordered to leave the supplies. None of the Iraqis would show up when we were there. Not even children. The imams would have them arrested or worse. You remember the saying: 'You deal with Americans, you die.'"

"I certainly do."

"Dalton and I were part of security. Terrible road. Insurgents thick in Fallujah by then—twenty-four different groups considered 'hard-core.' And of course even Saddam's enemies were starting to hate us. We'd been making lightning raids every day and there was always collateral damage, or so the Iraqis claimed.

"We had no trouble on the way in. We sat in that Humvee like a couple of nervous rats while the rations and first aid kits were loaded out. Dalton was always a little above things. Confident that he wasn't born to die or get blown up in this dirty little war. Beneath his calling. Looking back on it now, I think he was really, really afraid. I know I was. Our vehicle had just been up-armored with an add-on kit and some improvised stuff. Hillbilly armor. Which made it more prone to roll over. At any speed, that Humvee was a rollover waiting to happen."

Broadman stood and walked into the kitchen. I heard a refrigerator open and close. He was a slender man of average height. He moved slowly, the same way he spoke, with a hint of the spectral in the sunglasses, the tufts of white hair, the white cap, shirt, pants, and shoes. He carried himself with heavy deliberation, like a man much older than he was. Or, like a warrior wounded once and forever.

He came back, set a bottled water on the table in front of me, then sat again and twisted open one for himself. He picked up a remote from the sofa and pointed it to the front window. The blinds pivoted open slightly, allowing in more light.

"Pretty simple, really," he said. "They unloaded the boxes and we started back. We were point this time, not the rear guard. It's all about your eyes. You're looking for those roadside bombs hidden in anything that looks harmless and common—a ruined tire, a dead dog, a pile of trash, a blown-out vehicle that's not familiar. Anything not there before. The insurgent bomb makers were crafty. As you know, the bombs that worry you most are the ones you never see, the ones set off by cell phone, and that's what we hit. One of the big boys. Made by Rocket Man himself. You remember him?"

"Big news when we got him."

"We caught him at home, with a bomb schematic up on his computer screen. Anyway, they'd dug in the bomb after we'd passed through, dodging the patrols and the helos and the surveillance drones in broad daylight. Somehow. I used to think their Allah was a better god than ours, the way they could get away with things like that.

"The next thing the world blew up and I was upside-down. I saw the road through the windshield and I smelled the gas. Dalton had been blown out of the vehicle. His door was gone—armor and metal blown off at the hinges. A blessing, because the Humvee doors liked to lock up in a blast, trap you inside to be cooked. I couldn't get my restraint off. It was stuck and I had one shoulder dislocated and the other wrist fractured. They would not answer my will. I struggled in place, felt the gas on my legs. Prayed and screamed. The world went *whump* and the Humvee shivered, then Dalton was back inside but he couldn't get the damned strap off, either, because the latch had melted. He started sawing away at the restraint with his utility knife. The vehicle was fully engaged. Fire roaring around me. Like a pyre. Dalton kept crawling back outside for breath, then back in to help me. His hair was scorched wiry black. I remember that. Finally he just collapsed my bad shoulder all the way and pulled me outside into the dirt. I rolled around to put the flames out. Rolled over and dug my face into that filthy sand. I heard the sniper fire but I couldn't get my legs under me. Thought my nerves might have been ruined. Dalton ran to some K-rails for cover. I saw him when I was on my back. I was twisting like a dog to put that fire out, and he was upside down in my vision, running for the K-rails to safety. I felt abandoned. I knew it was just a matter of time until the snipers shot me or I burned up."

I imagined big, confident, above-it-all Dalton Strait proned out behind the big concrete barriers most people call K-rails. He'd gotten Harris out of the burning vehicle but no farther. Then barreled perilously through the sniper fire to safety. Did that make him half a hero and half a coward?

"We got air support and the snipers were blown to dust," said Broadman. "The convoy circled us, got Dalton and me into one of the transport trucks, and away we went. The pain was out of this world. It changed my life. I remember the corpsman giving me a shot of morphine and he couldn't figure out why I was still awake and wailing. He hit me with another pen and the next thing I knew I was in Germany."

When he reached for his water, I saw Broadman's cabled face and neck caught in a faint slat of sunlight.

"How did the pain change your life?"

"It made me realize you can crave your life and hate it at the same time. It was the beginning of my idea that character is not fate. The proof of that idea came later, when Dalton received the Silver Star for saving my life."

"Did you oppose it?"

"I wanted him to get it. I was learning to embrace the life he'd given me while detesting the man I'd been changed into. This . . ." He set the water bottle on the coffee table and opened his empty hands as if presenting himself to me for inspection.

I realized in that moment that Dalton hated himself.

"Dalton could have been anyone," said Harris. "The least of my problems was who pulled me from the fire, and if he could have done better. Could I do better? I doubt it. A burning man under fire cannot always defeat a military-grade body restraint that's been soldered shut by an explosion."

"So your fate was not your character? And Dalton's fate was not his?"

"Far from it. That is the brutal truth of life. Clearly exposed by war."

I thought of Dalton's eventual fate in Fallujah, the IED that blew his leg off just days after his act of "heroism." I recalled Jim Young's assessment of Dalton's later patrol behavior "went all the way to risky." I wondered if that was purposeful: atonement. What was Dalton's true character? Was it pulling Broadman from the Humvee, or abandoning Broadman in order to preserve his own life, or recklessly leading himself into the hidden bomb that took half his leg?

"What do you know about the missing wife?" Broadman asked.

"They were high school sweethearts," I said. "Married after graduation. Two sons. She's been gone since last Tuesday."

I told him about Natalie Strait's breakdown fourteen months ago, her gambling and spending enthusiasms, and I suggested that the Strait finances were possibly under strain. He used the remote on the blinds again, this time to close them tighter. I wondered at the agony of living with burned eyes in a bright desert. And more to the point, why Broadman had settled here.

"Do you suspect another psychological break?" he asked.

"I suspect abduction."

"Quite different from a runaway wife on a bender."

"Quite different."

"I've donated to Dalton's campaigns over the years," he said. "Modestly. He doesn't stand for my politics, but he's a brother and he saved some of my life."

"But no contact with him, since Fallujah?"

"None. Some memories you don't want to see, face-to-face." Again, his dry chuckle.

"What are your politics, Mr. Broadman?"

"I have none," said Harris. "It's liberating. It frees one up to begin at the beginning."

"The beginning of what?"

"All things."

Another moment of air-conditioned quiet. Broadman sat still, hands on his knees, a white apparition with a voice.

Then he slowly reached up and took the sunglasses off. Dark brown eyes in a face that looked like a heated thing, still melting.

"What did you bring home from the war, Mr. Ford?"

"I left as much as I could over there."

"But something always follows you back. It doesn't have to be a ruined face or a blown-off leg."

I nodded. And remembered the Jolan. Close and hot and just beginning to boil with hate. Door-to-door searches. All of us eager to find the Blackwater killers, and all of Fallujah turning against us, like a tide rising by the hour. Outside a small home, one of thousands, the smell of lamb and coriander and cumin. Interior dark, always dark. Sudden movement, face-close fire, muzzle flash, air thick with lead and gunpowder and screams. Brennan down. Avalos down in the doorway. By the time I got back to him, Avalos was still where he had fallen, floating in blood. It seemed to take us forever to shoot those insurgents. Forever to drag Avalos back inside, out of sniper sight. Forever to get his helmet off and pack the hole in his face with a roll of QuikClot, twelve feet of medicated gauze and even that couldn't fill the gushing space. He was staring at me with his one good eye when that eye fogged over and his body went still.

"I lost Avalos," I said. "A good man. We entered a dwelling and we met heavy fire."

"You lost him?"

"He was lost," I said. "And I was there. I replay those minutes sometimes. Fairly often."

"You replay it, looking for what you did wrong," said Broadman.

"Correct."

"If you don't find anything at first, you keep trying until you do. And when you find it, you play it again and again and again. The smallest thing. Something new, or something invented?"

"That's the method," I said.

"You torture yourself with a changeable truth."

I took a deep breath, shifted in my chair. "I would like there to be an answer. As to whether or not I am at fault."

"And to why it took you so long to do things."

"Yes," I said. I could feel my heart beating against my shirt. "Was I slowed down by fear? Was I afraid of what I would find? I heard that round hit him. It's an unmistakable sound. As you know. Even in all that chaos I heard it and in the periphery of my vision I saw him fall. I was that close to him."

I listened to the air conditioner hum in the half-light. Saw through the blinds the fractured images of children jumping into the swimming pool.

"Which leads you to the curse of the living," said Broadman.

"Why him and not me?"

"It should be embossed on our motto, right beside *Semper Fi.*"

"Sometimes I thank Avalos," I said. "Sometimes, he won't accept."

"In the dreams and nightmares."

"Sure. Less now."

"We're the lucky ones," said Broadman. "We have managed to move forward. Of course, we can't call ourselves lucky. That leads us back to the curse."

I offered him a somewhat formal nod.

"Please give my best wishes to Dalton," he said. "Tell him I bear no grudge for what he did. Or didn't do."

———

I sat in a bar called the Quetzal, just off of Christmas Circle in town. Ordered a double bourbon and knew there could easily be more. Drink up, get a room, fly home in the morning. I looked at that drink for a good long while before taking the first sip. When I took it, the bourbon was all there for me: strength, confidence, luck. There was a mirror behind the bar that aimed my face back. I raised the glass and sipped again. The TV volume was off as the news stars crowed from their red, white, and blue sets. I was glad for the silence.

Especially glad when Dalton's smiling image appeared beside that of head-scarfed Ammna Safar, then video of Dalton waving a fistful of papers at a group of supporters in what looked like a pizza parlor. The caption strip: "Campaigning California Assemblyman Dalton Strait of San Diego says his opponent Ammna Safar 'almost certainly' has blood relatives among Islamic State fighters in Syria, and is unfit to represent his 82nd district . . . Safar, who was born in the United States, denies the claim and has promised to file suit against Strait for defamation and slander . . ."

I wasn't sure if I wanted Dalton to be lying or telling the truth. Either way, after my talk with Harris Broadman, what could I possibly make of Dalton Strait?

As the bourbon spread through me, things began to expand. I smelled the wood smoke again from that day, the lamb and the cumin. I thought of Dalton and Broadman and Avalos, and the net of the war that had snagged us all. And the millions more. The Five. I tried hard to put us in perspective, cast us all as blips of light in the universe. But I couldn't. We're forced to see ourselves as the center of life. Because we have only one self with which to experience it. Just me. Just once. Just now.

I glanced back up into the reflected snout of Roland Ford, PI, and thought, *One foot in front of the other, man. You're okay. You're okay.*

I sat almost an hour. I'm always surprised how far a mind can wander and find its way back, how many memories can pass through one slim hour of life. Harris Broadman left me a text saying he'd call if he thought of anything that might help me.

I left the rest of the bourbon in the glass. The bartender gave me a look and I shook my head, dug out my wallet, left a nice tip.

———

Halfway to Borrego Valley Airport I got a phone picture and a brief message from FBI Special Agent Mike Lark:

> *Ramona FedEx security video of mail bomber. Return address bogus. Familiar?*

I pulled onto the road shoulder. My rental car shivered in the wind and a dirt devil spun its way through a meadow of past-their-prime wildflowers. The security video image was better than the earlier post office picture of the Fallbrook bomber. But not much. An average-build, dark-haired woman, hair loose and large Jackie O sunglasses. A plaid flannel shirt. The same in-a-hurry clench of jaw. Same woman. I'd bet on it.

I stared at her, letting the details sink in. Ten seconds later the picture and Lark's message vanished in a pixelated explosion.

FIFTEEN

The next morning, wanting to contact Kirby Strait, I was referred by Virgil to granddaughter Tola, who said that Kirby was "camping" on her property in the mountains near Palomar Observatory. She said that I was free to enter the property and told me a back way in, around the main gate that Kirby had elaborately padlocked. She said with a bright laugh that she'd order him not to shoot me.

"So much for Kirby's prison rehab," I said.

"Yep. And by the way, my previous invite to you comes with a twenty percent first-timer's discount at any Nectar Barn. I need to be present, though, so call ahead. You don't get the discount without enduring me."

Now Kirby Strait, six months fresh from the California State Prison in Corcoran, eyed me with clear reptile eyes and an engaging smile. Swim trunks and a knife sheath clipped to the waistband. He was lanky and tall and freckled, all prison yard muscle under a lopsided pompadour of red hair.

"I didn't do it," he said, standing in front of his tent.

The tent was an enormous rope-and-pole construction, certainly military surplus. A four-wheeler, an Indian motorcycle, and a pickup truck were parked along the shady side. A scoped long gun leaned against an oak sapling near the entrance.

"Kirbs?" asked a voice within.

"I heard about Natalie," said Kirby. "Bad news, peckerwood. You help me get some water, I'll talk to you. Because Tola told me I should."

He put on flip-flops and a work shirt, pointed to an array of mismatched plastic buckets in the shade of the huge tent. Near the buckets was a two-hundred-gallon cistern with a spigot and garden hose at the bottom, sitting on sawhorses. We each took two buckets and Kirby led us down a game trail to a swale of willows through which a small stream gurgled.

"Itty-bitty trout in this stream, if you can believe that," he said. "I catch 'em with a plastic colander and fry them up."

"Have you seen Natalie since you got out?" I asked.

He let the current fill one of his buckets, drew it up by the handle and set it on a flat rock. Took up the next.

"I haven't seen Natalie in twenty-five years, except on TV," he called back over his shoulder. "In spite of what

Virgil might think. He overestimates the wickedness in almost everyone's heart. Certainly mine."

"You have some history with her."

"Virgil tell you about that, too? Or Dalton?"

"Neither one. I'm a PI so I privately investigate."

"Well, ain't that quaint. I've run across your type in court. Funnier than cops, dumber than lawyers. Know-it-all little bastards."

"I stand six-three."

He looked back at me and shook his head.

"I found out that you and Dalton fought over Natalie way back when you were teenagers," I said. "Fairly serious. A concussion and stitches for Dalton. And later, a baseball bat and grandpa's hospital for you."

"Maybe Dalton bashed her over the head and dumped her," said Kirby. He rose from the streamside, set his sloshing bucket near the first. Dug a smoke and lighter from his shirt pocket.

I filled my buckets and found a place to set them down, my ribs still sore from last year's bout against six security men.

"Why would he do that?" I asked.

"Naw, he wouldn't. I can't think of a why. Dalton and Natalie always stuck things out together. As weak and gutless as Dalton always was. No matter how widely he spread his thankless seed. You couldn't get a pry bar between them."

I thought a moment about that. "You're my age," I said. "Married twice from what I learned."

"You circle like a lawyer."

"Just wondering if you could carry a torch for Natalie after twenty-five-plus years."

He smiled and picked up his buckets, his pompadour swaying in the breeze. "You cannot know the frozen cold in this man's heart. I was a kid when I tried to kill Dalton over Natalie Galland. When that failed, I grew up and said farewell to both of them."

"And haven't seen her since?"

"I made it clear the first time you asked."

We lugged the heavy buckets back to the tent, took turns upending them into the cistern, then headed back to the creek for another round.

"Ford, the thing about Natalie is she's a man magnet. She's pretty and smart and funny and she has that other thing. The extra thing. The thing that makes you want to stand next to her. Be in the same room with her. Call it whatever you want but she's always had it. Always known it. Hooking up with Dalton was a way to control it. And she's always been just a little bit crazy, too. Which appeals to men such as myself. And Dalton."

"You haven't seen him in twenty-five years, either?"

"When he came home the hero and all blown up I saw him at the VA a couple of times. I felt sorry for him. But he was always a spoiled little wretch."

"So he got what he deserved?"

"Looks that way to me."

I loaded my buckets with the cold, clear water. Chased out a small trout from his beat alongside a rock. Tried to balance out Harris Broadman's idea that even in war, character isn't fate, with Kirby Strait's notion that you get what's coming according to who you are.

I set the buckets down and Kirby waded in. "Do you hate him?" I asked.

"Not hate. Disrespect. He was always the favored. Always the baby. Always the privileged. Got the looks and the easy charm. Strong enough to finally whup my ass when he was sixteen. And did so. We're Jacob and Esau, except I don't think God can stand either one of us."

"There's this," I said.

When Kirby came ashore with his two dripping buckets, I showed him the picture that Natalie's sister, Ash, had recently taken with her phone, in which a proudly smiling Kirby Strait stood with one arm around his uneasy sister-in-law, Natalie.

"I was just out," he said. "Last Christmas. Family party."

"Slightly less than twenty-five years ago," I said.

Kirby gave me a nonchalant shrug. "Forgot about that one."

"Any others you forgot?"

"I might have kept up with Natalie a little more than I first let on."

"Privately?"

"I wish. She hasn't given me a real smile since 1995. Before the slam, every once in a while, I'd make up some kind of excuse to be where she was. Just to get a look and a word with her. That's funny, isn't it?"

"Not if it made you mad."

"I was never mad at Nats for one second."

Nats, I thought—Dalton's nickname for her, too. "Mad at Dalton?"

"Enough to hurt Natalie? Come on."

"You did try to kill him once."

"I was seventeen."

I let that hang.

"See? There you all go again—everyone looking out for poor Dalton—couldn't have been anything *he* would do. To me, the worst thing about him coming back crippled was I couldn't get a rematch. You can't kick a gimp's ass with a clean conscience. Especially when it's your brother—a spoiled little gimp like Dalton."

"When *did* you see Natalie last?"

"That picture. Christmas."

"Her car was found not far from here. Near the Tourmaline Casino."

"I didn't do it, just like I said. I've got an alibi and a damned good lawyer. And as of right now I've had enough of you."

We carried the water back up the rise toward the tent. When we cleared the willows I saw a young woman in shorts and a bikini top lying out in the grass on a beach towel. She took an elbow and shaded her eyes as we approached, dark hair falling.

"Charity, this is the famous PI Roland Ford."

"I just love Magnum."

"Lucky him," I said.

"Are you working a case, Mr. Roland?"

"I told you about Natalie," said Kirby. "That's what he's working."

"Any leads?" she asked.

"Everywhere I look."

"There's people in the trees that watch us, you know. Built into the bark. At night they turn into owls."

"Charity's a paranoid schizophrenic," said Kirby. "But in a good way."

She bounced up, threw a roundhouse punch that Kirby caught, folding her in close. "See you later, PI. I hope you find Natalie on some high-rolling bender in Vegas or Monte Carlo. Blowing all Dalton's money. In the company of some able gentleman who believes that she can do no wrong."

I purposely took a wrong turn on the steep two-track road leading out. More than curiosity, less than a hunch. Headed up mountain. Put my truck into four-wheel drive and steered around the ruts. The roads were furrowed deep by the winter rain. I found myself with no room to turn around so I kept going. Finally the road ended at a rise just flat enough to back into and reverse direction.

Before doing that, however, I took a moment to enjoy the view: six large greenhouses cut into the trees and arranged with the long sides of the structures facing west and east. Solar panels and generators. Pallets of soil and fertilizers. Growers call it a mixed-light facility—sun and man-made light—for rapid growth and high yields. Anything from orchids to cannabis.

I took my binoculars to the edge of the rise, glassed the greenhouses. Which was when the buzz of the drone reached me from the wild blue yonder. Scanning with the binoculars I found the crabby little thing in the middle distance, heading my way. I thought of the attack I'd survived last year, and how it had begun with a surveillance drone flying over me, like this one. And ended with six armed men who beat me half to death.

This time there were no quad-runners screaming across the desert toward me, just people approaching through the pine-and-oak forest growing high and dense on Tola Strait's property. Forty acres, she'd said, away from the light of the world, just like the observatory a few miles away.

They surrounded me. I held my arms out and opened my hands, slowly turning a full circle. A picturesque crew. Some with long guns, two with pistols on their hips. Two biker types, two Latinas with Sureño bandanas for scarves, a couple of California natives, and two outstandingly large Samoans. Eight in all.

One of the Samoans came close, dark eyes looking down on me from within his darkly mottled face. "ID," he said. His voice was a soft rumble.

I produced my license, which he read closely before handing it back.

"Everything down there is Indian owned," he said. "No county jurisdiction. No state. No federal. You are trespassing."

I showed him Tola Strait's Nectar Barn business card and his dark face contemplated it.

"She knows I'm here," I said. "I was talking to Kirby and got lost on my way out."

One of the women already had her cell phone out, staring at me as she held it to her ear.

"You better hope Tola's heard of you," said the big Samoan.

The Latina with the phone broke away from the group and walked to the edge of the trees. I could hear her voice but not her words.

"Cartel soldiers tried to take our plants last year," said the Samoan. "We killed two of them here, and Miss Tola made sure the rest got sent out of the country."

The Latina on the phone seemed to be listening more than talking now.

"Have you seen Natalie Strait lately?" If nothing else, I thought this question might disarm them.

"You just say nothing until we hear from Tola."

We stood in stubborn silence until the Latina on the phone was back. She addressed my interrogator.

"Tola says take him to the west gate and let him go."

They broke rank immediately.

"I'll miss each and every one of you," I said.

The younger of the Indians chose to ride with me, though I wasn't sure why. I was happy to be leaving, and in no mood to press my luck with these people, employees of Tola Strait or not.

The young Indian, Marcus, told me Tola was a great businesswoman and he was already making good money with her. He said she was the only Anglo they trusted in tribal business. He said the Nectar Barn was bringing in as much as a small casino, and much easier to operate. As I looked out at the mountains and rolling hills around me, I wondered where Tola's land ended and the tribal lands began.

The west fence was a stout construction of metal slats with a cheerless iron gate that stood open. Two greenhouse guards on horseback waited, with a third mount ready for my escort.

I put the truck into park, thanked Marcus for showing me the way out. He said I was welcome, and that a friend of Tola was a friend of his.

"Natalie Strait left her car out on the Pala res late that morning and got into a white Suburban," he said. "Two men with her. She looked afraid."

"What did the men look like?"

"One white. One black. Forties, maybe."

"How do you know this?"

"Indians all through there," said Marcus. "We talk."

I asked Marcus for his phone number and sent him a good picture of Dalton Strait.

"Ask your witness if this was the white guy," I said.

The picture chimed through to Marcus's phone and I watched him bring it up and study it.

"That's her husband," he said. "The politician. I'll ask my friends."

"This is important," I said. "I need this."

"Nice meeting you, PI Ford."

Ten minutes later Marcus texted me: "He doesn't think so. But he can't say for sure."

SIXTEEN

That evening I watched San Diego's *Local Live!* news out on the patio with the Irregulars, nursing one of Liz's "battle ready" manhattans. She substitutes amaro for the vermouth, claiming a thirty percent improvement in taste, though her husband, Dick, disputes the number. They've been married for forty-some years, and they live together on this property, though they rent the two casitas that are farthest apart. They drink freely, quarrel about everything, and spend almost every waking hour together. I used to think they were a poster couple for dysfunctional marriage, but now I'm not so sure.

Thanks to a generous former Irregular, the patio TV is not only flat and huge—seventy-five inches—but is modified to receive the densest of pixels and cleanest of sound. Almost wireless, and neat. Because of the TV's size, the newscasters on-screen are well-groomed giants, more detailed to us than we are to each other. The screen hangs from the western edge of the palapa canopy, so with some leaning or ducking you can peer under or around it to the pond, the oak savanna, the sky, sunset, or stars. We sit well back for our hour and a half of daily viewing. Mostly news; no regular entertainment, just occasional movies or prizefights. When the last person turns off the power, the TV tucks up under the waterproof palapa ceiling.

Local Live! led with Dalton Strait's bombshell claim that his opponent, Ammna Safar, was almost certainly related to IS fighters in Iraq, based on research done by the fledgling San Diego company HerediLink. The news anchor explained that HerediLink offered low-cost ancestry searches using DNA. A HerediLink spokeswoman admitted that her company was a Strait campaign donor. Then a brisk young Strait aide denied *directly* relating Ammna Safar to any specific Islamic State individual in Iraq—although many suspected IS fighters conceal their identities to protect blood relations in the United States. There were several "convincing" possibilities. He refused to reveal how samples of Safar's DNA were obtained. Which made me wonder.

Then a slightly blurry picture of a young girl and boy—eight or ten years old, by the looks of them— standing in a green field in soccer uniforms, grew into an epic portrait on our seventy-five-incher. An unshaven and wrinkle-shirted Dalton was next, saying that HerediLink had proven "genetically within ninety-nine percent" that the boy and girl were cousins and that the boy had very likely gone on to a life of terror in the Middle East, where records were poorly kept. The girl, of course, was Ammna Safar.

Frank sat to my left and Odile to my right, leaning forward to talk across me like I was furniture. Frank's mongrel, Triunfo, lay on the paver directly in front of us, giving me his full attention. A sleek black face with brown eyebrows and upright ears that flopped over up near the tips. He's taken an interest in me lately but I don't know why.

"Señorita Odile, did you see the future today?" asked Frank.

As a second-year illegal immigrant to the U.S., Frank worked hard to improve his English. I found him early the winter before last, living on the far reaches of the rancho, down in an arroyo, collecting water with a tarp, eating rabbits and quail he could snare. He was seventeen, skinny, and miserable. His father had been murdered in front of him and Francisco had fled his Salvadoran village under threat of death from MS-13. I honored the values of my nation by giving him asylum—a place to stay and a job. Which of course made me a criminal because Francisco Cuellar's asylum is not mine to grant.

"Well, I did observe parts of a client's future today," said Odile. "It's my job."

"Was a good future?"

"Frank, I've told you about psychic–client privilege."

"Yes, but I don't know this person."

Odile smiled and sipped her drink. Even sitting down at the communal picnic table, Odile is conspicuously tall.

She hunches sometimes, as lengthy women sometimes do. Catches herself and straightens. She has fair skin and rosy cheeks.

"She has three very good weeks to enjoy," said Odile. "A good job offer and no more car trouble."

"And then what?" asked Frank.

"You know I have a three-week maximum sensing the future. I'm trying to get stronger . . ."

Frank tapped his soft drink can on the table. "What kind of car does she have?"

"Come on," said Odile. "You know I won't give details like that. And Frank, you should pay attention to the TV now—something important is about to happen. Though I'm not sure what."

On the huge screen TV above me, the *Local Live!* studio anchors introduced their next feature.

"Ready to go ape in San Diego?" asked Dwayne Swift.

"All the way from the mountains of Congo!" said Jimena Callejas.

Then a cut to a *Local Live!* reporter at the San Diego Zoo with the newborn Belinda, a mountain gorilla. Although the size on-screen of an adult man, Belinda looked all baby, huddled deep and bright eyed in the arms of her Queen Kong mom.

"They ought to just leave them in the jungle, where they belong," said Dick.

"They're from the mountains, dearie. They look almost human."

"If you consider flinging your own feces at visitors human."

"You were a boy. You were taunting him."

Burt left the table, worked his phone from his pocket and walked toward the pond. A short-legged, top-heavy little man. The sun was setting, a showy orange ball dropping through gray clouds. I looked past Burt, out at the sun on the water and saw Justine in her rowboat and floppy hat, her fair arms on the oars, catching the rays all those years ago.

The *Local Live!* reporter, outfitted in hospital scrubs, paper cap, and sterile gloves, cradled Belinda in her arms as the camera zoomed in.

"Such a beautiful baby," she said. "Maybe she'll see her mountains someday! Back to you in the studio, Jimena and Dwayne."

Burt circled back to the table, setting up tomorrow's tee time, apparently.

Something went haywire on the *Local Live!* transmission, the big-screen picture in sudden free fall then fracturing into thick black bars like those in a slot machine. A roar of static, then silence and a fully black screen.

"Your cable sucks, Roland," said Dick. "Ought to rethink that satellite offer they keep making."

I could hear the "lazy landlord" tone in his voice. "I got satellite six months ago, Grandpa."

"This is much worse than a weak signal," said Odile. Her rosy cheeks had lost their color. Sitting bolt upright, she stared at the black screen, then closed her eyes altogether.

When order was restored in the *Local Live!* studio, three human figures wearing street clothes and hideous masks stood behind the news desk. On the left, a female wearing a disturbing Hannya mask from Japanese theater, in the middle a man behind a grotesque Iroquois tribal face, and on the right another male wearing a splatter mask from World War I. On the mega-screen they looked like players in a stage drama performed by giants.

On either side of them stood two black-clad, balaclava-hidden actors—one a man and one a woman—each pinning a *Local Live!* anchor facedown over the desk by the neck and holding a handgun to their respective heads. Jimena Callejas's hair had swept down over her face; Dwayne Swift was pale and bug-eyed with terror.

"God in heaven," whispered Liz.

"Sonsofbitches!" said Dick.

"No, no . . ." said Odile.

The middle figure, in the Iroquois mask—black haired, wild eyed, crazily baring his wide wooden teeth—raised a sheet of paper and began reading from it, voice lowered to doomsday bass by a voice changer.

"God in heaven," said Liz.

Burt and I commenced shooting with our cell phones.

"Allow us to introduce ourselves," said the Iroquois. A male voice, unrecognizable. "We are representatives of The Chaos Committee. You know what we have accomplished in the last week and a half. We wanted to give you a chance to meet us. Face-to-mask. Forgive our shyness but our anonymity is important."

It seemed as if all of Rancho de los Robles was holding its breath. I couldn't take my eyes off of him.

"The last week has only been our introduction, as we

have made clear. Injuring minor political slaves is not our goal. But now that you have seen us, we know that you'll be taking our devolution very seriously. We are serious because this is the nation we once loved and believed in and fought for in a thousand different ways. This is a nation born in chaos. Then destroyed by two centuries of greed, moral sloth, and the mass rape of nature. We must now return to chaos to be reborn. To reclaim our future. To devolve.

"Citizens, act with us. Lash out with fury! Destroy the masters in government—from city hall to the president. If you are an honest policeman, turn your guns on the wealthy who control you! If you are loyal military, bring us the heads of your officers! Death to the lockstep of parties and opinions. Only chaos can burn the weakness and corruption and greed out of this republic! Burn it brightly and completely. Compromise is surrender. Violence is victory. Chaos is God and God is Chaos."

Anchorman Dwayne Swift fainted, sliding down behind the desk as his ninja captor knelt out of camera beside him.

By now all of the Irregulars were standing and shooting with their phones.

Except Odile, who sat still as a statue, eyes wide. "Something worse is going to happen," she said. "I can't see it yet." She closed her eyes again and I could see her hands, clasped together and trembling on the picnic table.

"My brothers and sisters in arms," said the Iroquois Goliath. "As proof of our power and the power of our ideas, witness the Encinitas office of Representative Clark Nisson. Good night!"

The masks advanced on the cameras and the picture went spastic, then dark.

Burt stormed off toward the sunset, phone to his ear: calling Nisson's office, I presumed.

Odile stood, her eyes still wide and fixed on the television.

I changed the TV to the local PBS channel, which would be mid-broadcast with their nightly news hour.

And there she was, the familiar face from which we got our commercial-free San Diego weather. Another sunny spring day everywhere in the county, she said, then was suddenly cut off mid-sentence, replaced by the anchors at their desk, a man and woman of stolid professional calm and good cheer, now obviously distressed and trying not to show it.

"We have a confirmed report," said Rick Carpenter, reading off a teleprompter, "that a fiery explosion has rocked the Encinitas office of United States Representative Clark Nisson. We have no information on the cause of the blast, injuries, or damage. We do not know if Congressman Nisson was present. However—oh jeez—the terrorist group calling itself The Chaos Committee has apparently claimed responsibility . . . Donna, do we . . . Jimmy, is there any footage to go with that . . . no? None? Please, all of you at home, be patient, we're trying to get corroboration of this very disturbing development. Please stand by."

I hadn't felt that helpless since pushing the gauze into

Ernie Avalos's gaping face in that gun-smoke-clotted room in the old city of Fallujah.

Dalton picked up. He was drunk and morose. He'd been gaming, hadn't heard about the TV station takeover or the bomb sent to his congressman.

———

Late that night Mike Lark returned my several calls. Congressman Clark Nisson and aide Art Arguello were killed instantly when a firebomb exploded in the representative's office at 6:48 p.m. The bomb had contained a gel fire accelerant that had been blown throughout the office by the explosion. The fire had engulfed the small ground-floor office almost immediately. Lark and his brethren suspected another mail bomb, as was The Chaos Committee MO.

California's governor stated that the bomb was a terrorist act and declared a state of emergency at 7:30 the next morning.

SEVENTEEN

Tola Strait led me from the fragrant, spacious showroom of the Julian Nectar Barn to her office in the back. The skunky green aroma of marijuana followed us down a bare hallway, brightly lit. An armed and uniformed guard pressed a lock code into a wall keypad and the door slid open. He was a Native American, size large. Gave me a blank look on my way by.

The office was roomy and orderly: a brushed aluminum desk behind which Tola sat down in a task chair, a shiny concrete floor littered with Navajo rugs, brick walls hung with framed landscapes in oil and watercolor, and two Outlaw Iron Horse gun safes towering side by side on either side of a wet bar. A large digital scale on the bar top, away from the sink. A cowboy chic leather sofa along one wall, Pendleton blankets draped over both arms, and reading lamps at each end. A pink bathroom behind a half-open door.

And red-haired Tola, setting her cell phone on the brushed desktop. No business attire for her today. Instead, jeans tucked into cowboy boots, a crisp white dress shirt, and a red leather vest festooned with turquoise nuggets and leather tassels.

I sat across from her on a faux cowhide armchair.

"Thanks for looking at the Nectar Barn offerings, Mr. Ford," she said, nodding to the wall-mounted security video screen. "Though I'm disappointed you didn't pick out some good dope. I profiled you as a pump-me-up, high-energy cannabis user."

"On account of my laid-back nature?"

"You got it. One of those guys who toke up and run on the beach. Or hit the iron pile, or whatever you do to burn off the energy."

"Not my drug of choice," I said.

"It can take you up, down, or sideways. Ever tried it?"

"I giggled and couldn't walk straight."

"And the downside? Let me guess—loss of control over your surroundings. Paranoia and right-wing fantasies. An uncontrollable lust for ice cream."

"Peanut-butter chocolate," I said.

"We make an incredible edible—the Nectar Barn peanut-butter-fudge brownie."

"I wish you'd quit trying to sell me something I don't want."

"You just need the right hybrid."

"I know what I need, Ms. Strait."

An amused gaze. "I must have *something* you want, or you wouldn't have called."

"Natalie's been missing ten days," I said. "Complete silence from her, no credit card charges, no cell phone usage. Your grandfather fingered Kirby but I think Kirby's had his hands full. We know she's not on a manic-phase jag, or at least things didn't start off that way. Two men got themselves into her car, took her for a drive, then hustled her into a white Suburban not far from the Tourmaline Resort Casino. As you have probably heard from Dalton or Virgil, she wrote the word *Help* on the back seat of her car, in lipstick."

From a desk drawer she withdrew a pack of cigarettes and set them in front of her by the phone. Gave me a long steady study.

"This may be naïve," she said, "but why hasn't Dalton made this public? Why aren't the police high-profiling it?"

"He fears political fallout," I said. "And the police are doing what they can."

"The police have forgotten her."

"Forgotten?"

"Because of the bombs," she said. "A United States congressman and one of his aides blown completely away by The Chaos Committee. Did you see them last night, storming the station?"

"Everyone did. That was their goal."

"Not their main goal, though. Their main goal is to stop things. Like they said. So we can devolve. Natalie is one of millions of citizens who need help right now. Badly. But the police are all looking for the bombers.

They're distracted and paralyzed and Natalie isn't important."

I was about to make a crack about cannabis and paranoia but I saw that Tola had a point, herbally abetted or not.

"Okay," I said. "Good."

She slapped the cigarette pack against her free hand, aimed the two-cigarette offering my way. I accepted, she pulled the other one out, and I lit both of them with a Nectar Barn lighter from her desktop. It was heavy sterling silver, shaped like a barn, of course, with a push button on the roof that sent a flame jetting from a barn door that opened automatically.

Even in this well-lit office, from this clear angle, Tola looked enough like Justine to remind me of her. Same trim jaw and dubious eyes, same lurking good humor and subtle confidence. Same question-the-system attitudes, too: Justine a proud public defender of people like Tola.

"Had Natalie asked you for money recently?" I asked.

Tola shook her head.

"How about Dalton?"

"I loaned him fifty thousand dollars two months ago. No contract, just sister-to-brother. In this business, there's always cash sitting around, waiting to be spent or stolen."

"And before that?"

"Another fifty thousand late last year. When his campaign was kicking in."

"You know he's hugely in debt," I said.

"He has hinted at that. No hard figures. Mr. Ford—"

"Make it Roland."

"Roland, big picture is, I think what happened to Natalie is more personal than politics, or even money." She moved a Nectar Barn ashtray closer to me. "Very personal. Punishment. Revenge. Obsession."

The same three muses that had been barreling in and out of my mind ever since Dalton had walked into my office and told about his missing wife.

"Okay," I said, hoping to draw her out.

"Not okay. Because, if that's the case, when they've gotten what they want from her, then what? That's what worries me, Roland Ford. What will they do with her? I'd love to see a simple-minded ransom demand."

"It's been nine days," I reminded her.

She gave me an annoyed look, drawing lightly on the smoke.

"How about Dalton?" I asked.

She nodded as if she'd considered this before. "No. Dalton is weak, vain, and self-serving. But he's not wicked like that. What good does her disappearance get him? He can't even talk to the media about it."

I was surprised at the depth of her disdain for her brother. But it was not as deep as Kirby's.

"Did you take sides in Dalton's and Kirby's competition over Natalie Galland?"

"I was five. I thought Natalie Galland was the coolest, prettiest, most glamorous girl in the world. She didn't live in Buena Vista like us Okies. She was from fancy Ramona. Big houses in the hills. Kirby discovered her. I wanted Dalton to get her. Dalton was the kind one. Kirby not. Now I can see that she'd have been better off without either of them. Kirby will never change. But the war changed Dalton, Mr. Ford. Drastically and forever. Took the strength right out of him. He used to believe in himself. Now it takes an entire assembly district to make him believe in anything."

I imagined the Dalton of Fallujah, before the mine took out his Humvee and left Harris Broadman brutally disfigured for life. Dalton had been capable and well intentioned, at least. And after the IED that took half his leg a few days later? Well, maybe not. Maybe Tola was right. Maybe the war had left him an emptied-out young man whose only strength was the power of his office, the votes and money he scrambled for every two years. To prove his value.

Tola studied me curiously, tapping out her cigarette in the ashtray, which was shaped like a horseshoe surrounding a miniature Nectar Barn and barnyard. A tiny interior fan sucked the smoke into the nail holes.

"Have you followed up on Natalie's stalker, and the creep on the campaign committee?" Tola asked.

"The stalker admitted a crush on her in a police interview, and claims to have mended his ways," I said. "So far, so good, according to Dalton. The campaign volunteer is a slightly different story. Brock Weld. He didn't show for work at the casino the day Natalie disappeared. Claims he stayed home sick. Neighbors say otherwise. I have an associate digging a little deeper."

"An associate! So, you're like a league of private detectives?"

"Exactly. Each with his or her own superpower."

She smiled briefly. "I haven't helped you at all. Knowing that you were going to come here today, I thought about Natalie and my brother, and everything that's happened. Kirby, of course. I wish I could help you. But all I can do is offer you things you don't want."

I stubbed out my own half-smoked cigarette in the barnyard. Watched the embers fade on the green grass and the smoke snake down the holes.

"Like that half-used thing," she said. "See?"

"You've been helpful, Tola."

"But there's something else you want from me, isn't there?"

She held my gaze.

"I know a guy," I said. "Some years ago he loved someone and was happy, but it . . . ended. And when something reminds him of that woman and that time in his life, he's drawn to her. Like to a campfire on a cold night. That's where you came in."

A flat green stare. Impossible to separate from what used to be.

"By reminding you of Justine."

"Correct."

"I know what happened to her," she said. "We may look something alike, but we're so different. The noble legal mind and the drug pusher."

"I don't see either of you that way, but yes."

"Yes what, then?"

"You two are different," I said.

"But we both set off hardwired desire that draws you to us. Is that what you're saying, Roland?"

"I believe so, yes."

"So it's physical."

"It starts with that," I said. "I have a hunch that's nature's way."

"Which is part of your job. Following hunches."

"Less than people like to believe," I said.

I pictured Tola Strait marching down the hall of the Capitol building, toward her brother's office. And later, standing under the streetlamp on Sacramento's tree-lined Fourteenth Street not far from the Capitol, Zorro hat over her back and her arm draped casually over the craggy-faced man I'd seen in the San Diego FBI field office.

Tola's flat green stare became a smile, somehow private. She moved the Nectar Barn lighter one inch to her right.

"Well, that didn't quite come out of nowhere," she said.

"I tried to hide it."

"You're not much of a hider."

A sharp rap on the office door.

"Later!" yelled Tola.

"The eleven o'clock is here!"

"Later!"

"Yes, Ms. Strait!"

Her expression went from amused to serious.

"My turn, Roland. Ready? You remind me of absolutely nobody. You are not my type, as I understand my type to be. You don't connect with anything I've known or dreamed. But you've been on my mind since I saw you at Grandpa's. Not quite a lightning bolt, but a good, healthy shock. And I haven't been able to wash you out of my hair."

A flummoxed look.

"Which is not part of my program," she continued. "What I do is I compartmentalize. Put everything into boxes. Big as shipping containers or as small as thimbles. A place for everything and everything in its place. But I can't fit you into any of them. On less of a stoner's note, I spent more time getting ready for you today than I have for any appointment in recent memory. I didn't take a puff or a nibble because I was afraid I might miss something here. I felt as if I was preparing for something important. An audition. I've never felt that before, so strongly. And I feel good right now, sitting in this room with you. All sober and present. It's very unusual. For me."

Another long gaze from her. She fiddled with the lighter again, both hands this time, squaring it up before her, just so.

Time went by in the quiet of her office. She cleared her throat in an exaggerated way.

"The eleven o'clock is here," she said. "Stay and watch. It's fun."

EIGHTEEN

She entered something on her cell phone, waited a moment and entered something again. Waited a beat, eyes on the screen. Then pushed back her chair and walked toward the wet bar. Made a hard-right turn to one of the Outlaw safes, pushed a combination into the pad, turned the wheel, and swung open the door. With her back still to me she held up a pistol in each hand, fingers competently outside the trigger guards, waved them back and forth, then set them atop the big black box. Stepped away and turned to me with a game-show gesture to the safe.

The gun racks had been replaced by simple shelves as deep as the safe itself, about eight inches apart. All shelves except the top one solely occupied by bundled bills of varying heights. The top shelf flush-full except for the weapon bays.

"Kind of saw that one coming," I said.

"Another hunch of yours?"

"You don't need a hunch for cash the banks won't touch."

"Can't touch."

"How much?"

"Guess. Fifties on the top shelf only, twenties on the next three down, then one each of tens, fives, and ones."

I knew the values from my deputy days. Because counting bills costs traffickers too much time, they just weigh them. All U.S. bills weigh one gram. So, a pound of twenties is worth $9,080, a pounds of tens $4,540, and so on. The bundles looked fifty strong.

"I need a calculator."

Tola smiled, her face filling with pride.

"Five hundred forty thousand, six hundred and twenty dollars," she said. "The shelves aren't completely full, but almost. This is my central bank for all five Nectar Barns. Banks can't take it, the freebooters are too expensive, so I keep it here. Easier to defend one branch than five. Three armed guards here, round-the-clock. Good ones. I pay them small fortunes. I contract with two security firms. God knows what happens if they both show up at once."

Another knock. Tola pressed a code into the lock pad and the door slid open.

Under the solemn gaze of the door guard, two more uniformed men wheeled a cart with a strongbox on it into the office. One guard was very large and one very small. Both Natives—all muscles, guns, and radios. The door slid shut.

"Good morning, Ms. Strait," they said in near unison.

"My Strait Shooters! Feeling lucky today?"

"We're always lucky to be here, Ms. Strait," said the small one. "Sorry we're late. Hit a checkpoint on Highway 78, bomb dogs and National Guard, courtesy of the president himself. Everyone edgy about the bombers. Seeing those masks on TV."

I thought of Mike Lark's confidential tip on the Ramona FedEx being the point of origin for The Chaos Committee's second attack—on the county building in downtown San Diego. As of last night, had lightning struck twice from Ramona? Ramona was just down Highway 78 a few miles from here. Thus the federal roadblock. If last night's Encinitas bomb had arrived by mail, then The Chaos Committee was sophisticated enough to make a bomb either timed to match their *Local Live!* studio takeover or designed to be set off remotely. Both possibilities sent a cold tickle to the boxing scar on my forehead.

I also couldn't help but note the odd geographical proximity of the first two Chaos Committee mailings—both likely made by the woman wearing the big sunglasses—to key locations in the lives of the Strait family. Such as Fallbrook, where Dalton had first told me about his missing wife. Such as Ramona, where Natalie grew up and that Dalton now represented as part of the 82nd Assembly District. Such as Valley Center, also only a few miles from the Julian Nectar Barn, where Ash Galland last saw Natalie at breakfast. Such as the mountains around Palomar—also close to here—where Tola Strait grew some of her marijuana under armed guards . . . and her once fratricidal and felon brother, Kirby, was now encamped with a young woman. Such as sprawling Escondido, just twenty-seven miles from here, where Natalie sold BMWs. Such as Tourmaline Resort Casino, wedged between Fallbrook and Valley Center, and where Brock Weld, unappreciated observer of Natalie Strait, worked security. And how about the Julian Nectar Barn, where I now sat with Tola Strait and over a half million of her dollars?

She had taken up her phone again. A moment later the bolts within the strongbox hummed and the door opened one inch. She pulled it open, hinges wheezing open with stiff pneumatics.

She gave me an odd *this is what I do* look, then unloaded two handfuls of bundled bills onto the digital scale on the wet-bar counter. Pushed a button and turned to the guards.

"Thanks, men," she said. "Good work and see you later."

The big guy pressed the lock keypad and the door slid open. It closed on them a moment later, followed by the hum of steel sliding into steel.

She turned to me. "We'll have a one o'clock, a two o'clock, and a three o'clock today," she said. "Tuesdays, Thursdays, and Sundays."

"Business is good," I said.

"And it's about to get a lot better."

"How so?"

"Direct mail, baby," said Tola. "These stores will soon be quaint tourist attractions. Shipping will do for cannabis what Amazon did for everything else."

"Interstate, the feds won't allow it," I said. "Even with the Indians backing you."

She entered information on her phone, then set the bundles in the safe.

"One state at a time, Roland. How about California? Biggest pot market in the nation, not even close. Hand me some of those bundles, would you?"

I did. While I thought of Tola's late-night consorting with Heath Overdale, of Kimmel, Overdale & Schmitz, public relations consultants and lobbyists for the freight and direct-delivery industries. Direct mail, baby. And the craggy-faced older man whom I'd seen in the FBI's San Diego field office? Who did Tola Strait think he was?

"What are you going to do with even more cash?" I asked.

"Put it in the bank."

"Over the FBI's dead body."

"Got that covered, too. Almost. No dead bodies necessary."

Again I thought of the older FBI agent she had been late-nighting with in Sacramento. Was Tola working the agent or the other way around?

After the scale was turned off and the cash stacked, the guns put back, the safe locked, and the cell-phone notifications made, Tola Strait led me into the cavernous, high-ceilinged Nectar Barn.

The interior was rustic-hip, all distressed and antiqued lumbers, exposed crossbeams and metal joints and metal industrial lampshades. Sections for clothing—heavy on Nectar Barn–logo flannel shirts. An aisle of cannabis-helpful kitchenware—blenders, grinders, utensils, recipe books. Closer to the registers were the impulse buys: shelves of pipes, bongs, vaporizers, papers, clips, lighters. Drink holders and key chains, mouse pads. Skylights allowed a warm and glowing sunshine down upon it all.

We walked side by side around the customers crowded at the eight open registers. Long bakery-style shelves were filled with products, many marked with handwritten *Staff Picks* recommendations. Much earnest chatter about taste, strength, and psychoactive properties. Farther into the store were sections for packaged edibles, extracts, CBD-only pain remedies and vitality boosters, an Our Daily Bread shelf featuring all-organic, whole-grain, low-carb, no-sugar, gluten-free bread loaves with varying THC ratings. Vaporizer dosers and endcap stacks of canned High Country Brewers cannabis drinks.

Tola stopped and nodded. "Drinkables would put us on a level playing field with alcohol, but it tastes terrible and it's expensive. The THC takes forever to get through the digestive tract into the bloodstream. I know, I know—you'll stick with beer."

I noted the grim-faced armed guards in the corners, and the customers still coming through the door. All around was our America—polyglot and poly-racial, from baggy aging stoners to the slim-cut young, techies to athletes, artists to engineers, students to moms, rich to poor, Democrat to Republican to independent to disengaged, from the simple sober to the complexly loaded, the eagerly present to the permanently gone.

Tola walked me to my truck. She was a tall woman but

I slowed to match her pace. I felt a moment of authentic peace: a sunny day in May and a woman you're happy to walk with.

"May I be a little blunt?" she asked. Then giggled.

"Please do."

"Then you could smoke me anytime!"

I smiled as we continued.

"Sorry. It was on one of our Nectar Barn Valentine's Day cards."

"That's quite an offer," I said.

"It won't last forever."

We'd come to the truck. Tola Strait kissed my cheek and strode back through the lot, boots on the asphalt and sun on her hair.

———

Kissed and rolling down Highway 78, I got stuck in the same checkpoint the guards had been in. After examining my CDL, the burly, armored HSI agent pulled me into a makeshift secondary inspection turnout, where of course were discovered my sidearms, protection-modified 12 gauge, cameras, binoculars, flashlights, hiker's headlights, ropes, pry bars, sleeping bag, brilliant disguises—from costume mustaches and hairpieces to a Rolling Thunder Security windbreaker—and two days' worth of water and food, all neatly arranged in the oversized and locking toolbox in the truck bed.

Which went over poorly. In spite of my current enhanced PI photo ID card required by the state, my pocket license and valid CCW permits issued by the county, and my best manners, they made me sit and watch the near deconstruction of my beloved truck and its hasty reassembly.

I sat in the sun wanting to knock somebody out, but I couldn't decide who.

Dalton Strait on the phone:

"Roland, I need your help. The feds just indicted me and Natalie for misuse of campaign funds, fraud, and conspiracy. They say we swiped hundreds of thousands of dollars in donations and spent them to live the high life. Completely fake news and I'll prove it. It's all political. They're talking twenty-two counts and five years in the slammer for each of us. I'm having a press conference an hour and a half from now. I want you here at my house to take questions."

"Answer your own questions," I said. "I'm not talking to the press for you."

"You're on the payroll, Roland."

"Not that I noticed."

"Your money's coming, man. Just be here. I need you. Semper Fi, dammit."

And rang off.

Then, as if in answer to Dalton's call, a YouTube video arrived, courtesy of Harris Broadman, innkeeper.

His message said, "Thought you might enjoy this trip down memory lane. This is just a few hours before we hit the IED."

I hit the Play arrow.

A dusty Fallujah street of low, rectangular homes.

My beat for thirty days.

That soft glow to the dirty air. Bridges and sagging power lines in the background.

And resentful Iraqis watching the camera, which was moving along the road past them, apparently shot from a vehicle with some elevation to it. Broadman's Humvee?

Then Broadman's soft, calm voice:

"East Manhattan sucks, man. Here they are, thousands of people who hate us and want us dead. They cling to their customs and their sects and their ruined government because they're confused animals. They don't get that we'll be gone soon. So they fight because they're hardwired to fight. Like any animal. That's not an insult. We're all animals. I really can't wait to get out of this shit hole. Home to some warm women and cold beer."

I recognized Dalton's voice:

"Boy, ain't that the truth. I thought I was signing on to hunt terrorists. I didn't think they'd be hunting me."

"You're an innocent, Dalton. An innocent blockhead."

"Married to the prettiest woman in California."

"Don't lose your balls to a roadside."

"Not me, Harris. That's not in old Dalton's cards."

The clip ended and I played it again. And again, riding the video back sixteen years that seemed to have gone by in a moment. Back to my eager young man's desire to serve his country, and the innocence quickly lost. Back to the idea that you've been fooled and extremely lucky to have survived it.

The past being not even past and all that.

I looked out at the pretty plains along the highway, temporarily greened by rain.

Okay. Maybe it wasn't past, but it was behind me.

NINETEEN

The Strait home stood at the end of a rural road south of Escondido. It looked to be 1960s construction, a modest stucco two-story with a wholesome face and brown trim. The yard looked uncherished and the hedges needed trimming. A flagpole mid-yard, no flag. A FOR SALE sign. Around the home were several unbuilt lots and a few similar structures, as if these homesteaders had led the charge only to be abandoned.

Dalton stood in the doorway, a beer bottle in one hand and an apparently just delivered handful of mail in the other. He had his air of disheveled nonchalance. A small Bichon mix wagged its tail at me eagerly. The press conference was almost an hour away. I wasn't sure how hot a ticket it might be, given last night's bomb. Every media outlet I turned to—from local to national to the

BBC—was covering the bombing deaths of Representative Nisson and his aide. Would they have time for a humble assemblyman accused of financial misdeeds?

"I'm going to stand right in this doorway when the media asks questions," he said. "That way, they'll see I'm a just a humble blown-up war hero and family man, defending my home and wife against lies and slanted accusations."

"Raise a flag, shave your snout, and lose the beer," I said.

"Not a problem. There's a flag here in the foyer, would you mind? I'm going to go get pretty. Beer?"

"No."

"Come on, Freddie," he said to the dog. "Let's go get ready for the show."

While Dalton prettified upstairs, I carried a well-weathered United States flag to the front-yard pole. The pole had a clothesline, three pulleys, and a tie-down. As I hoisted the flag I noted the top ornament, a toilet bowl float painted gold. I wondered if Dalton was more patriot or scoundrel.

I sat in the living room and waited. Heard voices upstairs, three, male and argumentative. Freddie barked briefly. The living room was oddly dated for someone Dalton's age: Berber carpet, matronly overstuffed sofa and chairs, a black-lacquer-and-glass coffee table with untouched magazines and a faux Pueblan vase of artificial flowers. On the walls, framed floral paintings, mass-produced and mall-marketed, painful to look at. I wondered why the Straits' eye-popping credit card charges for the finer things in life hadn't included one item for their own living room.

I heard loud thumping on the landing upstairs, then a tall, beefy boy came pounding down. Lee, I knew from Dalton's phone photos, a college junior at San Diego State and part of the Navy/Marine ROTC program. He wore a lacrosse jersey, shorts, and cleats, and carried a red helmet in one hand and a defender's long stick in the other. Lee had short blond hair and an open, carefree face like his father's.

"Hey," he said, clomping to a stop on the Berber. "You find Mom yet?"

"Not yet," I said. "Any ideas where she went?"

"We never know with her," he said. "I'm going to practice."

He trotted past the plump sofa and recliner to the foyer tile, then out the front door. I saw the van waiting in the driveway.

When I looked back, another young man had already come down the stairs and stood at the landing, looking at me. The USC Trojan, I thought, younger, a freshman. Terrell. Shorter than his older brother, with something of his mother's engaging face. Dark hair and blue eyes. A *Seinfeld* T-shirt and lounge pants and the nubby rubber spa slippers oddly favored by the young.

"I'm a PI working for your dad," I said.

"I'm Terrell."

"How do you like USC?"

"It's okay. I'm thinking about moving back home to help find Mom."

"I respect that," I said.

"Dad told me to hang around and make a good impression at this press conference."

"You'll make a good impression."

He looked at me for a beat, uncertainty on his handsome face. "Do you think this was a psychotic episode? Another break?"

"I wish I could give you one bit of useful information, Terrell."

"So you have nothing, or nothing you can tell me?"

Nothing but a cry for help written in lipstick, I thought. And a lot of eyewitnessed hugger-mugger up near Valley Center and out by the Tourmaline Casino one Tuesday that by now must feel like a hundred years ago to this boy.

I saw the tension on Terrell's face, so unlike the annoyance on his older brother's.

"Are you close to her?" I asked.

He looked at me again with something of his mother's bright expression on the TV commercials. If Lee was Dalton's son, Terrell was clearly Natalie's.

"Well, she's my mom."

"People think highly of her," I said. "It's my job to ask around when things like this happen."

"Like an abduction?"

"We're not sure of that, Terrell."

"Why wouldn't they think highly of her?"

I considered this a good question. One of the several things that had been bothering me about Natalie Strait's disappearance was how lost in the shuffle she seemed to those who should be the most anxious to have her safe and back home. Such as her husband. And, apparently, Lee. *We never know with her.*

"People talk about this quality she has," I said, eager to get a clearer picture of the boy. "They describe it in different ways. How would you describe her?"

He looked down and slipped his hands into his pockets. Toed the carpet with his spa slippers. "I don't know. Um, I'm not that verbal or anything. I'm studying film. I'm going to be a moviemaker."

He vetted me again with Natalie's open charm, in absentia. "I made a movie that helped me get into school. It's about her. *A Day in a Life.* I'm into music, too, so the Beatles reference."

"I'd like to see it."

"It's not bad."

"Do you have a copy?"

"Probably a hundred. Right back."

He took the stairs two at a time. I heard banging, then some back-and-forth, across-the-house yelling with his father. The dog barking again. A moment later he handed me two plastic jewel cases and a brad-bound script.

"One disc is Blu-ray if you got it, and there's outtakes before the credits so don't miss those. Mom is much more interesting when she doesn't think the camera is on. And funnier. Like most people are. The script, too, if you want."

"I look forward to this, Terrell."

"Maybe it holds a clue."

I waited for the ironic smile and didn't get one.

"I'll do anything on earth to get her back," he said. "You need me, you call me. My numbers are on the script."

Half an hour later, Dalton, freshly shaven and golf-shirted, came down the stairs and gave me a brief salute. Then swung himself around the well-worn banister finial and limped into the kitchen. Heard him ordering his son to get him a beer before the vultures got here. A moment later he walked in with a fresh cold one.

"How do I look?"

"I'd almost believe you."

"I'll take almost."

"You'll need more than that," I said. "I read the DOJ indictment. They're throwing the book at you, Dalton."

"Um-hmm," he managed, upping the bottle for a long swallow. He wiped his mouth like a saloon gunslinger. "Thing is, they can't prove any of it."

I thought of Burt's non-grand-jury investigation, which had yielded plenty of damning evidence. "And what if they already have?"

"I mean in a courtroom, Roland. Whose side are you on, anyway?"

"What are you going to say about Natalie's absence?"

"I don't know. Hit at the plate. What do you think?"

"Our chances of finding her go up if people know she's missing."

He gave me an assessing stare. "More than one way to play it."

"This isn't play, my friend."

It wasn't play for me, either. The idea of being caught

and displayed through scores of media outlets did not sit well. Sometimes you need anonymity. You need a handful of aliases with business cards, websites, and phone numbers to back them up. You need to get yourself where you need to be with a story, a wig, a mustache, and a change of clothes. Even a pair of Jackie O sunglasses. A little can do a lot. But you can't do that if everybody knows you. Especially through the eyes of the media— social, news, whatever. Illogically, you're twice as memorable on a screen.

I settled on a Padres cap and windbreaker from the toolbox in my truck, and a pair of aviator sunglasses.

TWENTY

I stood behind Dalton on his front patio as he faced his questioners. There were more of them than I'd expected after the nearby carnage: network, cable, PBS, NPR, *Local Live!,* ProPublica, Politico, HuffPost. Print, led by Howard Wilkin from the *Union-Tribune,* who gave me an unthankful nod. I looked out to the street and saw their vehicles stacked back nearly to the intersection. Terrell stood beside me, hands folded in front of him, back straight, staring blankly ahead.

Dalton started with last night's bombing, the governor's state of emergency for San Diego County—which Dalton "absolutely" agreed with—and which would bring National Guardsmen and possibly federal money to "wage war on The Chaos Committee." He raised his fist: "We're going to hit them with everything we've got! The Chaos Committee will pay the full measure."

ABC: "But what about the federal charges against you, Mr. Strait?"

"I haven't read all the charges yet, but I don't have to. None of them are true. I am innocent on all counts. The indictment is a political move to keep me from being reelected. Questions?"

NBC: "Is it true that you and your wife spent over two hundred and eighty thousand dollars in campaign donations on personal expenses over the last three years?"

Dalton: "Absolutely not. This is the new DOJ bringing these charges. This is the deep state, hard at work. They're doing the same thing to the president."

CBS: "Why is your campaign treasurer reporting a current balance of only five hundred and thirty-five dollars when your reelection committee has taken in over three hundred and seventeen thousand dollars this year alone?"

Dalton: "We spent it. We're running a tough campaign. The question you *should* be asking is why my opponent in November almost certainly has terrorist blood relatives in the Middle East."

ABC: "Can you explain why campaign donations were used to pay for a golfing junket to Hawaii, a family vacation to Greece, and first-class airfare for Natalie's parents to fly from Los Angeles to Paris?"

Dalton: "Because we couldn't get a nonstop from San Diego? That was just a joke, Bethany. I repaid that airfare out of my own salary. Same with the Greece trip."

Fox: "Not according to prosecutors."

Dalton: "They are absolutely wrong. It's all political."

ABC: "But you told the Federal Election Commission that the golf junkets were charity events when, apparently, they were simply trips with friends."

Dalton: "War vets and donors—therefore legal all the way."

A murmur rose from the media, a collective rebuttal to Dalton's specious reasoning.

Howard Wilkin: "The Strait Reelection Committee claimed nearly a thousand dollars' worth of new golf balls were donated to the Wounded Warrior Project, but they have no records of such a donation."

Dalton: "Well, their bad."

Howard Wilkin: "Mr. Strait, the prosecution has released copies of Strait Reelection Committee credit card statements, with charges paid to various airlines, restaurants, and resorts for dates that you, friends, and family were present."

Dalton: "As I said, these charges are made up. Fake news. Why not focus on Ammna Safar's relatives? The DNA evidence? DNA is never fake."

Another ripple of protest from the reporters.

Politico: "Mr. Strait, why is Natalie not here to help defend herself?"

Dalton: "What was the question?"

Politico: "Why isn't Natalie here?"

I looked at the back of Dalton's nodding head, hoping he wouldn't look back at me or Terrell. Which he did. I saw the confusion on his face, gradually replaced by a cool, focused calm before he turned back to the crowd.

Dalton: "She's been missing for nine days. Foul play

has not been ruled out. I had been advised by the police to keep this a secret but I honestly think you should know. Maybe you can help me find her."

The reporters blitzed forward behind their mics and cameras, and their voices rose as if a volume knob had suddenly been cranked. A hundred flashes, a thousand blinking indicators. Facing the storm, Dalton raised his arms wide and waved his hands for order.

CBS: "Where was she last—"

Politico: "When did you last—"

ABC: "What is the evidence of—"

Dalton: "Two Tuesdays ago she didn't report to work at the dealership. They found her car out in Pala, where someone said he saw her with two men, being transferred from her car to another. No word from her. No ransom demand. My boys and I don't know what to do. We can't help but think something bad has happened. We're being eaten alive by worry. Please, all of you, look for her. She gets carried away sometimes."

ABC: "What do you mean by 'carried away'?"

Dalton: "It's just a saying."

Politico: "Hasn't she gone missing before, Mr. Strait? Approximately a year and a half ago? Before surfacing in Las Vegas?"

Dalton: "Affirmative. She suffered a psychotic break with reality. A mental glitch. Nats has been on medication since then, though sometimes she forgets or neglects to take it."

Terrell groaned softly.

NBC: "What's her diagnosis?"

Fox: "Which medication?"

Dalton: "Bipolar something or other. Not sure of the drug. I should also say that all of the Strait reelection donation books are kept by my wife, Natalie, as well as access to the checking account and campaign committee credit card. All campaign donations come through her and any expenditures are either made by or approved by her."

Howard Wilkin: "Are you saying your wife made these questionable purchases without your knowing?"

Dalton: "Very possibly. I can't speak for her. That's something we'll have to get to the bottom of when Natalie is safely returned. The most important thing is that she comes home and we win this election. Baby? Natalie? If you're watching this, only God knows how much I love you and miss you. And the boys, too."

Terrell turned an astonished face to me, and mine might have looked the same to him.

The noise of the twenty reporters and videographers rose even louder, a layered chorus aimed at Dalton. Dalton turned around again, smiling faintly, then back to the media.

ABC: "What is the evidence of foul play?"

Politico: "What is your relationship to Sacramento lobbyists McKenzie Doyle of Asclepia Pharmaceutical and Heath Overdale of Kimmel, Overdale and Schmitz?"

"Absolutely none of your business!" Dalton yelled out. "Don't throw me under the bus until all the facts are known. Talk to the San Diego sheriffs. Or here, talk to this guy—Roland Ford. He's the PI I've hired!"

Dalton pivoted on his good leg and swung back inside, artificial foot banging hard on the wooden porch.

Questions frayed behind me as I took Terrell by the arm, guided him inside, and slammed the door.

"How'd I do?" Dalton blurted out, headed for the kitchen. Terrell pounded upstairs without a word and I followed Dalton. From a bottle in the freezer he poured a generous vodka into a coffee mug, downed it, and poured another. Then led the way back into his living room.

"You just blamed your wife for twenty-two counts of fraud, misuse of funds, and conspiracy," I said.

"I didn't mean to, exactly. But it'll help them find her, right? It'll get the suspicion off of me so I can win this damned reelection, right?"

Terrell flew into the kitchen, grabbed a can of soda from the fridge, and headed—I guessed—for the garage. "Fuck you, Dad," he called back.

I heard a car door slam, a vehicle start, and the rolling thunder of an old garage door motoring up. Then the shouted questions and shouted answers from Terrell, followed by a screeching of tires and shrieks of alarm.

Dalton stared at the kitchen, from which his son's curse seemed to echo.

"Did I screw up, Roland?"

"Did HerediLink really get a sample of Ammna Safar's DNA?" I asked. "Or is that some fake news of your own?"

His boy smile. "One of my people went through her trash can at the curb early one morning. Tissues of God knows what, and wads of used dental floss. Red, the cinnamon flavored. Scout's honor."

Dalton set his mug on the coffee table, lowered heavily into the couch and rubbed his bad knee. I stood by the fireplace, looking at him while I considered walking off the job. In order to escape a devious child in a hero's costume betraying his wife and the public trust. While sucking down its money. More important, I wasn't sure he much missed his wife beyond her value in helping him win an election. Which in his mind might include her taking the brunt of blame for their shared foolishness and criminal dishonesty. I could see him making photo ops out of visiting her in prison.

"Dalton, you're disgusting."

"Oh, sit down."

"I'm good right here."

"Lee and me see eye to eye," he said. "But it's rough times for me and Terrell. He's a mama's boy, that's for sure. I suppose he gave you his movie?"

I nodded.

"It's really good. He adores his mother."

"Do you?"

"Sure I do," he said, rubbing his knee again and not looking at me. "What's that supposed to mean? Everybody does."

———

On my way home, Harris Broadman called.

"I had no real idea how much mischief Dalton has gotten himself into," he said. "But I watched his press conference on his Facebook. Is there anything I can do?"

I thought it was strange that Dalton's recent calami-

ties were enough to draw his old war buddy out of sixteen years of silence. But then, I can sometimes be a hard
and unseeing man. I reconsidered Broadman in light of
the press conference, imagining how it would affect him.
I imagined that these last sixteen years could have been
as hard on Broadman as on his failed rescuer—not as a
man burned by fire but as a man burning with a resentment he wouldn't admit. And couldn't put out. Maybe
Broadman needed to forgive Dalton for what he had
failed to accomplish in Fallujah the day their Humvee hit
the bomb. Every bit as much as Dalton needed that forgiveness.

"You two should talk," I said.

"Yes, I believe we should."

TWENTY-ONE

That night I drove to the Tourmaline Resort Casino to see Strait Reelection Committee volunteer Brock Weld, who had pricked enough worry in Natalie for her to tell her sister about him. His alibi for missing work on the day Natalie disappeared had left some of the other committee workers, and Burt, unconvinced.

IvarDuggans.com didn't have much on Weld: thirty-one, a white male, unmarried, a native of Miami. A business degree from San Diego State University. Employment as security in three San Diego hotels, two Norwegian cruise lines, casinos in New Jersey and Las Vegas, and now the Tourmaline Resort Casino. No criminal record. Last known address, Valley Center, California.

On my way to the casino, the radio news was heavy with the story of Natalie Strait. The evening news had showed pictures of her radiantly smiling face, culled from the BMW ads.

The Tourmaline is large and the grounds are lavish—with drought-encouraging fountains, drought-busting Southwest landscaping, and natural stone construction, all dramatically lit at night.

At the entrance I walked past four National Guardsmen in desert camo, field caps low, rifles slung over their shoulders. A bomb dog, alert and panting. Then through a temporary scanning station before I was allowed inside.

The Tourmaline Casino was surprisingly busy, given that a congressman and his assistant—representing some of these people—had been blown to death by a bomb not twenty-four hours ago. Maybe carnage encourages hopes of a miracle, or at least favorable luck. Special Agent Lark had told me the bomb maker had used short galvanized nails, which tore tender human flesh savagely and were difficult to remove without causing more damage, which mattered not to Representative Clark Nisson and his aide-de-camp, Art Arguello. Lark had also told me that the FBI's search for the type and origin of the package had slowed to a crawl—not enough of it left to work with. At this point, they were subtracting candidates by trying to determine which packages had *not* blown up. After the explosion, the congressman's large office suite had been fully engaged in fire.

I'm almost always early for appointments. Makes me feel ahead of the game. I played some blackjack at the $25 table, nursing a mostly ice bourbon to kill the time.

Managed to stay close to even, using the Revere blackjack system I'd learned as a high school kid. Revere has hard rules on splitting certain pairs, hitting the sixteens and counting the cards as best you can. Not easy in a chute with four decks. Pepper, the wispy-brown-haired dealer, gave me her *I know what you're up to* look.

The other two players at my table were a young couple, mid-twenties, dressed up and having fun. Making bold plays to little avail, much volume when they won.

Pepper got hot as blackjack dealers often do, drawing improbable cards at impossible times, politely annihilating the table as if it was just part of the job. Hit two blackjacks in a row, allowing us to almost break even on the insurance.

The couple gathered what was left of their chips and headed off, leaving us alone at the table.

"I can't believe how crowded we are after what happened last night," she said.

"It must have to do with hope."

"Everything does. Ready?"

I nodded.

"I'm hot, as you know."

"I can see that."

Pepper dealt me a king and a six, a perilous hand that Revere says you should hit against any face card unless the deck is rich. She showed a jack of clubs and the chute cards were close to neutral by my less-than-practiced count. Peeked at her hole card for a blackjack ace.

"My son and daughter were watching the TV when it

happened," she said. "I mean the takeover thing of *Local Live!*"

I scraped the table felt with two fingernails, caught a five. My lucky night. Pepper turned over a ten, paid up on my twenty-one, and scooped away her losing cards with a competitive glance my way.

With a terse sweep of hand over the chute, two fresh cards appeared before each of us, her up card a two.

"And I picked up the remote to change the channel, but I couldn't," she said. "So the three of us watched the whole thing. The terrifying masks. The horrible things they ordered us to do. The guns on the newspeople's heads and poor Dwayne Swift fainting and slipping down. They didn't fall asleep until early morning, my kids."

"I'm sorry they had to see that."

"Now I can't stop seeing the masks. I look at a player and I see the mask that most resembles them. I feel like a terrible person and a terrible mom. Want a card?"

I had a fourteen, remembered my Revere, and held against her two. She flipped her hole card ten, drew a jack of clubs for the bust.

"You've changed the luck," she said. "I'd tell you to keep striking while you're hot, but that would be giving advice, which we cannot do. But . . ."

We split a few hands. No one joined us at the table. A not-unpleasant hypnotism fell over us, two souls, two roles, the play of rules and luck, the significance of the wager, the subtle indicators of fate. And the dust of a bomb settling down on a land seemingly so far away.

At the agreed time, Brock Weld came down the stairs and into the Cavern wine bar. The bar was dark, built of rough stone into which diamond-shaped bottle racks were fitted. TV turned to the local news.

The security man was straight from central casting—muscled and hard faced, in a black, well-cut suit and a wire mic in one ear. He moved lightly on his feet.

I thanked Brock for agreeing to meet me on short notice and attempted Chargers, Padres, and weather small talk. No takers.

"The bombs have us all on high alert," he said. "How can I help you?"

"Dalton Strait hired me to find Natalie. You know that she's been missing for nine days now?"

"I know she hasn't been at campaign headquarters," he said. "I saw part of the Dalton press conference."

We watched in silence as *Local Live!* aired video of Natalie Strait from the BMW ads. The more I saw of her on TV the more I felt her spell. Or maybe it was the danger I knew she was in.

Brock sent the waitress away without an order. We studied each other's faces. I saw a young man of sturdy constitution and staunch beliefs. A man absolutely sure of himself. I don't know what Brock Weld saw in mine.

"As Dalton noted in his press conference today, there's suspicion of foul play," I said.

"Can you give me any details?" he asked.

I told him about her breakfast with her sister, her

missed lunch with Virgil Strait, her BMW being found out in the ruins of the farmworkers' camp. And the two men escorting her from her vehicle to another. I left out the lipstick.

"That's all I have. But Dalton mentioned you as a volunteer of note in his campaign."

I saw a bitter disbelief in him. "You're here because Natalie spoke of me?"

"Yes," I said. "Natalie was alert to you, Mr. Weld. According to people I've interviewed, she found you bold enough to mention as a person of concern. More than once."

"Concern."

I nodded and held his dark-eyed stare.

"Let me set forth some facts for you, Mr. Ford. One, I'm not close with Dalton Strait. I originally volunteered for his campaign because I thought he was a good representative for the district I live in, and where my place of business is located. We have big issues here—the Pala Reservation's interests, the casino's wealth, land-use, water, and fire-abatement concerns. The marijuana industry. Complicated things. I believe in a strong military and strict immigration enforcement. I'm pro-God, pro-life, and pro-gun. Dalton Strait has been on the right side of things. For the most part. But the more I work with him, the more I see that he's self-centered, impulsive, and destructive. As you saw in his press conference today. I'll continue to volunteer because I believe Ammna Safar would be far worse."

"What's your relationship with Natalie?"

Weld was sitting bolt upright but managed to straighten even more at the question.

"At the office, strictly professional," he said. "But over the months I had questions about her bookkeeping. I mentioned that some of the income and expenditures looked shaky."

"And?"

"She's a sloppy bookkeeper, Mr. Ford, but she's a proud worker, and she basically told me to mind my own business."

"Which would be in line with an indictment for criminally spending donations," I said.

"I'm not surprised by the charges," he said. "I'm disappointed. If this plays out, she could spend time in prison. It's hard to think of her in the slammer. All that energy, charm, and good nature."

"So you and Natalie are professional coworkers at the office," I said. "What about outside?"

He nodded as if anticipating the question. "I volunteer sixteen hours a week there. Saturdays and Tuesdays. I started back in November. The office is small and slightly chaotic, so we worked closely. Once a week I'd have drinks after work with her and some of the others. One day it was just us, and that was fine with me. I told her I thought her husband was a foolish child, incapable of satisfying a woman of her intelligence and beauty. And if she ever thought about having some adult male company, I was very interested."

"A direct approach," I said.

"It's the only one I ever use."

"You're a single man, I take it."

"You must know that from IvarDuggans," he said. "The Tourmaline subscribes, too. It helps to know who's losing big money in my casino, and if I should be worried about it."

Noted.

"How did she react to your proposal?"

"She laughed it off. But I could tell that I had found her truth. Her face flushed, so much like a girl. Neither of us ever mentioned that general topic again. Or that night."

"Back to business, then."

"Absolutely," said Weld. "I never ask for anything twice."

"Did your coworkers pick up on all that?"

"Ask them, Mr. Ford."

"What do you think the criminal charges will do to his reelection?" I asked.

"We had a flood of new money come after his press conference today. I expect more."

I asked him if he'd had any communication with Natalie since she disappeared that day.

"None. I would have told you that already."

"How often did she gamble here?" I asked. A gamble of my own, but favorable odds.

"Occasionally. She actually does well."

"Did she play here before you two met at campaign headquarters?"

"Yes," he said. "I'd seen her playing here before volunteering. I never approached her."

"Until working together?"

He nodded impatiently.

"What's the talk around the campaign committee office?" I asked. "So far as Natalie's nine-day absence?"

"Until the press conference today, Dalton had been making excuses," he said. "Family obligations. A long overdue reunion with friends in Hawaii. A lacrosse tournament up in Santa Barbara with her son. These were usual things for her. No one seemed concerned."

"What did you make of her being suddenly gone?"

"I sensed trouble immediately," Weld said. "It's a critical time in the campaign. Safar has a six-percentage-point lead, up a full point since last month. That's big, with only six months left."

"There's a lot of trouble to sense these days."

"After the station takeover and the bomb last night, I called Dalton on his personal line. I thought The Chaos Committee bomb qualified as an emergency, since all of their targets have been San Diego politicians. I told Dalton he should get the best protection he could afford for the next few weeks. California can't offer twenty-four-hour security to every one of its senators and assembly persons, so I told him to hire a private company. I recommended two."

"And?"

"He said you were handling it."

I held his gaze and shook my head. Which earned a minor smile from Brock Weld. I thought it was time to put what pressure I could on him, though he seemed like the type to welcome it.

"I heard that you were home sick the day Natalie disappeared."

A stubborn look. "A fact."

"Why didn't you quiet down King?"

"You talked to my neighbors?"

I shrugged.

"I was with a friend. It's complicated and don't ask me for a name."

I let that complication hang in silence, hoping it might unravel. Weld drummed his fingers on the table.

"Mr. Ford, you might think about adding some protection hours for Dalton Strait. He's a perfect target. The Chaos Committee isn't going to stop. I see unquestioned intent in them. Devotion to cause. A workable cause. Tear down everything. Tap into the popular outrage. Use violence to undermine authority and launch a country into chaos so that order may be restored."

"Straight from the anarchist playbook," I said.

"History tells us it can work," said Weld.

Another silence into which I was hoping Brock Weld might let something fall. Instead he folded his hands on the table and bored his gaze into me as best he could.

"Mr. Ford, I've got one hour here before I can go home and forget about bombs and indictments and a woman I'm worried about. Let me know if I can be of any more help in finding Natalie. I doubt that she's been spending campaign donations behind Dalton's back. He's enough of a coward to blame things on her."

We stood.

I thanked him for his time, found my way to Terrace

Café, where I could sit outside, have dinner and a drink, and watch the Tourmaline Resort Casino employees' parking structure. Waited out the hour.

It was just after eight when Brock Weld came walking toward the structure with a young man and woman. Her suit was black and her blond hair was up. The man wore a black moto jacket and carried a helmet.

A moment later Moto Jacket came out on a black-and-orange Kawasaki, heading down the ramp, keeping down his engine noise for the casino guests. Then Weld and the woman. They exited into the wash of the entry light just as she was shaking out her hair in a pale, shiny wave. Brock Weld's complicating friend? He turned off the ramp in a white Suburban—the same type and color vehicle into which a worried Natalie Strait had been escorted by two men—almost ten days ago, a few miles from where I sat.

TWENTY-TWO

Late that night I carried leftovers upstairs to my home office, poured a thoughtful bourbon, and cued up Terrell Strait's *A Day in a Life*.

The namesake Beatles' song played softly as Natalie Strait stood in her kitchen, cooking eggs and bacon in large skillets. She wore a dowdy plaid robe and a Padres ball cap snug over her thick hair.

I followed along on the script.

The handheld camera swept abruptly from Natalie to Dalton and Lee at the table, to the family dog begging at Natalie's shearling-booted feet, then back again to Natalie.

The opening credits rolled.

A DAY IN A LIFE

PRODUCED AND DIRECTED BY TERRELL STRAIT
WRITTEN BY TERRELL AND NATALIE STRAIT
MUSIC BY THE BEATLES AND TERRELL STRAIT

STRAIT SHOT ENTERTAINMENT

INT. KITCHEN MORNING

Natalie turns from the skillet to the
camera, mugging happily.

NATALIE

Breakfast, as we all know, is the
most important meal of the day.

INT. KITCHEN MORNING

Camera pans to Dalton at the table in a
business suit, puffy eyed, a newspaper atop
his place setting. Lee sits across from him
in a lacrosse jersey, phone in hand, thumbs
working.

DALTON

(to camera)

Terrell? You sure this is necessary
right this minute?

TERRELL

(offscreen)

It's a day in a life, Dad!

LEE

You suck, Terrell. Mom, is it ready?

NATALIE

(spatula at the camera)

But why is it the most important
meal? Because the whole family's
together for probably the only time
all day. This is family central,
baby, it's what I signed up for, so I
make it count!

LEE

(not looking up from phone)

I never signed up for this.

NATALIE

I did! I was seventeen when I told
your dad I'd marry him.

DALTON

Honey, really. I'm late already.

The dog bounced up as Natalie swung a big skillet
off the stove top, pirouetting once on his bandy hind
legs.

Next, a smash-cut to the Escondido BMW dealership,
where a smartly dressed Natalie swings open the door of
a brand-new 5 Series sedan and gestures to the camera to
have a look inside. By then, *A Day in a Life* had given

way to a cheerful island-style ukulele that must have been
Terrell.

EXT. BMW DEALERSHIP MORNING

                    NATALIE

    This is my favorite interior. Camel.
    It goes best with a dark exterior,
    such as charcoal gray or black. Guys
    buy the outside, chicks buy the
    inside. The last place anybody looks
    is under the hood. It's too
    complicated and all they want is
    power. Wouldn't be here at BMW if
    they didn't.

                    TERRELL
(offscreen)

    Is it hard to sell one? That sticker
    says seventy-eight thousand, eight
    hundred and eighty-five dollars.

                    NATALIE

    I'll work out the price. It's what I
    do. But right now, Terrell, you just
    sit yourself in the driver seat.
    Road and Track calls this car an
    instant classic. High praise from
    the car gods. Yes indeedy.

Then another cut to Natalie at the wheel of a BMW convertible, hair flying beneath a BMW of Escondido baseball cap, car engine whining, video trembling, cars and buildings zipping past the windows.

I was surprised by her concentration. Grip firm at nine and three, gloved fingers nimble on the paddle shifter. She kept the RPMs high. Didn't look away from the road and said little. Squint lines on her face. Gradually, the camera came close in and I realized that Terrell was treating his subject with the same absolute attention that Natalie was giving the road. The ukulele seemed to serenade her as she drove.

Next came a sequence of Natalie at a desk, dressed as she had been for the car shoot—a flattering black business suit and a turquoise blouse. At first I thought this was her dealership workstation but the campaign posters on the wall behind her said otherwise. Distorted guitar came in.

Terrell had positioned himself across the desk, his camera and his mother at eye level. Gone was her chipper breakfast demeanor and her sales-pitch energy for moving Bimmers. This Natalie had gravity, not joy.

```
INT. CAMPAIGN HEADQUARTERS AFTERNOON


                    TERRELL
(offscreen)

     Your husband is a California state
     assemblyman. What are you doing for
     his reelection campaign?
```

NATALIE

Politics is ninety percent about
raising money and ten percent about
spending it smartly. This is what I
try to do for Dalton Strait.

TERRELL

Does it take more than money to win
an office?

NATALIE

After money, attention and anger get
a candidate elected. Attention for
himself, and anger aimed at his
opponent. I'm talking about everyday
anger, the anger that's in the air
we breathe. This anger is up for
grabs and the candidate who directs
it toward his opponent will almost
certainly win.

TERRELL

That seems very strategic. You seem
to have given this some serious
thought.

NATALIE

I've been Dalton Strait's chief fund-
raiser for four elections. I knew
nothing about it at first, and

```
really, I did it the same way I do
everything—by the seat of my pants.
I also believe what Mom told me
years ago. She said, Natalie, do
things like they count a lot or they
won't count at all. Counting meant a
lot to us Gallands. It meant do
things that matter. It meant don't
waste anything. Ever. We never had
an extra dollar.


                  TERRELL

Like at breakfast today when you
said to make it count if you sign up
to raise a family?


                  NATALIE

Yes! It's so nice to be interviewed
by someone who actually listens!
```

Their conversation continued as Terrell's camera zoomed in and slowly panned across his mother's desk. It was almost covered by handled boxes of mail, mostly letter-sized envelopes. Natalie's out-box was almost full as well.

I saw vividly that a mail bomb addressed to the Strait Reelection Committee might very likely have been opened by Natalie.

I paused the video and considered. She had gone missing only one day after The Chaos Committee's first mail bomb had exploded in city hall. In some ways, she would be an even better target than Dalton. She was a perfect victim of terror: innocent, unsuspecting, and easy to attack. Like anyone else working on a reelection campaign.

The camera pulled back to show Natalie gesturing at the mail with a look of pride on her face.

                    NATALIE
     (holds her right index finger to the
     camera)

          Paper cuts from the mail I open.
          We're being outspent four to one
          this time around. But look at this.
          These contributions come from the
          moms and pops of this district, the
          seniors, the working people. We've
          got plenty of retired military, and
          Dalton works hard for them, too. It
          takes faith to put a check in an
          envelope and send it off. You have
          to believe it's going to count!

                    TERRELL
          There you go about counting again,
          Mrs. Strait.

Natalie's smile changed from a deployed campaign gesture to a spontaneous display of delight. And pride at a mother's job, well done.

The next few minutes of video followed Natalie from the reelection committee headquarters to the supermarket, then on to a gym and a huffing workout on the stationary cycle. She pedaled away, talking about her childhood in Ramona, her young girl's dreams of having horses and maybe falling in love with a cowboy, her great affection for her sister, Ash—short for Ashley—and how they'd walk home from high school with a group of friends. Which was where she'd first seen Kirby Strait.

NATALIE

(still on the workout cycle)

> Kirby was this gangly redhead with a
> great smile. Totally full of himself
> but he had this way of making you
> feel noticed. Maybe even special. He
> started showing up on our way home
> from school, so us girls went
> another way and he'd be there, too.
> He just showed up at the house one
> day with a handful of flowers he'd
> pilfered from the neighbors. Mom and
> Dad couldn't stand him. Said the
> Straits were lowlifes. Like we
> Gallands were born better. We still
> didn't have two nickels to rub
> together. When Dalton came over with
> Kirby one day, Mom and Dad tried to
> tolerate him. Me? I was interested

```
            in him right off. Dalton was the
            opposite of his brother. But the
            Straits had that reputation. The dad
            got shot and messed up in the Better
            Burger holdup later. Archie. Such a
            nice guy.
```

Natalie churned along, breathing hard and wiping her face with a towel, hair up and skin shining. Her widow's peak sharp and slanted like an apostrophe. A muscled young man stopped to say he saw her hustling a new red M3 on TV and he was going to come buy it from her. She gave him a splendidly dimpled smile, said she'd be in tomorrow at eleven so bring that checkbook. He smiled, too, but mostly at the camera.

Then dinner at the Strait household, minus Lee, who was at practice. Dalton ate almost wordlessly, lost to his phone, a large goblet of red wine at his place; Natalie looked tired doing dishes alone, glancing occasionally at the camera while Freddie repositioned himself for prime begging angles.

The next cut was abrupt and startling:

```
INT. STRAIT LIVING ROOM NIGHT
Mom sits alone in the living room, facing
the fireplace. She wears the same flannel
robe in which she cooked breakfast. Freddie
lies beside her. The lights are off but
there is a good fire and her facial
```

features are clearly dramatized by the
flames and surrounding darkness.

TERRELL
(offscreen)

>   Mom, can you talk to me about the
>   darkness and the light?

NATALIE
(in the moody firelight we see that Natalie
is pensive and subdued, her hair down and
long)

>   Oh. Well. So different, Terrell. But
>   they're two halves of the same
>   thing.

TERRELL

>   Of the same person.

NATALIE

>   Tell me what you've seen. In me.

TERRELL

>   Your light. Like earlier today when
>   we filmed your life. It's obvious.
>   People see it. But on other days
>   there's no light. Only darkness on
>   your face and in your spirit. Then,
>   you vanish.

NATALIE

I have bipolar disorder, which
always includes a manic-depressive
subset. The manic is the light.
Depression is the darkness. These
are my names for them, not
scientific ones. The light and
darkness have been here my whole
life but in the last few years they
have been more pronounced. I've
always tried my best to hide them.
It's easier than it might sound. Your
father didn't quite get that
something was wrong until about a
year and a half ago when I had this
break. They call it a break.

TERRELL

What breaks?

NATALIE
(petting Freddie)

You turn inside out. You lose your
usual behavior and most of your
memory. I went to Las Vegas and
gambled away lots of money. I drank
in excess and abused some
prescription painkillers for my
knee. There might have been other

misdeeds but I don't remember them.
Just that everything was so dark.
Like it was taking place at night.
Like there was only night all day
long, even in a bright place like
Las Vegas.

                    TERRELL

Have you had another break since
then?

                    NATALIE

No. I have medication and take it
every day. When I feel the darkness
trying to get into me, I dispel it
with strenuous exercise, hard work,
and hot baths. When I feel the light
around me I try to grow it with a
sunny attitude and gratefulness for
all the beautiful things in my
life. Such as Freddie and Lee and
you, Terrell. I love you all very
much.

                    TERRELL

And dad?

                    NATALIE

Dad, too. So much. Of course.

By then, Freddie had awakened and climbed into Natalie's lap. She lifted him from the couch to the floor. Then studied her son with a weary expression.

                        NATALIE

        How did I do?

                        TERRELL

        Just beautiful, Mom.

The last scenes of *A Day in a Life* briefly took us back to the kitchen, where the movie had begun. But there was no Natalie, no family, no Freddie, and no sound, except for the Beatles' "A Day in the Life" playing faintly in the background. Just the empty breakfast nook, places set.

Ditto the BMW dealership, campaign headquarters, the gym, the market, the Strait dining room, and finally the living room, now with a cold fireplace. No Mom. A day in a life emptied of life. I wondered at young Terrell's patience in refilming these sets without humankind—his vision of a world without his mother.

The outtakes that Terrell had mentioned weren't labeled as such but I saw the change in her. Natalie was more relaxed and humorous at home in her living room or on the back patio than at work, or at campaign central. She had a self-deprecation that was winning, calling herself a "spaz" without reservation or condemnation, and she seemed to look on most people and things with an optimistic and blameless eye. Maybe from seeing the weakness in herself, I thought. In how fragile a mind can be.

TWENTY-THREE

The next morning Dalton and I sat at a long table in the conference room of the Valley Center sheriff substation. Facing us was Lieutenant Lew Hazzard of the Special Enforcement Detail, and homicide detective Tony Proetto. Hazzard was tightly packed into his uniform, thick arms surrounding a folder on the desk. Proetto wore jeans and a golf shirt and a baggy blazer. Hazzard eyed me with the same robust hostility he'd offered when I had watched the CSIs work Natalie Strait's dust-covered BMW X5 out on the Pala Reservation. Proetto was distant.

"We found some interesting things in your wife's car," said Hazzard. "And got some solid information in our field interviews. And a call on the tip line just after your conference yesterday. No smoking gun, but we know more now."

"Good, Lew, good," said Dalton, looking at the lieutenant and fiddling with the cuff buttons on his dress
shirt. "What exactly?"

"You're sure about the PI being in on this, sir?" he said
as if I wasn't there. Then a ham-faced assessment of me.

"Pretty damned, Lieutenant," said Dalton. "We fought
in Fallujah together."

"I'm aware of that."

"I actually don't have all day, Lew."

"We appreciate you being here," said Proetto. "We'll
keep it short. A witness saw two male subjects getting her
out of her BMW and into a white Suburban—out there
on the reservation, where she left her SUV. A black man
and a white man."

Brock Weld? I wondered if they'd found Marcus, the
young man I'd talked to while being escorted from Tola
Strait's marijuana farm. Maybe he'd come forward, trying to help.

"We already know that," said Dalton. "But how did
two men get into her Bimmer in the first place?"

"A woman called our tip line after your press conference," said Proetto. "Our luck. Tuesday morning she saw
a late-model blue SUV and a larger white SUV with a
flashing red light, both on the southbound Valley Parkway shoulder. Looked like they'd just pulled over. She
saw a brunette white woman behind the wheel of the
blue SUV. She saw a white male subject standing at her
window with a clipboard or a citation book. She saw a
black guy driving the white SUV. And one passenger,

maybe. It all went by in a flash. It was around nine-thirty, not long after Natalie left the restaurant. That's the direction she'd be heading for work in Escondido. The BMW was in front, indicating she'd pulled over and stopped for what she assumed was law enforcement. When we asked if the white SUV had a law-enforcement emblem she said no, it did not."

Hazzard gave Dalton a placid, blue-eyed stare. Proetto watched Dalton closely, but I could read no emotion on his face.

"And not long after," said Proetto, "as we know from Mr. Ford, Natalie Strait is seen out in Pala with two men—one white and one black—exiting her BMW and getting her into a white Suburban. Natalie had gotten there in the back seat of her own vehicle, likely followed by the Suburban that pulled her over. But we found no signs of struggle in her car. No blood, no abraded tissue or skin, no clots of hair or damage to the interior."

"She didn't write 'Help' in lipstick just for the fun of it," said Dalton. "Maybe they had a gun. Maybe she figured cops are cops and you do what they say. Maybe they *were* cops."

Hazzard absorbed the cop possibility with a stoic expression. Straightened the folder on the table before him and tapped it with his fingers, as if this finalized something. Proetto nodded noncommittally.

"Assemblyman Strait, do you and Natalie own a horse or horses?"

"Nope."

"Do you or your wife own clothing or crafts or decorations or accessories or art or furniture or anything that might contain horsehair?" he asked. "Specifically, horse-*tail* hair?"

"No. Not that I know of."

"Does she transport friends, relatives, or business associates who might be around horses?" asked Hazzard.

"I suppose it's possible but I really don't know," said Dalton. "Why?"

"Because we found horsetail hair in her vehicle. One fiber—black, thick, and straight. Cut at both ends. Some kind of adhesive at one end. Someone in her BMW very possibly brought it in. Maybe part of a belt. A purse. Some accessory that makes use of horsetail."

"You mean a woman kidnapped her?" asked Dalton.

"Why not?" asked Hazzard. "And men can have a horsehair bracelet, or accents on a coat, right? Again, we assume a third person—someone driving the white Suburban when Natalie was transferred to it. The FBI is looking at the hair for me, but it's going to take time. A lot of time, with The Chaos Committee out there sucking my up resources."

Dalton sat back, shaking his head, likely scrolling through his memory for horse-owning acquaintances.

"Mr. Strait, do you own a dog?"

"Freddie," said Dalton. "He's Natalie's. She found him running loose one day, dirty and hungry, no tags. Doesn't care for me, but he votes Republican."

"We found a fair amount of short, curly white hair in her car," said Hazzard.

"That's him," said Dalton. "He doesn't shed much."

"Where does he ride?"

"Jumps the seats. Bounces all around. He's a maniac."

"Did you get any prints from the BMW that weren't Natalie's or Dalton's?" I asked.

"I'll get to that," said Hazzard. Then did. "They lifted two nice fingerprints off the child-proof door and window toggles. Not Natalie's prints, and not yours, Mr. Strait."

The driver's, I thought, keeping Natalie from getting away.

"No," said Dalton. "No reason for Natalie or me to use the child-proofer with grown boys."

"We sent them to ATF and the FBI," said Hazzard. "But again, The Chaos Committee is slowing things way down."

Dalton made a fist and touched it lightly to the table. "The California Assembly's job one is to find those bastards and get 'em in the ground."

I wondered if Dalton campaigned in his sleep.

"Yesterday a cop up in Adelanto got shot in the back, long-distance," said Hazzard. "Going to be okay, but another in Fresno got shot at, too. Two cops in one day. That happens just about never in this state. Proof that there are fools out there, taking these Chaos assholes seriously."

Hazzard looked at Dalton, then at me, placid blue eyes in an angry pink face. "So put as many of them in the ground as you can, Mr. Strait."

"You know I will," said Dalton.

"I'll help any way I can," said Hazzard.

"Then give me your vote in November, Lieutenant."

Hazzard nodded his big head.

"Otherwise it looks to us that the interior of your wife's car was wiped down for prints," said Proetto. "We found an unusually small number of everyday latents. They found small shreds of paper snagged on the dash and armrest controls—like a paper towel would leave."

Hazzard slapped open the folder, stared down at the top sheet. "Okay. Natalie wrote 'Help' in lipstick on the back of the front passenger seat. She was cool and smart and got away with it. In their hurry they apparently never saw it. She also left this in the map pouch that 'Help' was written on."

He took out a sheet of printer paper and slid it to face Dalton. A close-up photograph, enlarged. The focus and color both good. Against a dark background I saw a faintly shining circle with a faceted pyramid attached.

"Her bridal set," said Dalton. "A carat and a half combined, white gold."

He stared down at the copy. "Another signal to us," he said. "Another warning."

Dalton lifted the paper for a different angle. A grunt's stare, a thousand yards foreshortened. And a long moment.

"We also got the recent destination settings from the navigation unit," said Hazzard. "Which are right here."

He set another photocopied picture in front of Dalton, the X5 computer screen in its recent-addresses mode:

COSTCO WHOLESALE, San Diego

CAHUILLA CASINO, Anza

ASCLEPIA PHARMACEUTICAL, San Diego

FEDERAL BUREAU OF INVESTIGATION, San Diego

LEAH & TOD FINE JEWELRY, La Jolla

"So?" asked Dalton.

"Anything surprise you at all?" asked Hazzard.

"Like what?"

"I'm asking you, Mr. Strait."

"Well . . . she uses the navigator for practically everything. Even if she knows how to get there. A crutch. She likes that lady with the English accent."

"Why would she go to the FBI?"

Dalton shrugged.

"Or Asclepia Pharmaceutical?" asked Hazzard. "It's a regional office. They don't sell any drugs out of there."

I wondered if Natalie had been having a look at McKenzie Doyle.

"Funny name, Asclepia," said Dalton, blushing.

"From the Greek god of medicine," said Proetto. "Zeus killed him for raising the dead."

"I'd have given him a raise," said Dalton.

"Why would Natalie drive to the regional office?"

"Come to think of it, she was applying for a job there," said Dalton.

Another ham-faced glance of suspicion from Hazzard to Proetto. "She wasn't selling enough BMWs?"

"She was looking for a better earning opportunity," said Dalton. "She's good at sales."

"And her visit to the FBI, was that a common thing?" asked Hazzard.

"Not that I know," said Dalton. "But it's possible the feds were talking to her behind my back. The goal of the charges is to keep me from being reelected. As you know."

Proetto leaned forward. "We went back through the navigation memory and saw Natalie made three other trips there in the last six weeks."

"You'll have to ask them why," said Dalton. "Odds are, they were trying to get some dirt on me."

"Dirt?" asked Hazzard.

"Read the papers, Lew," said Dalton. "How thick are you?"

A glare from big Hazzard.

"Mr. Strait," said Proetto, "in one of our earlier talks here, we established that you were in Sacramento the day your wife went missing. Am I remembering that right?"

"Yeah, so?"

"And what time did you fly out of Lindbergh?"

"Early morning. I don't remember the exact time. I already told you that."

"Just checking the timeline," said Proetto. "Because this witness who put Natalie with the two men out in Pala, getting her from one car to another, he said one of them looked like you."

"You showed him a picture?"

"Routine, in a case like this, Mr. Strait," said Hazzard.

"Well, he might have looked like me but he *wasn't* me," said Dalton. "Jesus, you guys . . ."

"Do you have a record of that travel? An airline or hotel receipt?"

"Of course I do—it was assembly business."

"We're just nailing down the details," said Proetto. "Get me a copy of that receipt and we can move on to the things that matter. No hurry, Mr. Strait. I know you've got an awful lot on your mind these days."

Dalton stood. "I hope you sonsofbitches know I didn't have anything to do with Natalie's disappearance. You're smarter than that, right?"

═════

Dalton sat in heavy silence as I drove us toward Borrego Springs and our Fallujah reunion with Harris Broadman. Stared out the window for most of the way.

As we dropped down into the valley he checked his phone, returned a call and some text messages.

"I'm looking forward to seeing Harris," he said. "Kind of nervous, too."

"It was his idea," I said.

"It's the right thing. Sometimes, you have to go back."

TWENTY-FOUR

The parking lot of the Bighorn Motel wasn't as busy as before. The bungalows around the pool sat patiently in the mounting May heat. According to the Bighorn website, the wildflower bloom was all but over.

Standing at the locked front door, I pressed the intercom button and waited.

"Good morning," a young woman said, her voice familiar.

I told her we were here to see Mr. Broadman.

"I can see if he's available."

"Open the damned door, honey," said Dalton. "It's hot out here."

We stepped inside to the same cramped, poorly lit, slightly dusty office I remembered. The counter with the bowl of mints and the things-to-do pamphlets organized and upright in the rack.

And Cassy, the pale girl with the thinning hair and the mini-mic clipped to her plain smock dress. Today's was baby blue. Behind her was the taxidermy cabinet and the closed door to her room.

I introduced myself and Dalton. Dalton shook her hand and said he was running for reelection in the 82nd California Assembly District.

Cassy's soft gaze drifted to me. "I remember you, Mr. Ford."

"It's nice to see you again."

"It's nice of you to say so."

I heard a hint of Texas in her voice that I hadn't heard before. She stepped back into the shadow of the preserved desert animals and let the shoulder mic pick up her voice. Told an invisible someone that Misters Ford and Strait were here.

A moment later, Harris's soft, calm voice came through the wall speaker. "Bring them around to nineteen, Cass."

"Yes, Mr. Broadman."

Cassy led us from the cool lobby and back into the midday heat. Along the covered walkway, past bungalow six, where Broadman and I had first talked. Past the clean, empty swimming pool then left down the second leg of the horseshoe, and left again to bungalow nineteen, the last unit of the third wing. Cass had led us the long way around but kept us, and her own delicate skin, out of the ferocious desert sun.

As before, the door was cracked and Broadman told us to come in.

Broadman had given up his all-white wardrobe for

conventional jeans and desert camo boots, a tan San Diego Veterans Writers Group T-shirt, and what looked like his everyday service cap from Fallujah, faded and frayed by the war. Like we were, I thought.

He unbent from the couch, slowly crossed the room and gave Dalton a brief hug. Shook my hand. It was the first time I'd touched him and I was surprised by his grip, cold and strong.

The living room was much different from the sparse, mid-century modern look of bungalow six. I wondered why Broadman occupied two units in the same motel. This unit was warmer in spirit, homier. Better light. It reminded me of the Midwest—with knockoff colonial rockers and a wood-framed sofa that could have come from a Sears catalogue in 1965, a braided oval rug, a dated entertainment cabinet anchored by a portly TV and shelves of vinyl record albums. I remembered that he was born and raised in Kenton, Ohio. Broadman was roughly my age, just old enough to have grown up with things like these around him. If these furnishings weren't Broadman's from boyhood, some effort had gone into re-creating that time. The walls were lined with wooden bookshelves and cabinets brimming with framed family photographs, award ribbons, trophies, and war memorabilia.

Broadman took up the center of the couch again, and Dalton and I sat facing him across a low maple-finished coffee table with scalloped edges and cloth doilies. A bottle of Rebel Yell bourbon sat unopened on an *American Rifleman* magazine from 1989 and the three glasses sat perfectly centered on their doilies.

"You still drink that shit?" asked Dalton, smiling.

"Not anymore," said Broadman. "It's for you guys."

"God knows we put some of that away," said Dalton.

I remembered that quality spirits were hard to come by in Iraq. One of our sergeants had a stateside supply line of budget vodka and that was as good as it got. Beer was better anyway, if you could keep it cold. Sleep was best of all, if and when you could get it.

Dalton considered the fresh bottle for a short beat. Opened it and poured himself a shot. Broadman and I declined his offer.

I sat quietly as they caught up on family and careers, knowing that the pull of their combat is what had brought them here. Though I had fought the same war, my battleground was different and they could have been talking about a world apart. My world was the Jolan, in the oldest part of the city, thought by the Iraqis to be insurmountable by U.S. troops. Dalton and Harris met their fates in East Manhattan, insurgent-heavy, difficult to get in and out of, often not even patrolled by the Fallujah police.

So they fell into their war stories, first an informal roll call of their combat brethren living and dead, then on to specific patrols and firefights that, like most war stories, they delivered in one-two punches of the gruesome and the comic.

I lapsed into a semiprivate reverie of my own, peopled by men I'd fought with and laughed at and overheard talking loudly into their phones to loved ones back home. Jason and the guitar his pet rat lived in. Amin, the terp nobody fully trusted. And of course I thought of the ones who had died. They still occupy my dreams.

As do my memories of the Five. My unfortunate Five, whom I've never mentioned to any civilian, even Justine.

I thought of the door-to-door searches that had me juiced with adrenaline, trained to kill and amped on the idea I was about to die. We entered a home or a business in what they called a three-stack: first the corporal, then a sergeant or sergeant-major, then a private. The corporal was me—too big to be ideal for the job, but fast and good enough with a gun. And good to hide behind, as we liked to joke.

"So, Roland, how many hajis did you kill?" asked Dalton.

I eyed him through the gun smoke of a living room reeling with bullets and bodies.

"Five."

"Come on. Five confirmed? You never told me that. *Really, Ford? Five?*"

I nodded through the smoke. Saw a boy run screaming down a hallway into the back of the house. Or was he a small man? Someone behind me shot him. I don't know who and I didn't ask.

"No wonder you're so fucked up. Here, have a drink." He poured into my empty glass.

"I'm good for now, Dalton."

"I only got one. Harris, two," said Dalton.

"And you're the only one who still swills the booze," said Broadman. "I see those ads of yours on TV and I think, that old jarhead drinks too much. It's the bags under your eyes."

"They're known as character bags at the Capitol."

Broadman smiled, teeth white, eyes brown in the surly red flesh.

"Yet I carry the weight of an entire assembly district on my broad shoulders," said Strait.

A beat of silence, uneasy and eager to be broken.

Dalton took another drink, then set his empty glass back on the doily.

"When that bomb went off I thought we were all dead," he said quietly. "The world went red and I was eating road dirt. Thought it was the first place you had to wait to get into heaven."

Broadman nodded slowly, set his hands on his knees but said nothing.

I thought they might want some privacy for this. I went to one of the wall cabinets, pretending polite interest, but my ears were tuned to the conversation behind me.

Family pictures. The Broadmans. A midwestern interior circa 1985, not unlike the room in which I stood. Two boys and two girls. Mrs. Broadman looking pleasant; Dad in a Levi's jacket, a trucker's cap, plenty of hair.

"And I just couldn't get that knife through the nylon, Harris. I'd hack until the flames got too hot, then I'd fall outside into the rifle fire. Then I'd climb back in and hack away again. It just would not cooperate. The harness. The fire. Good Christ, it was hot in that Humvee. I could smell us burning."

"You could smell *me* burning," said Broadman.

"Yes, that's what I . . . meant to say."

"I saw you take cover behind the K-rails. Leaving me for the snipers or the fire."

I heard Dalton pour and drink. Went to a bookshelf. Mostly nonfiction on fat subjects—science, nature, history, and biography. Darwin to Durant, Carl Sagan to Jared Diamond. Some obscure books, too, whose titles I didn't recognize. A few I did know, such as the *Complete Works of Malatesta, Volume IV*. I remembered Malatesta from nineteenth-century European history class at SDSU, Professor Nicolas Falbo presiding. Malatesta being an Italian political prisoner and activist who wrote voluminously.

"I was coming for you. Then the gun truck arrived and the Spookie blew the Wollies away. I helped the corpsmen get you into the truck, Harris. I was there. I took fire for you."

"You left me in the road to die."

"I needed thirty seconds to rest."

"Fire can eat a pound of flesh in thirty seconds."

"I don't see it that way."

"There's no other way to see it."

I turned to see Dalton leaning forward in the chair. Back hunched, his elbows on his knees, a shot glass in one hand and his head down.

"I won't apologize," he said. "I tried to get you out, and I failed. But I can't carry that around the rest of my life. I'm not strong enough."

"I expected more from you."

"Then or now?"

"Both," said Broadman.

He walked slowly to a window and turned the shutter wand. I wondered why he didn't have a remote, as in bungalow six. The sunlight laddered through and caught his molten face and the clear dark brown of his eyes. Looked out for a moment, then cut off the light again. Turned to Dalton.

"I didn't ask you here for an apology. The opposite. I want to apologize to you. I've been silent and bitter for all of the sixteen years I've been forced to live since that day. I'm not strong enough to carry that any longer, either. I've unburdened myself of much, Dalton—love, joy, nature's pleasures. Even art and music and other human escapes. Surrendered my belief in our nation and my faith in our gods. Now I surrender my resentment of you. I apologize for hating you so long."

A long silence as the invisible weights of blame and forgiveness shifted on their invisible pulleys.

I wondered if Harris Broadman had furnished this— his second home—to resemble a time when his world was comfortable and good. The world of the child he had once been. So that he could recline into a beautiful past while he surrendered his tormented present.

Dalton was still hunched in his chair, elbows out and head down.

"Well, of course you know I'm going to accept, Harris."

"Good. We are now square. And can proceed in our lives."

"I'd like that."

Broadman creaked over to the couch and sat back down. "PFC Strait, I'm concerned for Natasha. Are you any closer to finding her?"

Dalton straightened, put his glass back on the coffee table. "Natalie."

"I beg your pardon."

"But no. I don't think we're closer. Are we, Roland?"

Well, I thought, *maybe, but not in ways I could discuss right now*. In just the last few hours, I'd heard police suspicion of a mismatch between Dalton's words and his abduction-day airline flight. And now Dalton's new best friend, Harris Broadman—after despising Dalton for sixteen bitter years—was expressing concern for Natalie's well-being. Those two interesting details, plus my boxing scar, which was now itching vibrantly on my forehead.

"We're closer," I said.

An affirmative nod from Harris, fire-battered lips pursed and his eyes luminous brown—nearly copper colored—in a slat of light. "If I can be of any help."

"Thanks," said Dalton. "That means something to me."

"What can I give you, Dalton? What on earth do you want?"

"Natalie back."

"Something I can give. Something I can do."

Dalton squeezed his knee thoughtfully. "Lemme think on that, Sarge."

Broadman walked us the long way around to where we had parked outside the Bighorn lobby. He stood in the shade, listening to Dalton's loud campaign pitch, so I rang myself inside the office to pick up some brochures.

Cassy came from the back. I got a brief glimpse of her quarters again, the IV drip station in the far corner facing the chair and the TV.

"I wanted some maps and brochures," I said.

"Take what you want."

"One of each, maybe?"

"There's plenty."

"How do you like working for a war hero?"

"He doesn't pay much, but I trust him."

"Trust him to what?" I asked breezily.

"Not try anything aggressive."

"That's important," I said, removing the pamphlets one at a time and setting them on the dusty countertop.

"And I enjoy being valuable," said Cassy. "There are some things Mr. Broadman can't do because of his health. I understand that. I have cancer and I'm fighting it, but sometimes I can hardly get out of bed. Same with Harris, but it's not cancer."

"So you help each other out."

"All the time. Little things to keep this place running. Run to the big box in La Quinta to pick up lightbulbs. More floor cleaner. The market. The bank. There's three of us women so Mr. Broadman can concentrate on his studies and writing."

"What's he study and write?"

"I don't know. I've seen some of the books he reads. Old historical books. European mostly."

I took pamphlets for the metal sculptures tour, the

Borrego night sky tours, and the poisonous dwellers of the desert program.

"It's good to care about other people," I said. "The way you care for Mr. Broadman."

"Do you think I'm a simpleton?"

"No, why?"

"A statement like that sounds like you're talking to a child."

"I'm just making small talk while I clean up on the brochures."

"It's too hot out here by now to do most of that stuff anyway," she said. "I'll get you a bag."

She handed me a brown paper grocery bag from somewhere below the counter, and I swept the brochures in. Then began selecting more, scanning the graphics for promising topics.

"Do you have any favorites?" I asked. "Of these desert things to do."

She gave me a pale appraisal, pushed a lank length of hair back behind one ear. "I like the wildflowers but they're gone. Pictograph Trail is a nice hike. Especially if you like native culture, which I do. It's on the cover."

She tapped a brochure. I saw the venous catheter port high on her arm, an always ready portal for chemotherapy. A surgically implanted port implies a long haul and I wasn't sure if that was a good thing or a bad one.

"I enjoy Harris's company," I said. "He's got that subtle sense of humor."

"Not much of one, though," Cassy said.

"Kind of a homebody, is he?"

She gave me another doubtful look. "He gets out. Almost every day."

"That his silver Tahoe out front?" I nodded toward the window.

"Yeah. And don't ask me where he goes. He tells me that we all own the rights to our secrets. I think his are from the war. Obviously."

"And yours?"

"Oh, no special secrets. I'm all about world peace. My little world, anyway."

"What's your last name?"

"Weisberg. Harris told me the politician hired you to find his wife."

"I'm looking."

"Abduction terrifies me. I dream about it even though it's never happened to me. In the dreams, I'm claustrophobic. I'm enclosed by immovable dark things. Oh, don't miss Hellhole Canyon. A good hike. I don't see why they gave it such a terrible name."

She leaned over the pamphlet rack to find one, set it on the new pile. I slipped the Hellhole Canyon brochure under the others and scooped them all into the paper bag.

Held up my best picture of Brock Weld and his consort on my phone. Fishing.

She studied it.

"I've never seen either of them."

"Thanks for looking," I said. "Peace, Cassy Weisberg."

"You too."

TWENTY-FIVE

As we climbed out of Borrego Valley toward his campaign headquarters, Dalton worked his phone: posting, talking, tweeting, returning media calls. Half-lit by bourbon, he mumbled his replies as he posted them, so I got the gist. The cops had rattled him and Harris Broadman had set something loose in him, and now Dalton's reaction was to put his foot on the gas.

Most of the interview requests he passed on to his reelection committee, but he returned one to Fox News and expanded on the idea that "mentally disturbed Natalie could easily have spent some campaign donations on personal stuff because it's so damned hard to navigate the fed rules anymore. And these allegations against me are nothing but a political hack job by Democrats who want to run the last Republican out of state office. Just ask 'em—they'll *tell* you that."

Etc.

"It's crazy, man," he said, ending the call. "You tell the world your bipolar wife might have blown a few campaign dollars for a round of golf with contributors, and people go bonkers. I'm getting way more media than before—*everybody* wants me! They can't get enough dirt. And guess what? The money's flooding in again big-time, right after my press conference. Speaking of which."

Dalton shoved himself up in the seat, worked out his wallet, and pulled a thick stack of bills. I heard him counting them off.

"Here's the eight hundred to get us started," he said. "Even though that was days ago. I'll have the rest but . . . it might be a while. I'm good with this, Roland. Hope you are, too."

"I enjoy being shorted by my clients."

"Shit." He broke the wallet back open.

"Forget it, Dalton. Pay me when you can."

"You know I will."

"I don't know what you'll do."

"*Really?* After all this?"

"Hang on to your money," I said. "For now."

Dalton put his wallet away then fished a flask from a coat pocket.

I declined.

He took a draw. "So, there's a lot of people saying I can't just blame this indictment on Natalie, that I'm a real bastard for trying to do so."

"It looks bad, Dalton. The way you talk about her bipolar condition. It makes you sound like a pig."

"I do bring home the bacon."

"There you go again."

"Want to be my campaign manager?"

"No. Someone's had your wife captive for ten days and you're joking."

"Heroes cry on the inside."

"Any idiot can say stuff like that."

We came down the mountain from Valley Center on Cole Grade Road, a fast road with long views. It was late morning and the ceanothus was blue against the green slopes.

Dalton set his phone on his leg, took another swig, and let out a soft groan. "I borrowed money to buy that bridal set. If you bought the engagement ring and the wedding ring as a combo, you saved some shekels. To be honest, I was really proud to give them to her. We were just stupid in love. You've been like that?"

"I have."

He gave me a look. "It kind of started a civil war in my family. Marrying her. My older brother, Kirby, was the one who introduced us. He wanted her bad. Half killed me when I told him she was going with me. Dad and Tola were pulling for me, mostly because Kirby was unstable and they really liked Natalie. Mom and Grandpa, though, they were for Kirby all the way. Thought I'd betrayed a brother. Broke a Strait bond. Maybe I had. Hell, I was fifteen. Later Kirby did what he did to Dad and everything changed."

"Which was?"

"Big fight. Dad just a little slower than he used to be. Kirby, way strong for his age, and mean. A good fair fight until Kirby used one of his kung fu moves and tripped Dad back hard with his foot. Well, they say the Lord moves in strange ways and He sure did that night. The back of Dad's head hit the river-rock barbecue pit so hard it sounded like a pistol shot."

I thought of Archibald Strait, healthy looking but apparently unconscious in his hospital bed, catching some sunshine in Virgil's rock fortress living room.

"That's not the story Virgil told me," I said.

"He prefers the Better Burger robbery story."

"I'm surprised you all could pass it off for so many years."

"Surprised why? East County is Strait country. We write the stories."

Which was the first thing we new East County deputies were told when starting out in that vast, hard country. I was one of them only briefly. But back then I hadn't realized quite how true it was.

"Because of who she is, Natalie always has men after her," said Dalton. "Women like her always do. It's not looks. It's not even behavior. It's attitude. An unknowable thing. A certain kind of man senses that in her and the rest is simple nature. He *knows* what he wants and where it is. That's what got me to marry her. Love her."

Echoes of Kirby.

I thought of Kirby and Dalton, Brock Weld, and the guy at the dealership. I pictured the robust and attractive woman I'd seen on the car commercials and had to admit that even on a screen Natalie Strait had some not-quite-visible attractant.

"Nats knows this and uses it," he said. "Sometimes, she pretends to be flirting, sometimes not. Either way, I understand how she's coming across to these guys. How it's affecting them and what they think their options are. Which has put me in the protective-husband position a lot. Not something I aspired to. It takes energy. Jealousy can creep in. Worst emotion in the world. Makes you do crazy stuff. You are always in the wrong. Makes you second-guess. Your leg. Your dick. You. Gets you where you live."

We came down the grade and headed for the campaign headquarters in Escondido.

"I lost a nut in the blast," he said. "My favorite. There's some ugly scars. And some nerve damage, but the doctors say the damage is in my head. I'm okay that way but not perfect. I've hardly told anyone that."

I didn't see any point in telling him that he'd said as much to me, drunk, in the Sacramento men's room.

"It sounds like I'm complaining about her, but I'm not," said Dalton. "If I could go back, and know what's ahead, I'd do it all over again with her. She's like . . . a diamond you find, and when you get it home you see the flaws in it and they make the diamond even more valuable. More one-of-a-kind."

He took another draw and propped the flask on his half-natural, half-manufactured knee. Let the flask top swing loose on its chain. Rolled up one sleeve of his business shirt, switched hands on the flask, and rolled up the other.

"I want her back, Roland. Not out there in a world that can hurt her. I know you're trying. She's trying, too. Asking for help. Leaving her rings in her car as a way to communicate with me."

"We're going to find her," I said.

"Ten days. It's got to be some kind of record."

The Strait reelection campaign headquarters stood in a stately neighborhood of '50s-style homes, some now converted for commercial use. A law office, an orthopedic surgeon, an architect. Pepper trees and trophy citrus, salvaged and proudly groomed. A boulevard from Southern California's past still trooping into the future.

A uniformed private security guard stood outside the front door, armed but essentially defenseless against a mailed bomb.

As we stepped in, Dalton's unannounced visit sent a visible charge through the faithful. In the halting of tasks and the turning of faces and the pause of conversations I saw that nearly all of the people here were at least as old as the neighborhood, as much a part of the past as the trees outside. He was their young one. They drifted toward him subtly, more drawn than moving with a purpose.

He proceeded into them with greetings and handshakes, hugs and slaps on shoulders. Familiar comments, smiles, and confidential laughter. Dalton grabbed a donut from a pink box, turned back to me, and waved me over.

He stood on a folding chair, a big man with a mop of curly brown hair and a donut in one hand, his cuffs rolled up and a strangely serene air around him. I realized that this was Dalton at his happiest. His most whole again. Surrounded, supported, and followed. Standing on their shoulders to dream his dream.

"I apologize for making excuses about Natalie," he said. "Any minute I expected her to walk in here. You know how stubborn hope is. But she didn't. I knew from that first day that something was very wrong. That she needed help. I didn't want you all to worry."

Silence. Not a question from Dalton's loyalists. Not a murmur.

"I apologize, too, for the false and malicious claims that my own federal government has brought against me. You all know how honest I am, and what a stickler Natalie was for keeping the books right. These charges represent a new low in American politics and I vow to fight those charges with all my might."

"Yeah, Dalton!"

"Kick 'em right back, Mr. Strait!"

"We're all in for you, Dalton!"

He hopped down, finished his donut, threw some hugs. Let them take selfies with him.

Half an hour later we were headed through Escondido toward Dalton's house.

"Hey, Roland, park in that Chevron lot right there, by the air and water pumps, will you?"

I pulled into one of the parking slots by the pumps.

"I don't need air or water," I said.

"Me neither." He took another long draw off his flask. "I need certain things a man in my position is denied. It's a heavy burden. I think you'll understand."

He pocketed the flask and got out, just as a black Lincoln limousine pulled alongside me. The black-suited driver stepped out and opened the rear door for Dalton.

"Good morning, Mr. Strait."

"Morning, Joe."

"Another beautiful day."

Dalton looked back at me, waved and nodded before getting in. Beyond him, deep in black leather, sat Asclepia Pharmaceutical representative McKenzie Doyle, a recessed spotlight aimed at the phone on her crossed knee, readers down on her nose, looking at me without expression.

TWENTY-SIX

Lark had agreed to meet me later that afternoon at the Duffytown shooting range. I told him I had some information on Dalton and Tola Strait that he might find interesting. This was enough to get me one hour with my friendly neighborhood FBI. It was also true enough, though the larger truth was that I was planning an ambush.

Duffytown is a mock town on a navy base, part modern and part Old West, named after an old San Diego sheriff—a good place for law enforcement training. Targets jump out at you from doorways or windows if you want them to, or you can just take old-fashioned range practice if you'd rather.

The place was bustling, befitting the bombing death of a local congressman. All manner of law enforcers squeezing off rounds. The rattle of automatic fire. A pair of fighter jets out of Miramar roaring low overhead.

We shot conventional—life-sized paper silhouettes on retracting cables at ten, twenty-five, fifty, seventy-five, and a hundred feet. Lark used his .40-caliber Glock and I used my vintage .45 Colt Gold Cup, a gift from my father.

I have 20/10 vision, a genetic gift. One hundred feet is a long shot with an open-sight handgun, good eyes or not. A trained *pistolero* will put eight out of eight shots in the black all day long at a hundred feet. A street cop who qualifies four times a year at twenty-five feet because he's required to, won't.

On this clear spring day my eyes were sound and the rhythm found itself and I beat ultra-competitive Lark in our first round. Six of eight in the black for PI Ford; five for Special Agent Lark.

He set his earmuffs on the bench and examined his target with tense disappointment. Poked his fingers through the outside-the-silhouette holes from behind, as if he could make them disappear.

"Mike, tell me about the craggy-faced old agent who interrupted us in your conference room that day. As you know, he was with Dalton and Tola Strait in Sacramento Monday night after Dalton's bill got shot down. Heath Overdale was there, too—the freight and shipping lobbyist."

Lark looked at me, all suspicion. Anger, too, at the risk he'd taken by bringing me into his San Diego field office, and how the simple opening of a conference room door had blown a cover. I remembered the annoyance on Lark's face when the older man had looked in.

"Back off, Roland."

"Why?"

A long consideration from Lark, wheels turning. "What put that idea in your head about Sacramento?"

"I was there."

"We've worked hard to get him in place, Roland. Don't fuck it up."

The next round, Mike shot first and toggled the target back to us. Six clean holes in the black. One in the center circle. He blew on his upraised barrel like a gunslinger and set his pistol on the bench.

I brought up the Gold Cup, took a deep breath and let it out slowly, settled my weight evenly, and enjoyed the God-given blessing of my vision. I shot unhurriedly. As Wyatt Earp once noted, fast is fine but accuracy is final. The trigger's sweet spots presented in rhythm, weighted and cam-like within the heavy Colt. As the silhouette sailed back to us I could see points of sunlight through the paper. Seven in the black—one just at the edge of the bad guy's right shoulder—but enough to win.

"What's Crag Face's pitch to Dalton and Tola?" I asked.

Lark's look was cool anger. He could do little more than trust my professional ethics, and our untested, young friendship.

"A California Department of Business Oversight regulator with holes in his wallet and his morals," he said. "Maybe willing to look the other way on Tola's wannabe credit union partners. His favorite foundation funds literacy on Southern California Indian reservations. The second she offers it cash, that's a bribe and we've got her."

I wondered if Tola had been sufficiently fooled by Crag Face to do something so reckless. Her familiar attitude toward him suggested that she might have.

"And if Dalton is willing to sweeten the pot by throwing in a no vote on credit union oversight in return for a campaign donation from said foundation, we get two for one," said Lark. "We snag a drug pusher and a vote-peddling assemblyman."

I was suddenly sick of Lark and his feds. Of their separate laws and pugnacious power. I thought they should leave California's problems to California, rather than compound them. Go entrap someone else. I said nothing. But Lark and I knew each other well enough for him to read my mind like an open map.

"Roland? I still carry the federal handcuffs in San Diego. So if you blow our cover to Dalton or Tola, you'll qualify to wear them."

I didn't have to tell Mike that his FBI wouldn't be able to prove such a thing if I simply whispered in their ears.

"Your call, Mike, not mine."

"Are you personally interested in Tola Strait?" he asked. "I've seen her."

"She showed me around the Nectar Barn outside Julian."

"And?"

"I thought she might hire me to move some cash but she didn't. I was glad. It looked like an easy way to die."

Lark gave me his hard-guy look, somewhat softened by his awkward haircut.

"Her cash comes from federal crimes," he said.

"Her business is legal in the State of California," I said. "And you put people like Tola Strait in danger by not letting them bank their money. She's sitting on safes full of time bombs. Her growers were attacked by cartel gunmen last year and had to shoot their way out of it."

"Poor little felons."

"I don't see it that way."

"Then we agree to disagree," said Lark. "If Dalton and Tola suddenly turn a cold shoulder to my man, I'll have to have a talk with you."

"I can't make them fall for his bullshit, either, Mike."

"I wonder. Maybe we can help each other. Even dogs can share the spoils."

I didn't say so, but I'd never seen dogs share anything, especially spoils.

Instead I asked him about their progress on The Chaos Committee.

"Representative Clark Nisson had eighty-seven letters, twelve oversized envelopes, and seven packages delivered to his Encinitas office the week leading up to the bombing," he said. "That we know of. Almost half of those items came through twenty-eight different U.S. post offices, the others from private carriers. The bomb contained a powder accelerant and the fire destroyed almost everything evidentiary—paper being paper—part of The Chaos Committee's intention, no doubt. But we've got no positive point of origin. Which leaves us mountains of surveillance video to view, along with all the internal tracking information. All to locate a suspect we can barely make out on the outdated surveillance video. If, of course, she even mailed it."

"Jackie O," I said. "Mailing bombs from Fallbrook and Ramona. Gaming the postal workers and FedEx employees with phony names and return addresses."

"Washington is frantic for an arrest," said Lark, an edge in his voice. "We've sent her image to every post office clerk and carrier in the county. To hundreds of FedEx and UPS employees. To every media news outlet there is. She's been all over the social platforms. Last night the president tweeted that every U.S. citizen should be on the lookout for her. Well, that's all great but we've got scores of thousands more tips, possible sightings, and positive identifications than we can follow up on. And they're still flooding in."

Lark wasn't exaggerating. I'd seen Jackie O everywhere the last few days, from the mainstream media to the corners of the dark web.

"We've computer-flagged all post office mailings addressed to government workers in California," he said. "The obvious ones, that is—mayors, city councilmen, supervisors, state legislators, judges, commissioners. Anyone elected or appointed to federal positions. A huge job. But there are thousands of cops and firefighters we can't flag. And The Chaos Committee promised more and bigger bombs—*soon*."

"What can I do, Mike?"

Lark reloaded his gun and jammed it back into the

paddle holster high on his right hip. Gave me a small but joyless smile.

"Joan always said to watch out for you and your favors."

"You and Joan have gotten plenty from my favors."

Once again, what hung before us was that terrible night when Joan Taucher was lost to both of us, suddenly and forever.

"I've sent you all the surveillance video we have from the postal service."

"I'm still catching up with it."

"I'd like you to look at the private carrier video also. Some of it's good. Some not."

"Send it, Mike."

He gave me a tired and harried look. "But mainly, Roland, you can help me by standing behind my agent's cover if the opportunity arises. Maybe even pursue such opportunity. In your usual subtle fashion. And along the way, I want you to let me know what Dalton and his sister are up to. If you can find it in your heart to defend the Constitution and help us hated feds."

TWENTY-SEVEN

After dark, I found a place in the Tourmaline Resort Casino parking tower. Took the stairs down to the employee level, located Brock Weld's white Suburban, and attached a GPS tracker to the bottom of the trailer hitch. The powerful magnet clanged with an echo. I turned it on and a few minutes later was sitting in the Terrace Café.

Just as he had the night before, at ten minutes after eight o'clock Weld came off his shift with the same two coworkers. Again, the younger man wore the black moto jacket and carried his helmet. They disappeared into the employee parking garage. As before, Moto Jacket came out first, easing his burping rocket down the ramp. But tonight the blonde came out next, alone and at the wheel of a yellow Mercedes two-seater. Last was Brock Weld in his clean white Suburban.

I turned on my tracking app, laid my cash on the tray, and headed out.

Easy tracking with the Vigilant 4000, the best $299 a PI can spend. I have three. With one-second real-time reporting you can follow far behind and still track the target on a three-color map with a flashing indicator. On your phone, of course. The only downside is that the whole contraption runs on cell signal, which can be spotty and sometimes nonexistent. You can program the app to give you a complete two-week driving history, nailing down the bad actor/cheating spouse/runaway son or daughter without having to follow him or her all over town. You can use it to set up a geo-fence that notifies you when the unit enters a certain area.

Highway 76 to Cole Grade Road, through Pauma Valley. In sunlight a beautiful valley, heavy with orange groves, rimmed by hills. In the moonless night a dark expanse, with Weld's white Suburban easy to see up ahead of me. He turned right on Valley Center Road, again on Lilac, then Via Clemente. I hung back and drove by his house a minute later, saw the Suburban in the driveway and the house lights coming on inside. The neighbors were just lights on a hillside road, neither distant nor close.

I found a turnout in the trees, pulled up tight to the fence, cut the lights and engine. I've modified my truck to be one hundred percent lightless and silent with the engine off—no anti-theft warnings or bluffs, no interior indicators or beeps. Blackout windows, exterior chrome replaced by matte black metal. Reflectors likewise.

I set my wristwatch in a cup holder to defeat reflection. Pondered Brock Weld's domicile. It was a small, rectangular, flat-roofed adobe with iron grates over the windows and faded peach paint. Baja California all the way. Gravel instead of grass, with columns of ocotillo and sticks on fire reaching up past the roofline. A cracked asphalt driveway, pricked by weeds. Scattered pots mostly without plants, an empty hose reel leaning against the living room wall below the window.

Always interesting to compare the animal to its lair. Brock's minimalist groundskeeping contradicted his sharp personal grooming, apparent physical strength, and swift opinions. The home had the look of the temporary. But so did Weld himself. A man used to motion. Fit, armed, and ready to engage. I thought back to the IvarDuggans bio— security work for cruise lines and casinos.

The faint ghost of movement behind the curtains. Then again. No flicker of TV light yet, and I had the feeling that Brock Weld was getting ready to leave. My lucky night. Or not. The last time I'd followed a hunch and tracked someone into the night, I'd ended up battered, broken, and about half-dead.

An inner house light went off, then another. When Weld came out his suit had been traded for jeans, white athletic shoes, and a baggy red hibiscus-print Hawaiian shirt.

He went west out Valley Center Road onto Highway 76 again, but east toward Palomar Mountain. Past the Rincon Indian Reservation and the observatory exits. It was black out there that time of night. A barn owl, white in my headlights, lifted a mouse from the road and churned up into the darkness. I hung back and let the Vigilant 4000 track my prize.

Past the La Jolla Indian Reservation, past the glistening black water of Lake Henshaw. Weld sped by a fat motor home and I tucked in behind it for the fast stretch to Highway 79.

A quick five minutes later, my phone map showed Weld turning northeast on Highway 79. Interesting. Because Highway 79 would lead him to S2, which would take him to Borrego Springs.

Beautiful, wild Borrego Springs.

Harris Broadman's Borrego Springs.

The scar on my forehead itched and my mind bounced merrily along in front of me like a bird dog working a meadow. Zigging and zagging, checking the cover, looping back and checking again.

A few minutes later, for the second time that day, I turned onto S2. Then watched the Suburban start the long gentle grade toward Montezuma Valley and Borrego Springs beyond.

Bringing to mind the molten-faced innkeeper Harris Broadman, who was pulled not quite to safety from his burning Humvee during the battle for Fallujah by the young, terrified grunt Dalton Strait.

Bringing to mind Natalie, Dalton's lovely, unstable wife, abducted, in credible danger, and recently indicted by a federal grand jury for misuse of campaign funds— along with her philandering husband.

Leading straight to the aggressive Brock Weld, who had bluntly made himself available to coworker Natalie and had no certifiable alibi for his whereabouts the morning she vanished.

Maybe Brock Weld was now on his way east to some other desert destination. Maybe to the Salton Sea, one of the most polluted bodies of water in the state. Or to one of the poor, dust-bitten desert towns that surround it. Perhaps headed south to Mexico or north to Las Vegas, driving hundreds of miles out of his way to get there. Maybe he was leading his friendly neighborhood PI on a snipe hunt. Or into an attack even worse than the one I had stumbled into last year.

I watched the road and checked the phone screen every few seconds. Up the grade, through the rising plains of Montezuma Valley, then the long, steep drop to the bottom of the desert floor.

Welcome to Borrego Springs.

Eighty-two degrees and a brisk breeze shivering the creosote. Far ahead, Weld went right onto Palm Canyon. I kept well back, used a plodding old VW van for cover. Watched the Suburban on my phone screen, moving slowly toward Christmas Circle, where he went south on Borrego Springs Road, toward Harris Broadman's Bighorn Motel. I doubted the apparent coincidence of encountering the Bighorn Motel twice in one day.

But then, Weld passed the Bighorn.

Five and a half dark and breezy miles later, he pulled into La Casa del Zorro, the swankiest resort in this part of the desert. I drove past, saw his Suburban parked near the lobby and Brock Weld swinging down from the driver's seat. A quarter mile down I U-turned and pulled into the resort just as the white Suburban turned onto the self-parking road.

I'd stayed at La Casa del Zorro before and I knew the layout: quaint casitas with private pools; a good restaurant and bar; tennis courts and verdant grounds under graceful palms, all especially beautiful at sunset. La Casa del Zorro had a romantic air, like the masked Zorro himself, robes and slippers and private hot tubs. Thus, popular with couples. I thought of Tola Strait in her Zorro-style hat that night in Sacramento, perhaps trying to strike a deal with an FBI agent posing as a state regulator.

I looped back to the restaurant lot, parked, and rolled down my windows. Nice breeze. Nice angles for my camera. The restaurant was busy on this Friday night. I tried to coax some news from my radio but FM got me faint music and AM nothing but static. Watched my phone screen as the Suburban came to a halt. It took a moment for the Google map to load but when it did I saw that Weld's Suburban was parked conveniently for any of four casitas on a cul-de-sac bordered by a wall, with open desert beyond. The image was aerial and reasonably clear.

Twenty minutes later, Weld came from the lobby, dressed as before but carrying a silver aluminum briefcase. His coworker from the Tourmaline was with him, still dressed in her dark work suit, hair down and lifting in the desert breeze. It was just after ten o'clock. She'd made good time in her little yellow sports car. They stood at the turnout, Weld with an almost palpable air of annoyance. Looked at his watch. I got some decent pictures with my G9. A moment later a black Yukon with blacked-out windows pulled in and stopped. Weld and the woman climbed into the back passenger-side seat. In the brief moment before the door shut I saw the shape of a driver but no detail.

Following the Yukon without the Vigilant 4000 considerably upped my chances of getting busted in a tiny town with no traffic to hide in this late. So I cautiously followed, up Borrego Valley Drive to Palm Canyon Drive, then left, back toward town.

I slowed and pulled over, watched the taillights disappear.

Tried to imagine what Brock Weld and his companion were doing here in this desert. I had no idea, and thought less of myself for the failure of imagination. But I'm not paid to be imaginative. I'm paid to find things other people can't. Such as Natalie Strait. She was the center of this, she had led me to all four of these people— indirectly, of course, without having ever spoken a word to me. Unless you counted *HELP*, written in lipstick on the back of her car seat.

I headed for home, alone in my truck with the scattered pieces of a puzzle on this moonless night, somewhere in the San Diego County desert. Waiting for the pieces to fall into place, as they sometimes do if you stare at them long and hard enough.

Tried again for radio news; not quite back into range.

Which was when my phone went off. Burt's name and number and a text message with video attached:

> **This just in.**
>
> **10:59 P.M.**

The video was brief, clear, and concise:

The three familiar grimly masked actors and two balaclava-hidden operatives standing against a white interior wall. The Chaos Committee in all its deranged and hideous glory.

This time the splatter mask spoke, in the same digitally altered doomsday voice as the Iroquois tribal mask had used during the *Local Live!* studio takeover.

"We have sent another gift to another government thug in beautiful, deluded California," he said. "A woman. She cannot be protected. Strike your matches, great state! Burn the disease from this once holy cloth. Burn the government to the ground. Violence is justice. Chaos is purity!"

I called Burt. He'd already talked to Dalton and his campaign headquarters about opening any packages or even mail, especially those addressed to female workers. He'd counseled the Irregulars to stay in rather than go out tomorrow and not to open any unexpected package from any carrier.

I drove fast into radio range, switching from station to station, trying to piece together the chaos.

California Governor Gavin Newsom has furloughed all nonessential state workers for at least two days and will deploy National Guards to search state offices and mailrooms for bombs . . . KNX News Radio has learned that police and sheriffs are being assigned to some city halls, county offices, and courtrooms . . . Police officers were shot and killed in Fresno, Oxnard, and Oakland less than an hour ago, bringing the state total to six since The Chaos Committee released its call to violence . . . dozens of harmless packages apparently mailed to elected officials . . . widespread tagging of Southland churches and synagogues . . . library fires set in Hayward, L.A., and Adelanto, heavy damage, officials say . . . impossible to determine who is responsible . . . continuing reports of car fires and gunfire throughout the state, Rudy, but the number-one fear here is looting. None of that, yet, thank goodness . . . So, KFWB's thanks to the millions of fine people in California who are reaching out to help or at least staying home and away from this unprecedented social upheaval . . .

━━━━

I stayed up late in my home office that night, plugged in to the TV, the radio, my computer, and phone—whatever might shed light on the threatened Chaos Committee bomb and the no-longer-simmering violence.

Talked briefly with Lark, Dalton, and Burt.

And later, with Terrell Strait. I'd been thinking about him since Dalton's misfired press conference. Where Terrell witnessed his father selling his mother down a river.

"It looked like I was on his side," he said over the phone. "I hope Mom didn't see it."

"She knows you better than that," I said.

The boy was grimly determined that his mother was okay, that she'd walk out of "her latest episode and back to us when she's ready."

He asked for a report on his dad, whom he refused to

call. I filled him in as best I could. Terrell said he was back at school, packing up to come home for the summer.

It was well after two o'clock. Nowhere near sleep, I sat back down at my desk and considered the newly arrived brown paper shopping bag. Courtesy of Cassy Weisberg, for carrying my many tourist brochures. Upended it over the scarred and venerable desk, a gift of the Timmerman clan, as part of their wedding gift to their daughter and me. I felt a tinge of guilt over wasting so many good pamphlets as a way to keep Cassy talking. What should I do with them now? Return them and say I'd gotten what I needed?

I fanned them out on the table in no order and with no purpose whatsoever. The night sky tours and the hiking trails maps looked promising.

The Bighorn Motel pamphlet pictured the motel in younger days. The parking lot full, kids thick in the pool, moms and dads in '50s fashions and coifs, sipping colorful drinks. I wondered what had drawn Broadman to a desert like Iraq's after the terrible thing that had happened to him there. I wondered, too, at a man so disfigured that he felt more comfortable hidden than seen, going into a business that brought in strangers by the carload.

━━━

In the wee hours I logged in to IvarDuggans and paid my way into the facial recognition program to run my best photo of Brock Weld's Tourmaline companion.

Her name was Gretchen Deuzler. The IvarDuggans

photos of her were five and eight years old, respectively. A handsome woman, blond then brunette. Age thirty-one, born in Denton, Texas, to a mining engineer and a college math professor. A degree in hydrology engineering from Arizona State. Member of the fencing club. I saw that she had worked as a blackjack dealer on some of the same cruise ships and at the same time as her consort Brock Weld. Tracking her bio against the hard copy of his file, I saw that Gretchen had moved into security work for the same casinos in New Jersey and Las Vegas, again simultaneously with Weld. So, based on shared employment, they'd known each other for at least thirteen years. She'd worked briefly for the United States Post Office. She had never been married and had no children, according to IvarDuggans. She owned a home in Escondido, was certified as a scuba instructor and as a small vessel boat captain by the Coast Guard.

Gretchen Deuzler's father was also a former president of the West Texas Blasters and Demolition Union.

Which would no doubt have given him—and maybe his daughter—easy access to restricted explosives and related materials: blasting caps, fuses, timers, high-nitrogen fertilizers.

Which sent a cool bristle of nerves down my neck.

In this age of anger and violence.

In this age of chaos.

I finally fell asleep while watching Lark's surveillance video of possible Jackie O's mailing the bomb that killed my congressman and his assistant.

TWENTY-EIGHT

Memorial Day morning. Tola Strait opened one of the Nectar Barn safes, entered a second code on her phone, and waited for the go-ahead. A two-combination Outlaw—a hard code to get it open and a cell code to disarm the interior alarm sensors. A moment later she set the two handguns on the safe top, then turned and looked at me.

"Thank you for taking this little job. You must be very busy with all the violence in the world."

"I don't love the idea of you moving a hundred thousand dollars in cash from one place to another."

"The Strait Shooters are terrific but today I wanted you. Sometimes a girl needs a different kind of company. But you're not cheap, my friend."

"Not for this kind of thing."

"Have you ever killed a man? In work, I mean, not war."

I nodded and caught the hard approval on her face.

"Well, none of that today!"

"Do the Strait Shooters know about this?" I asked. Holdups of the kind I feared are often inside jobs.

"Yes, and I trust them with my life. And yours."

Our destination for Tola's dope loot was the California side of Buena Vista, a small town split roughly in two by the U.S.-Mexico border. I had my suspicions about the Buena Vista Credit Union. For one thing, it didn't show up on my Internet search. For another, why would it be open on a national holiday?

But with a hundred thousand dollars under my watch, I wore my Gold Cup in its paddle holster in the small of my back, and a .410/.357 ankle cannon, deadly, small, and smooth. I thought back to Friday and how well I had shot with Mike Lark at Duffytown. But everything changes when your target is firing back at you.

We loaded the bundles of cash into two large rolling suitcases made of some textile that resembled stamped leather. They were light and probably strong and looked like Mexican saddles—handsome and ornate.

"Cold feet?" she asked.

"I get sullen on Memorial Day."

"I know that feeling."

"How do you know it?"

"I'm an East County Strait. We like big hats and big emotions."

I couldn't argue that and didn't try.

We loaded the two suitcases into the back seat of my truck, exactly $50,000 in each heavy piece. On the

passenger seat she set a stubby coach gun I recognized—
a Charles Daly Honcho 12 gauge—three very short
barrels and a pistol grip. For bad guys after the strongbox. Sling swivels fore and aft, easily concealable under a
coat. Designed for short-range killing. Tola high-fived
me and kissed me on the cheek.

"There won't be trouble," she said. "But the possibility makes me feel alive."

I held open the door and watched her climb in. Jeans
and red cowboy boots, a tucked-in snap-button satin
blouse the same green as her eyes. Red bangs and a ponytail under a big straw Stetson.

"Here we go, Rolando!"

———

From Julian we headed south through the mountains of
Cleveland National Forest to Interstate 8, then east into
the boulder-piled mountains where I'd called on Virgil
Strait and for the first time laid eyes on Tola. We climbed
up the steep curves and switchbacks, from San Diego
County to Imperial County then back to San Diego
again. The temperature rose with our long descent and
the interstate flattened into the desert.

Back straight, hat tilted off her forehead, facing the
bright day outside her window, Tola set a hand on my
knee.

"It seems so long since I've done something happy
and simple," she said. "I claw all day to make money.
After work I catch my buzzes, maybe hang with friends,

usually stay home and read a book before bed. Watch something. It's harder being legal. Mostly legal. Back in the good old days, everything you did could get you prison time. Or worse. An adrenaline high from dawn to dusk. I saw some people go down bad and I always figured I was next. But now I'm legal. Somewhat. I can enjoy this drive and not even miss my morning dose. I can enjoy my company."

"You still have a sawed-off shotgun in easy reach," I said.

She gave me a smile and I saw Justine as I'd seen her for the very first time, at a dismal county-employee holiday party at the downtown Hyatt. One smile that changed two lives. I wanted to switch off my memory box but I wasn't sure how. Or if I should. Justine vanished as if she'd read my thoughts.

"Tell me about Buena Vista Credit Union," I said. "It didn't turn up on my searches."

"Just chartered last month," said Tola. "I met one of the partners through Dalton."

"The credit union will accept your money?"

"If it comes through a recognized Indian tribe. I loan the Nectar Barn cash to certain of Granddad's native friends. They repay the loan to my accounts with my own cash—after taking a handsome percentage. The CU will take a handsome percentage, too. I'm an LLC so my accounts are all business banking, and the words *Nectar Barn* appear nowhere on the docs. At last, Tola can pay her taxes. Indians happy, governments happy. Everyone wins. A little curvy but technically legal. A state regulator for the southern district is helping us . . . well, *understand* the rules."

Crag Face himself, I thought, *Lark's man, waiting for Tola to offer him a bribe to look away.*

"What about the feds?" I asked.

"Buena Vista Credit Union doesn't belong to the Federal Reserve. Thus, open today. And it's regulated by the California Department of Business Oversight. Which is where my regulator friend comes in."

"Friend."

"More like a counselor."

"Do you trust him?"

Tola gave me a matter-of-fact look. "So far. I have to, Roland. All this legalized marijuana business is shadow land. So many things are new and unwritten. The law contradicts the law. Talk about chaos. Trust is all you've really got."

"I fear for you."

"Why? What do you know that I don't?"

"I know there are DEA and FBI investigators all over the country looking for ways to bust the pot market big boys. Of which you are one."

"Don't call me a boy," Tola said. "And I'm more than aware of that. I have good instincts about whom to trust. They've kept me alive for thirty years."

"Smart people are the easiest to fool."

"They think they're too smart to fail?"

"Yes, you do."

"I've considered every facet of my business, every

which way," she said. "Then I've thought it around, over, under, and back again. It's going to work. Everyone is ready and everything is in place. Every 'i' dotted and every 't' crossed. Now I just have to trust *me*. That I put it together right. That it's absolutely going to work."

"Are you expecting your regulator friend to be present today?" I asked.

"Why are you so interested in him?"

"Maybe I'm helping you dot an 'i.'"

"No. He won't get near this until he wants something."

"What's he after?"

"He has a foundation that he claims does noble work for American Natives. He's let me know about it. No solicitation yet. I know he needs money. I know his marriage is falling apart and he's drinking hard and fast."

"Don't offer."

She lifted her sunglasses, gave me another searching look, but said nothing. Then pulled her hat down and looked back out the window.

———

Tola's three Native American business partners—I found out later they were Cahuilla, Luiseño, and Kumeyaay Indians—were young men, casually dressed and helpful. At least two of them were armed. They carried the suitcases from my truck into a long-abandoned stucco home that stood inexplicably alone on Luiseño land.

A Mercedes Sprinter and an unmarked armored car waited on the broken concrete driveway, both facing the road. The armored car driver was barely visible through the bullet-resistant polycarbonate windshield. His partner waited in the shade of a paloverde tree with an open-sight AR-15 cradled in his arms.

In the living room, I stood behind Tola and watched the four of them sign documents. I could see that some of the papers already bore signatures and notary stamps, now being falsified to anyone who cared.

All of the players seemed to know just what to do, so there was little discussion, and little small talk, either. The Chaos Committee was mentioned—no bomb today but one man had heard of another peace officer being shot, this time in San Bernardino. Virgil and Kirby were referenced, briefly. Dalton, of course. And the new Nectar Barn being built near the Sycuan Casino. A sense of grave accomplishment seemed to hover in the room. A fence lizard appeared on a glassless windowsill, looked our way, did four push-ups, then wandered back out.

When the papers were signed and divided, two of the men rolled the suitcases onto the driveway and into the armored car.

Tola shook hands with each young man, then got into my truck and closed the door. The Sprinter led the armored car toward the road, tire dust drifting east.

Tola turned my face to hers, leaning in close. Her hand was surprisingly cool and her breath was warm.

"Follow the money," she said. "My heart's pounding right now, Roland. You're my rock."

TWENTY-NINE

The wall is old-school—vertical iron columns spaced wide enough to see and talk through, ten feet high, no concertina. Because the city predates the wall by over a hundred years, its historic downtown, retail, residential, and industrial neighborhoods are divided roughly in half. Small shops, rough cobbles, and dogs. People meet along the wall, trading news and gossip and shopping bags of goods and produce. They talk energetically and touch each other through the rough iron bars.

I spent some time here, helping Charlie Hood, a friend who'd taken the job of chief of police on the American side. His was not an easy assignment, with Buena Vista being a plaza perennially contested by drug cartels, and Hood himself a troubled soul. I hadn't told him I'd be coming into his jurisdiction with the outspoken marijuana maven Tola Strait. The less people who knew about this, the better.

The Buena Vista Credit Union was located in the newer outskirts of the U.S. downtown, in a humble strip mall home to two restaurants, a photography studio, and electronics shop from which Mexican and American pop songs blared, and a women's boutique with colorful dresses on racks outside the entrance.

Inside, the building was brightly lit and smelled of new carpet and paint. A counter with three tellers but no customers. On one side of the tellers was a steel gate leading to the vault, on the other side an open seating area built around two impressive wooden desks. No managers on duty. Hand-painted oil copies of Diego Rivera paintings on the walls hung almost straight, potted artificial saguaro cactus with strings of LED lights, magazines on the coffee tables. All three Indians seated and waiting.

The armed guards, each with a machine gun in one hand, pulled the luggage into the desk reception area, then stopped and looked at the Indians for direction.

From an open doorway beyond the desks came a stout older Latino in a gray suit, white shirt, and a red tie, who stopped, considered us briefly, then waved us to follow. With him was a young woman he ignored. He introduced himself to each of us as we walked past him into his office—Robert Calderon, general manager, my pleasure to meet you, please have a seat.

His office was spacious, with hardwood floors and a low ceiling. A wooden desk even larger than the ones out front and plenty of chairs. A sophisticated digital scale, apparently new, sat on the immense desk. Tola and the Indians sat in a line before the desk, the guards retreated to stand on either side of the doorway. I loitered near the guards and their rolling treasures, near the door, another hired hand. PI Ford. Has guns, will travel.

Then a flurry of folders with metal top-clips, distributed by Señor Calderon's assistant, the documents signed by all parties, notarized by the woman, who then collected and arranged them on a far corner of the big desk. I detected that she felt this ugly business was beneath her. Next she pulled a sturdy metal cart with plump pneumatic tires into position to her boss's left.

The guards rolled the suitcases to the desk, and at Calderon's nod, tilted them onto the floor, unzipped them, and began handing the bundles to him. He in turn handed several randomly chosen bundles to the notary, who counted the bills with blistering speed and placed them on the cart. Calderon himself weighed the others.

When he was done, Calderon sat down again and slid to Tola a wooden presentation box, open to reveal three tooled-leather checkbooks, six packets of checks, and three elegant-looking pens. He set a business card inside and swung shut the lid.

"It's so nice to deal with professionals," said Tola, to no one in particular. Polite assents. She looked back at me with a demure smile.

A few minutes later, deep in the shiny steel vault that smelled faintly of burning metal, we watched Calderon and his never-introduced assistant transfer the bundles to the racks.

Back outside in the bright Imperial County sunshine, we loaded the empty suitcases into my truck. I set Tola's security shotgun and my uncomfortable ankle cannon in the steel utility box and locked it.

"I'm starved and coming down," said Tola. "There's a great place to eat on the Mexico side. If we use the pedestrian crossing, we won't get stuck in the traffic."

She requested a shady table in the courtyard restaurant of Hotel Casa Grande. Potted palms, eye-shivering violet bougainvillea, a central fountain in which a pair of spotted towhees splashed. As we were being seated, Tola remarked on the English translation of the hotel name, as pertaining to Kirby, and their old running joke about how much longer he could manage to stay out of the "big house."

"As it turned out," said Tola, "not that long at all!"

We drank a small pitcher of margaritas. Tola paid cash from a fat roll in her purse, turned her face up to the palm-slatted sunlight, and closed her eyes.

"I am content right now," she said. "To be imagining pleasant things behind my rose-colored eyelids. And I'm proud that I remind you of somebody you loved." Her eyes were heavy on mine. "I got us a good room here. We can continue this discussion inside. Or not. *Está bien?*"

"More than fine."

═══

Twenty emotional, pleasure-soaked hours later we were back in the truck and heading for Tola's pot-growing acres near Palomar Mountain. She consulted the visor mirror and said she looked like a tart, well used.

The highlight reel kept playing through my mind, courtesy of three or four hours of sleep, if that. We made love as soon as we closed the room door, a trail of clothes marking our way to the bed. Followed by a tender, more civilized event. A nap and a time-out for shopping, dinner, and later some Nectar Barn "Love Bomb," which lived up to its name. Our third engagement took place in a downy time warp that seemed to last hours, followed by our hysteria over the room's focal oil painting, a basket of canna lilies appearing to levitate above a table rather than rest upon it. The French-milled soap just floored us. Tola laughed like a scrub jay. You had to be there. We came together again deep in the morning, sleep-deprived and delirious. At sunrise when I tried for another rematch, Tola locked herself in the bathroom and told me to grow up.

I felt taken from and added to at the same time.

In the truck she rambled about girlhood days in the Imperial Valley, how she ran away for San Diego at sixteen, got a job at Taco Bell and a weekly rate room at the Southern Hotel. The job paid $7.25 an hour and no tips, but they'd only give her thirty hours, so the $200 room left her twenty-five bucks for everything else. Wouldn't have penciled out for long. She'd been eating nothing but Taco Bell until Virgil and Kirby found her a few days later and brought her home. She'd actually put on weight from all the rice and beans and tortillas, had real boobs for the first time, she said. Her mother hadn't showed for

Tola's homecoming. Mom had divorced Archie by then and had long shed the duties of motherhood.

"I'm extra hard on Mom because she didn't like me," said Tola. "But Dad thought I was a rock star. Daddy's little girl all the way. When Kirby did that to him I was nine years old and riled up enough to want revenge. In the end, the planning did me in. I just couldn't decide what to do to him—poison him or let the brake fluid out of his motorcycle or maybe just shoot him in the knee-cap. After a few weeks of that I realized, well, he's my brother and it was an accident and I'd never seen Kirby that depressed and disgusted as then. He was punishing himself. So I let it go. It felt good to forgive him. Blood forgives, for better or worse."

I steered up the mountain toward her property as a black-and-white helicopter hovered in the blue a mile away. Found the shortcut around Kirby's elaborately padlocked gate, bouncing my truck onto the rutted road with a metallic grate of shocks. In the distance I could see Kirby's gigantic military tent billowing slightly in the breeze, the Indian motorcycle, the four-wheeler, and the pickup truck all where I'd last seen them.

The tent door flap blew open and closed and open again. No rifle in the sapling.

And the young woman, Charity, working on her tan again, looked uncomfortable on her towel in the little meadow.

"Get the guns," said Tola.

I'd already swept my binoculars from under the seat.

Saw the bloody body of Charity on her beach towel. Flies and meat bees already at their tasks. Saw the glint of brass in the grass and more near the lilting door flap. Gave Tola the field glasses, hopped into the truck bed, handed her gun through the back window, and loaded the legal ten shot shells into my own security weapon. I saw the helicopter hovering far out.

"You can stay here," I said.

"Wrong."

"If you're not used to this kind of . . ."

"Roland, I'm going in with you. So go."

"Follow me and keep the trees between you and the tent."

"Okay."

"Keep your finger off the trigger until you're close enough to hit what you're pointing at. Never bluff. The shot spreads out wide and fast with that barrel."

"I know, I know exactly what shotguns do."

The willows along the creek were big with foliage from the winter rains.

We kept to the streamside, rocks slippery but the gurgle covering our noise. Made a wide, slow circle around the meadow where Charity lay dead in her blood-drenched swimsuit.

Up close to the tent I could see that the big cistern had taken fire, leaked, and soaked the ground around it.

I motioned for Tola to stay, then hustled to the tent, pulled open the flap, and ducked inside, head low, gun up and scanning. Fallujah. If it's armed, it's over. Tola suddenly behind me just like Avalos, damn her. Bullet tears in the far wall, leaking sunlight. Brass on the floor and a throw of blood drops on the tent wall beyond the air mattress. No sign of Kirby or his rifle. A long gash in the north wall, where Kirby had likely slashed and dashed.

We tracked the blood drops and footprints on a rocky trail that led uphill into the forest. I guessed at least three sets of prints. The blood and prints vanished at a branching game trail, a matted pathway and no wider than the deer that made them. We picked up footprints again but no blood and I wondered for the first time if whoever was bleeding—likely Kirby—wasn't critically wounded at all, and had maybe even found a way to out-scramble the killers. In the distance, the helicopter circled and lowered.

The forest grew taller and darker and the game trail faint. Steep enough to pull ourselves upslope by branches. Both of us breathing hard and I felt the weight of my legs, not from strain but from nerves. Fallujah again, hardwired into my memory.

The trail widened. Onward with a sinking feeling. You see the punch before it's thrown. Avalos used to see things before they happened, saw the canal footbridge blowing up as we crossed it and two hours later coming back across the un-blown-up bridge, the IED blew it in half. Now drying blood on an oak leaf, just hours old, the same age as Charity's. Buzz of my boxing scar. Dread sharpening.

Then through the trees I saw a clearing bathed in sunlight, a tawny cloak of oak leaves over boulders of black basalt. Beyond the clearing stood a thicket of cottonwoods, dense and pale trunked.

"I see . . . him," said Tola.

Just then my eyes found Kirby, too. Half-hidden within the glimmering cottonwood leaves, his white naked body dangling straight as the crowded trunks in which he hung, head cocked sharply and purple faced.

We cut him down wordlessly, laid him out on the rough rocks. Tola cried and kept touching his blood-matted red pompadour.

Certainly they had carried rope just for this purpose. His hands had been bound with a black-and-white New Generation bandana.

Holes shot through his skinny body like in the old outlaw pictures, but not just a few holes. Scores of them. The modern language of the automatic. *Postmortem cartel insults*, I thought. *More than insults. Warnings.*

"The real target is me," said Tola. "I'm bad for business."

"So are your growers, Tola," I said. "We should get over there right now."

"I'm not leaving him here."

"Help me get him into the truck."

"I thought of everything. I thought I thought of everything."

"You can't think of everything."

"It was Calderon. I know it was Calderon."

We wrestled her brother into the bed of the truck and tied a blue tarp over him. I cut loose his hands and put the cartel bandana in the big locking toolbox.

═════

The San Diego County sheriffs were all over Tola's pot grow, only two miles down-mountain from Kirby's tent, as the crow flies.

Tola's breath caught as we topped the rise and looked down on the vehicles and deputies. The helicopter waited, blades still. Uniforms and windbreakers, men and women moving amid the knife-sundered plastic walls of the greenhouses. Lights and frost heaters thrown to the ground. Through my binoculars I could see the plants, scorched black and limp. *Flamethrowers,* I thought, *much faster and more dramatic than Roundup.*

The deputies moved with purpose, a sense of aftermath and order, Tola staring down at them with blood-shot green eyes.

I eased the truck over the crest and began the long, rutted descent.

THIRTY

Late that evening, Dalton's black BMW X5 came barreling up the long drive toward my house. The Irregulars and I watched from under the palapa, where we were finishing dinner.

"I've never met my legislator," said Dick.

"Corrupt," said Liz. "He's hiding behind his missing wife."

"I feel that his wife will come to harm," said Odile. "I see her slouching in the shadow of a dragon in the desert sun."

Since the explosive debut of The Chaos Committee two weeks previous, Odile's visions and prognostications had become more pessimistic. She told me that The Chaos Committee's actions were affecting the behavior of almost every cognizant citizen who consulted her. Even children. Only the mad were immune. She was beginning to dread her consultations because of the "darkness of our times." She asked me if I thought people would be better off not knowing their immediate futures. She could not change her findings, but she could pause or even cease her practice. Find a new calling. I didn't have an answer for her.

As Dalton's vehicle approached, *Local Live!* filled my enormous-screen TV with "Massacre Near Palomar," in which three state-licensed marijuana grove workers were gunned down and burned with flamethrowers. And two more individuals—"possibly campers and not believed to be involved in the cannabis industry"—were apparently shot and killed. Evidence at the scene pointed to the deadly New Generation cartel, which was known to be battling the Sinaloa cartel. The massacre was seen as part of a larger New Generation strategy to control all drug distribution within the United States. Legalized marijuana was the Achilles' heel of all the drug cartels, said *Local Live!*

Hours ago, when the news crews had been allowed in to see the Palomar crime scene, Tola had done her best to speak to the reporters. She said that all of her workers were U.S. citizens or legal immigrants working in a state-governed agricultural industry. One of the deceased was a Native American.

"And most importantly, they're good people," she said. "Good souls. Until the banks will take our legal money and cartel gunmen can't cross our borders and get automatic weapons, this kind of thing will happen again."

I couldn't see through her sunglasses on the TV, but

her voice was shaking with grief and fury. At the time of her interview I had been squatting down behind one of the sheriff vans.

Just as she finished on *Local Live!*, Dalton clomped from the darkness into the patio light, out of breath and sweating hard, and slapped a nine-by-eleven clasp envelope on the picnic table in front of me.

"Hi, y'all," he said to the Irregulars. Shook each of their hands and looked them in the eye. "Sorry to interrupt. Uh, Roland, this was in my mailbox when I came home an hour ago. I ripped it open and knew you should see it. Cut myself on the metal."

He loomed over the table eagerly, showing us the blood-marked bandage on the side of a knuckle.

I noted the jaggedly torn envelope, the bent clasp still attached, the smear of blood.

The Irregulars crowded behind me as I slid out a sheet of printer paper and set it on the table. The message had been printed in a common roman font:

I will tell you how to save your wife. Until then, suffer quietly as America suffers. Your last full measure of devotion will be required. If you show this evidence to law enforcement, you will never see Natalie again except in your memories.

I upended the envelope and out slid a shirt, neatly folded and wrapped in plastic, as if fresh from the dry cleaner. Light blue and long-sleeved by the look of it. Blood on the plastic.

"It's Natalie's," said Dalton. "I recognize the glass buttons. Damn the world, Roland—they've *got* her."

Ash Galland, on what her sister had worn to breakfast the day she vanished: *a light blue satin blouse the color of her eyes.*

"Why did you open it?" asked Burt. "You must have seen how foolish that was."

Dalton gave Burt a *fuck you, little guy* look but said nothing.

I righted the empty envelope before me and read the sender's name and return address. Heard the catches of breath from the Irregulars behind me. Handwritten block caps, right slant, neat.

JUSTINE TIMMERMAN FORD

RANCHO DE LOS ROBLES

48 OLD HIGHWAY 395

FALLBROOK, CA 92028

"What?" asked Liz.

Odile shook her head. "What does this mean?"

"Who did this?" asked Dick.

"Someone trying to get personal with Roland," said Burt. "Someone trying to anger and distract him."

A moment of silence fell over us as Natalie Strait's image filled the TV, *Local Live!* updating us on week two of her disappearance, a sidebar to the Palomar massacre, as part of the Strait family misfortune that had seemingly followed them for decades.

All eyes on Dalton.

"Any dinner left?" he asked.

=====

Burt and I sat up late in my upstairs office again, saying little while we viewed more hours of Mike Lark's surveillance video on my desktop monitor. Some of it crisp and clear, and some of it muddy and useless. Jackie O? Nowhere to be seen.

I felt the anger creeping up on me. If none of Lark's battalion of eager *federales* had been able to spot Jackie O, how could we?

What if someone else in The Chaos Committee had mailed the damned bomb? Lark had professed faith in my luck and eyesight, and in our friendship, but I sensed he'd recruited me less as an able-eyed volunteer than as an informant on the Straits.

I left another message for Tola. Rang off uneasily, the scar on my forehead tingling. I sipped bourbon against the bloodshed of the day.

"What worries me most about Dalton is how little he cares for Natalie," said Burt. "And how much leverage and publicity he's enjoying. All the while carrying on with big pharma's dreamy lobbyist. Maybe the sheriffs are onto something. Maybe he's behind Natalie's absence. Look at the benefits—it frees up his love life, increases his sympathy votes in November, and makes it easier to blame her in court. She can't even defend herself. What's to keep him from hiring out the kidnapping, putting you between him and the cops, mailing himself Natalie's blouse as a diversion? Invoking Justine as a way to confuse and divert you?"

I paused the video and thought about that. All of it credible and possible.

I asked the obvious. "Did he have her killed?"

"If he arranged her abduction, her death would solve certain problems."

I grunted, stood, looked out at a western sky pricked with stars. Felt like I was trapped in a cage with high black walls and a faraway lid with little holes in it to give me air and hope.

"The question is, *would* he?" said Burt. "What kind of man is Dalton Strait at his core?"

"It depends who you talk to."

"I'm talking to you, champ. You fought a war alongside him."

I told Burt what I'd learned about Dalton's behavior in Fallujah, regarding Harris Broadman and the burning Humvee. That his battlefield heroics were in question, and his alleged Silver Star heroism had left a man badly scarred. And that by one commanding officer's account, Dalton's Purple Heart was earned through bad judgment and reckless conduct.

"But if you sit down with him one-on-one," I said. "When he talks about Natalie, you get a different version of him. He loves and adores her. They've spent well over half their lives together. She's someone he . . . admired and wanted to be worthy of."

"So, his love appears real," said Burt. "Just as his heroism does."

"I don't think he'd have her abducted or killed."

"Semper Fi, Roland."

"Faith has nothing to do with it, Burt."

I resumed the video, trying to concentrate on the surveillance footage, but my mind was picking back through every minute of the last two weeks that I'd spent with Dalton—reevaluating him, looking for a different angle or something I'd missed, re-vetting my own interpretations when Dalton had left me unclear or doubtful. I knew Burt was half right. The marine in me wanted Dalton not to have done such things.

Then I was back in the green meadow where Charity had died. And in the groves of cottonwoods where Kirby had been hanged and mutilated, and in Tola's grow with the bullet-riddled, flame-thrown humans and plants left heaped on the ground with equal disregard, and the sliced panels of sun fabric fluttering in the breeze.

My eyes locked on the monitor, where another dark-haired woman mailed another package. UPS, Portland, Oregon, according to the footer. Not Jackie O.

And so on, into the late hours.

After Burt retired, I soldiered on, seeing no one very much like our prize.

I called and woke up both Dalton and Virgil with concern over Tola's whereabouts and well-being. Dalton said he had no idea where she was and her grandfather said she could take care of herself. I reminded him of the lopsided slaughter on Palomar.

I finally crashed on the office couch, landing in dreams of Tola Strait and gunfire. I'd never been around Tola and gunfire at the same time and later I wondered if it was a premonition. I wondered a lot of things.

My phone rang loud in the timeless dark.

"I'm at your gate," she said.

THIRTY-ONE

The next morning, Lieutenant Hazzard and Detective Proetto sat in their Valley Center station interview room, Natalie Strait's blue satin blouse in its blood-touched plastic wrapper on the table before them. Beside it lay the torn envelope and the sheet of paper.

"Why didn't Mr. Strait bring this to us himself?" asked Hazzard.

"Off to Sacramento early this morning," I said.

"Convenient, like the video of his shackled wife that only he has actually seen. Because it self-destructed on his phone."

I shrugged but said nothing.

Proetto used a pen to bring the torn mailer closer.

"Dalton's prints and blood are on it," I said. "He lost his patience, ripped it open. Handled the blouse through the plastic. At least he didn't touch the garment. The evidence techs might have a shot at some hair and fiber."

Proetto held up the envelope by one corner, worked his pen into the torn opening, gave the mailer a good shake.

"The lab found another horsetail hair in Mrs. Strait's BMW," he said. "Which now makes three. Thick, black, cropped at both ends."

Hazzard eyed me unhappily. Proetto poked at the plastic-covered blouse with his pen.

"Dalton gave us run of the house last week and we found nothing there that correlates to horsehair," Hazzard said. "No belts, jewelry or accessories, purses, crafts or works of art. No clothing or furniture containing horsehair. Natalie doesn't ride horses recreationally. Which leads us to the abductors. And makes me wonder if there might have been some activity in that vehicle. A struggle, maybe Natalie trying to get out, she got a handful of—whatever was made of horsehair. A necklace or bracelet. Even a rope, maybe."

I tried to think of another, unrelated, source for decorative horsetail hairs in Natalie's SUV. Drew blanks on top of blanks.

But if the horsehairs didn't come from Natalie herself, then her abductors were a very possible source. So, what did we know about these abductors? Little. According to witnesses, two men and a woman. No good physical descriptions. There was no suspect or even persons of interest. Except in the mind of Hazzard, focused on Dalton himself. My own short list was long indeed: a world full of people looking to take down Dalton for a multitude of transgressions. Brock Weld? What evidence did I have on him except an admitted attraction to an attractive woman, a disdain for that woman's husband, and a creaky alibi for the morning Natalie was abducted? But what use would either of them have for horsetail hair?

I considered Hazzard's ham face and small, aggressive eyes. I understood why he disliked me, and why he was in a hurry to convict Dalton Strait. I wondered what else was stoking his anger. The abduction of an innocent woman? The Chaos Committee itself?

"Thanks for bringing this in," said Proetto. "I'll walk you out."

"Just a minute, hoss," said Hazzard. "Were you up in the Palomar Mountains yesterday with Dalton's sister?"

"I was."

"What was your takeaway?"

"A warning to Tola from the New Generation."

"With Kirby in the dirt, that's one less Strait we have to worry about," said Hazzard. "They're vermin, you know."

"Vermin come in all shapes and sizes," I said.

A shrug and a stare.

Proetto walked me into the bright morning.

"I don't know what's between you and Haz, but you seem to bring out the asshole in him."

"It's the shot I didn't take that day in Imperial Beach."

Proetto went quiet for a moment. Then, "Hazzard wants it to be Dalton—the abusive, cheating, self-centered male. An elected official, no less. It's the narrative of the day."

He had a point. I still wasn't buying in on Dalton, but said nothing. Proetto had steered me away from Hazzard for a reason.

"Dalton never got on that Sacramento flight, the

morning Natalie was abducted," he said. "He flew to Orange County instead. Then headed up to Sacramento that night. When the dealership and campaign people and her own sons started wondering where she was, Dalton didn't answer or return their calls."

My first thought was: *Orange County, home of Asclepia Pharmaceutical and McKenzie Doyle.*

"You're not throwing in with Hazzard on Dalton, are you?"

"Not all the way. But why did he lie about where he was that morning?"

"Something about a blonde."

"The rumors are true?"

"At least one of them is," I said. "Dalton is reckless and contradictory, but I don't think he mailed that blouse and letter to himself. He didn't have her abducted. But I'm losing traction here, Tony. Can you get me some? I'm doing my best to help you out."

Proetto gave me a long look. "Brock Weld's alibi just got worse. The neighbors say his dog barked all day, which it only does when he's gone. He says he was home the morning Natalie disappeared, laid low by the flu and with headphones on. Didn't hear the dog. And get this: Brock Weld is a Tourmaline Casino security employee. Also known as Brock Weld by the Strait Reelection Committee. But his real name is Brock Holland. He did a year for hacking into a credit rating database and assaulting the cops who arrested him. Maybe there's a harmless reason for an aka and a bad alibi. Maybe there isn't. He's currently on a two-week paid vacation. We don't know where he's gone. Let me know if he comes up in your net."

Holland had a nice portfolio, I thought. Tech and violence. He'd been bold enough to proposition his boss as he volunteered on her husband's assembly campaign. While consorting with a casino coworker. A sexual opportunist? Maybe. Natalie had refused him. Maybe he just wasn't smart enough to fool her into bed. Time to deploy his violent side?

═══

Back in my truck, I consulted the Vigilant 4000 for the real-time location of Brock Holland's white Suburban. It was currently still in the same Casa del Zorro parking spot where I had last "seen" it on Friday night. Which made sense if Holland had chosen Casa del Zorro for his two-week vacation. Fun in the sun with your beloved. Play tennis, read by the pool, a good restaurant. Bike around the desert in the cool early mornings on complimentary Casa del Zorro bicycles.

However, during those four days, the SUV had made three round trips to the same address in San Ysidro, California, a district of San Diego that lies on the border with Mexico. Rough and hectic San Ysidro—not a place associated with romantic getaways, poolside hours, fine dining. Yet Brock Holland—or at least his vehicle—had spent almost eighteen hours there.

A few minutes on Google Maps and a brief talk with

a Realtor friend and I learned that the address in question was the National Allied Building, a fourteen-thousand-square-foot, two-story building in the warehouse district. Legal ownership in dispute; number of tenants and lease arrangements, if any, unknown. Not currently listed on CoStar, LoopNet, or CityFeet.

"Not unusual for that part of the border," said my friend. "Watch your step."

In my downtown Fallbrook office I dug out Brock Holland on IvarDuggans.com.

Like his alias, Holland was thirty-one and a native of Miami. And he had done security work in local San Diego hotels, two cruise lines, and casinos in Las Vegas, as claimed by Weld. Holland had no degrees but he was crafty enough to fool IvarDuggans.com and his Tourmaline employers into believing he was someone else.

Instead of college, he graduated through a series of lesser crimes—mail fraud, impersonating a city official, malfeasance. Minor jail time, community service, and fines. But finally upped his game by hacking into a credit rating company with criminal intent, and assault-upon-an-officer charges. Followed by the year in Chino Men's. He'd been clean since his release in 2015 and had been off the radar ever since, hiding behind Weld's cover.

I thought about telling Proetto where to find his man, but decided not to. I wanted to keep Brock Holland's secrets to myself for now.

And get a look at another one of Holland's secrets— the National Allied Building—where he'd been spending so much of his hard-earned vacation time.

THIRTY-TWO

San Ysidro was bustling that afternoon, retaining its title as the busiest land border crossing in the world. The warehouse district sprawled low and metallic within sight of the border itself, two high fences of chain link with tangles of concertina overflowing the top, shining in the spring sun.

The National Allied Building was two-story I-beam steel construction, with vertically corrugated walls. Sparsely windowed and—according to the graying white paint—fifty years old. Three roll-up doors that I could see, one at ramp level and two to the ground. The domed acrylic skylights of decades past. An office door. All huddled under a sagging crisscross of power lines.

I parked and checked the phone. The Vigilant 4000 had Brock Holland's white Suburban still parked back at La Casa del Zorro in Borrego Springs, a two-hour drive away. If I was going to be observed while making my professional rounds here in San Ysidro, it wouldn't likely be by him.

I locked up my truck, grabbed my briefcase, and headed toward the building. I was resplendent in a blue blazer, a white shirt, and a yellow necktie. Business cards in the jacket pocket. The briefcase contained booklets of various boilerplate lease agreements, pencils and legal pads, a measuring tape, a calculator, and my permitted .45 Colt Gold Cup, tucked into the laptop slot. I was Robert Franklin, Century Group Brokers, Commercial Realty Division, Los Angeles, license #396248.

I pressed the front door buzzer. The door was sun-blasted bronze-toned glass and the built-in intercom speaker grille was rusty. The camera screwed into the metal wall above it was newer and clean. The company names and their suite numbers were framed in an acrylic directory, the letters severely faded. Some had fallen off altogether. The lid of the mail slot was rusty, too, and the general air of the place was vacancy.

Wrong.

A man's voice through the speaker asked me who I was here to see. I said I was a broker looking at warehouse space for clients from L.A. Held a business card up to the camera.

Then a buzz and the clank of a dead bolt obeying orders.

"Come in."

I pushed through the heavy door and into an industrial lobby: a wall-to-wall counter with a double-wide pass-through and a stout, block-faced man standing be-hind it, hands on the counter, expression doubtful. Dark hair and eyes. He wore a black T-shirt with a graphic of a woody full of surfboards and a palm tree on the front. We introduced ourselves and shook hands and I handed him the card. His name was Pete Giakas.

"There's nothing for lease here," he said, looking up from the card.

"I need something private and secure," I said, setting the briefcase on the counter as might a man with pa-tience and time to burn. "My clients don't deal directly with the public."

"Neither do most of us," said Giakas. "Special-order stuff. Not much public coming and going. We have a mold maker, a dune buggy welder, a direct-mail printer, two telemarketers, and some others on the first floor. Second floor is a guitar teacher, printed circuit boards, and import-export."

"Long-time tenants?"

"Depends what you mean by long. The PCB and import-export have only been here a couple of years."

"And you?"

"Going on twelve. I'm the senior tenant and the un-derpaid receptionist. I collect the mail off the floor and pile it on this counter. I tell the other tenants if someone comes by when they're at lunch or away."

"What is your business, Mr. Giakas?"

"T-shirts. I do the silk screens, sell them at swap meets. Surf culture always sells in San Diego."

"I surfed once upon a time."

"I fish off the pier."

"What's the square-foot rate here?" I asked.

"Ten-eighty on a one-year lease. But that was two years ago."

"And who is the building owner? It's not on any of the listing services."

"I've never met the owner and I have no name for him or her. Very private. I have an email address and that's all. Don't ask me for it."

"No, I understand."

I took a moment to look around the unkempt lobby: ancient nicks and scratches on the counter, a battered linoleum floor circa 1960, a half-filled wastebasket in one corner, the sun-reflecting bronze windows giving it all a faint butterscotch cast.

"Mr. Giakas, may I speak briefly to the tenants working today? With an eye for a future vacancy? This place really does seem right for my clients. I won't be a nuisance."

Giakas studied me.

"Only some of the tenants are here today. The direct-mail printer in unit six is hell on wheels. Maria. And the second-floor people aren't in today. I'll be in unit four if you need me."

He lifted the pass-through and held it up as I took up my briefcase and entered a warren of hallways and suites.

I heard parakeets shrieking in their happy way. Smelled someone's lunch, heard the steady thump of music from First Class Molds, paused outside the Direct Solutions Mail Company, from behind the glass front door of which a large Medusa-haired woman stared at me.

I nodded and continued on. Sand King Welders had a cardboard clock set to three o'clock dangling at eye level on the glass window insert. Beyond it I saw the simple reception area: a gray metal desk with a gray metal chair on either side, colorful posters of tricked-out dune buggies, ATVs, and off-road three-wheelers on the walls.

The telemarketers were both in, doing business in offices that faced each other across the hall. Of course they were on their phones. It took me a moment to surmise that they were sisters—almost certainly twins—running two similar companies headquartered not twenty feet away from each other. Same Vietnamese faces, same dark eyes, same bangs. They offered identical smiles and similar waves of hand as I passed by.

"May I help you," a woman's voice demanded.

I turned to see Maria, the Medusa-haired direct-mail printer, standing in the hall behind me, hands on her hips. A short, wide woman. Black lipstick, heavy eyeliner and makeup, a sequined black pantsuit and bright white running shoes.

"Yes," I said. "I'm a commercial broker. Trying to find a unit here for an L.A. client."

"No space available now. That's why there's no sign out."

"I was looking for October of this year."

She shook her head. "Not possible. All the tenants are very good here. We like the rates and the building. No crime. No one bothers us. Upstairs are the new people. Very unfriendly. Talk to them if you want. It might be good if they're leaving."

"Are the upstairs PCB company and the import-export

companies one and the same, or two different tenants?"
I asked.

"The same unfriendly faces. They turn away. Won't
look at me. Men and women."

"How many?"

"Four men and three women."

"Is there a couple? The man is well built and likes
Hawaiian shirts. The woman is blond and pretty."

"Who are you?"

"If so, they're my clients," I backfilled. "I thought
they might come down here and try to strike a deal on
their own. Thereby cutting me out of my commission."

"They come and go," she said.

"White Suburban and a yellow sports car?"

She nodded, eyeing me hard.

"Mr. Giakas seems like a reasonable manager," I said,
hunting as always but not sure exactly what for.

"Calls himself the manager," said Maria. "Throws the
mail behind the counter. Might or might not tell you if
you've had a customer come in while you're gone. I'll tell
you something about him. He makes good T-shirts and
keeps parakeets in his shop. And he has the same thing
for lunch every day: Better Burger. Are you interested in
direct mail for your company? You're a good-looking
man. I can get your face in front of a hundred thousand
potential customers for a lot less than you think. I know
how to target. I design and write and print, even post, if
you want. Flyers aren't like those online ads that get
blocked and deleted. They stay right in front of people,
right up to the time they have to pick them up and throw

them out. Then there you are, smiling at them from beside the coffee cup stain, giving them one last chance."

"I'm interested. Do you have a card?"

She drew the card from I know not where, held it toward me between two extended fingers. Black nail polish,
fingers glittering with jewels set in silver.

I gave her one of my own cards, thanked her, and me-
andered down the hall and around the corner.

The mold maker briefly looked up at me through a
glass door. I saw that the thumping music came from a
boom box set on the office floor beside him. He sat on
a folding chair next to a floor heater, a large wooden easel
on his lap and a pencil in one hand.

Past a sculptor working in clay.

And a wholesaler of Mexican guitars, which hung from
his ceiling.

Then onward to a glass office door on which an image
of Jesús Malverde—patron saint of narcos—had been
skillfully etched. Malverde wore his usual neat Sinaloan
mustache, knotted scarf, and stony gaze.

Above him, in frosty letters:

Raul Santo
Private Investigator

And below Malverde's etched gaze, just a few yards
from me, clearly visible through the door glass, sat a man
with his boots up on a desk, eyeing me knowingly.

I'd been made and there wasn't a thing I could do
about it but close the door behind me.

THIRTY-THREE

Mr. Roland Ford, what a pleasure to meet you."

"All mine, Mr. Santo."

He stood and we shook hands. He was thickly built, medium height, with a head of black curly hair falling to his shoulders and a trim mustache. Malverde in need of a haircut, I thought. He wore a black guayabera with white embroidery, jeans, and a gold bracelet of interlocked serpents on each wrist.

"What brings you here?" he asked, plopping back into his chair. "Please, sit."

I didn't. "A tip on a stolen identity case. It fizzled, so I'm on my way out."

"But out is *that* way," he said with a smile, pointing vaguely toward the lobby. "Which of my fine neighbors here had your interest?"

"Please, Mr. Santo."

"Of course, of course. Our curse is our curiosity."

"Well said. I'd appreciate it if you'd keep my real name to yourself. Today I'm Robert Franklin, a commercial real estate broker. Like I said, it was a dead end anyway."

I handed him a card.

"And you must be looking for industrial space here on behalf of a client in Los Angeles," he said.

"Good guess."

"When I work in Los Angeles, I am sometimes the Realtor Ron Montero representing clients from San Diego."

"We PIs are a cagey crew," I said.

"Judging by your presence at his press conference, I'd say you've been hired by Assemblyman Strait," said Santo. "My wife is addicted to missing-persons stories, so she forwards the highlights to me almost every day."

I nodded.

"Natalie Strait is still missing?"

And nodded again. Santo sat back and crossed his thick fingers over his ample gut. "I am saddened by the slaughter in the Palomars yesterday. Dalton Strait must feel surrounded."

"By?"

"Misfortune. Natalie. Kirby. His many legal troubles."

"Have you worked for the Straits?"

"No, never."

A quick flash in which I understood much. Tempted as I was to show Santo a picture of Brock Holland and Gretchen Deuzler, such a gamble could sink me if this PI with the narco-saint emblem on his door was in any way tied to them. They could be friendly, for all I knew. Certainly the opportunity was good, right here in this strange building. And in the larger sense, the New Generation Cartel had hundreds of eyes, ears, and guns in this jammed quarter of the border. El Chapo's splintered Sinaloans did, too. And all the meth freebooters. A Malverdean PI would certainly be a temptation to any of them. Even if Santo was independent of Holland and the killers who had taken five lives in the Palomar Mountains, a report of my presence here in the National Allied Building might be valuable to someone.

"You have had some big adventures," said Santo. "I saw you on the news when the terrorists hit San Diego. When the FBI woman was killed. And before that, when the helicopter was shot out of the sky and crashed on your property! You are the only celebrity PI I know who is not a TV character."

"I liked it better when I could waddle around the world in secret," I said.

"As a real estate agent or an insurance salesman! As a bird-watcher in naturalist's clothing and the big binoculars strapped to your chest. As a Hollywood producer. Those are disguises I've used before. No one recognizes me, but I've never been famous."

"Thanks for your help, Mr. Santo."

"How did I help you?"

"By keeping this between us professionals."

"Why not? What else would I do in this age of The Chaos Committee? Even we privateers must stick together."

===

I toured the rest of the first floor with a leasing agent's air of critical optimism. Caught a sharp glance from Maria, another disinterested look from the mold maker, then wandered to the far southeast part of National Allied. Aging elevators spook me so I took the stairs to the second floor. At the landing were double doors with glass windows.

The left window announced in crude stick-on letters:

Native World Import-Export
Appointment Only

And on the right:

Sandpit PCB
No Admittance

The sandpit being a grunt nickname for Iraq.

The same unfriendly faces being Maria's analysis of the people here.

No intercom. No surveillance camera visible. Two companies trying to be ignored. Not the business model I had come to know.

I moved closer to the glass and looked in. The lobby was lit by fluorescent tubes behind opaque plastic ceiling panels. Jittery light, yellowing plastic, dead flies. The room was spacious, and mostly empty. Three metal desks with little on them, chairs in tight. Another double door on the far wall, leading back to the guts of the operations.

I heard the distant rhythm of the mold maker's music. The slamming of a door. Brakes whining outside. Tried the doors.

I sized things up. I wanted in. Santo was right: our curse is our curiosity. And so much of National Allied to be curious about, starting with Brock Holland's presence here for extended hours over the last four days, very possibly right here in this upstairs Sandpit/Native World suite. Four men and three women. Unfriendly, making no eye contact. By appointment only, or just plain no admittance. Don't forget Raul Santo, a narco-drawn PI who I saw as a fat black spider centered in a web and having his eight legs within reach of so many relevant things. Such as the drug trade that enamored him. Such as Brock Holland and Gretchen Deuzler. And other unfriendlies at whose door I now stood. And maybe even, through Brock Holland, Natalie Strait—about whom Santo had directly inquired.

Things sized up, I set my course.

Made sure to shake hands and say goodbye to Pete Giakas. Thanked him again for the tour. Took the scenic route to my truck, noting the old-school National Allied alarm system fed by a single 120 VAC line nailed high under the eaves of the metal wall with plastic fasteners. Saw the fire ladder, elevated eight feet off the ground to discourage the casual user.

Drove downtown for lunch at the Waterfront, one of my old haunts with Justine. Talked to Burt, Dalton,

Lark, and Tola. Swung by a big-box store for an extension ladder.

Then circled back to National Allied near sunset, parked away from the lot and watched through my binoculars as the tenants left the building for the day. Watched a white-and-green Badge Security car make its round. When Pete Giakas came out and locked up I checked my Vigilant 4000 app and saw that the white Suburban had left La Casa del Zorro and was on its way southwest on Highway 78, headed in the general direction of San Ysidro.

After dark I parked in the empty National Allied lot. Waited for Badge Security to complete its next drive-by. Twice around the building, a two-hour patrol. Easy money.

When it turned out of sight, I got into the big storage box in my truck and donned my black Rolling Thunder Security windbreaker. The jacket boasts threatening yellow letters across the back, federal style: RTS. I put on good leather gloves, a black RTS ball cap, and a hiker's headlight, which I left off for now. Then took up my new extension ladder. Battle rattle, baby. Let's do this.

I unhurriedly carried the ladder around to the rear of the National Allied Building. Rolling Thunder Security just doing its job. In the good darkness of the building's back side I scaled the new ladder to the rusting built-in and continued up, not wasting a second. The broken rib from last year lodged a complaint, as did the torn tendons in my calves, but not enough to slow me down.

I paused at the security electrical line but the odds

were with me that I shouldn't cut it. I knew that there would be sensors wired to the building's exterior doors and windows, but not likely the rooftop skylights, where any pigeon or seagull could set one off.

Once on the roof I stood, got my balance, and used the headlight to follow the insulated metal screws toward my destination—the old domed skylights near the peak. The screws are the only way to safely walk a metal roof: walk on them and you'll stay positioned on the strong steel purlins inside. If you stray, you'll get a dented roof or worse, depending on your weight and how fast you're moving.

I settled on both knees in front of the old acrylic skylight. Pulse up; vision clear. Turned off the hiker's headlight. Checked the Vigilant 4000: white Suburban still possibly on its way here, a little less than an hour out. Looked down on San Ysidro from two stories up, the lights and cars, the signs and pedestrians, Interstate 5 jammed with traffic.

Let my eyes get used to the near dark—there's never quite full dark in a city with a million people in it.

Then leaned forward to the acrylic skylight, cupped my hands around my eyes, and gazed down into the heart of this unusual enterprise.

Of course the decades of weather had dulled the acrylic to an opaque window. The surface hadn't been washed in some time. And the domed shape distorted the contents below. I was surely looking down on the Sandpit PCB side of the space: two long workbenches set up in a V, with two backed stools near the apex. The surfaces of the benches appeared neatly kept but sparsely furnished. Bench vises. Articulating lights and magnifying lights. Toolboxes, lids down. A soldering gun with its power cord wrapped around its handle. Screw clamps large and small fastened here and there along the inside edges of the benches. Glue guns. Spools of wire. And of course boxes of printed circuit boards, lined up and easy to see like vinyl 33s in ancient record stores. It was too blurry to see what stage of completion they might be in, or for what application they were being created or modified.

Still on my knees, I straightened, looked out at the twinkling city, then did my best to rub some clarity into the worn skylight. The leather gloves helped but no amount of elbow grease could increase the visibility much at all.

Once again I leaned forward. Went macro: small kitchen and dining area in one corner, a bathroom with the door open, a television mounted on a wall arm, cables neatly bundled down to the outlet.

I rocked upright again and, recalling the lobby layout, looked out across the roof and tried to calculate where the skylights over Native World Import-Export might be. Pretty straightforward: the import-export business was east of Sandpit PCB, which meant to my right. Twenty feet? Thirty? Not far from where I was, but how best to get there by following the internal beams of the building?

I stood and let the blood back into my legs, calves burning with old pain, rib aching. Turned the hiker's headlamp on and followed the screws back downslope to the roofline, across approximately twenty-five feet of I-beam truss just beneath my feet—arms out for balance, the delicate metal skin of the roof to my left and thirty feet of free fall to the parking lot on my right. With the city lights blinking all around me I followed another line of screws, nimbly and lightly as I could, leading me safely back up to the desired skylight.

I knelt again and rubbed the time-frosted dome with my gloves. Squinted down at the murky tableau: an attempted retail showroom, perhaps, with what looked like rustic wooden flooring and walls. There were various display cases, set out without apparent order, arranged willy-nilly, some windowed and others not. A few looked empty, others filled with brightly colored items—dolls, toys, carvings maybe? One had fallen over to spill what looked like colorful pillows to the floor. Then, an entire wall of slouching bookshelves, the titles impossible to read. Paintings on another wall, hanging crookedly, maybe primitive in style. And a rack of elaborate spears, points upright, festooned with feathers and leather straps, amulets and gewgaws I could not identify. Rugs, possibly African; a semicircle of large stone heads, possibly Mesoamerican; animal hides piled high like carpets in a Persian rug store.

The wall farthest away from me was dense with rustic wooden ladders festooned with what looked like rugs and weavings. I couldn't even guess the cultural or ethnic origin, not through smoky acrylic and the poor light. A small congregation of totems looked out from the far corner.

Native World Import-Export indeed.

I stood and checked the Vigilant 4000. Brock Holland's clean white Suburban was still on course for San Ysidro, about ten minutes away.

Arms out for balance, I stepped carefully along the eave strut to the emergency ladder and back down to the extension. Hit solid ground, which felt sure and dependable after thin metal. Retracted the new ladder and headed for my truck. Parked again, half a block down, with a good view of the National Allied lot.

Eight minutes later the white Suburban swung into the lot and took a space right in front of the lobby.

Brock Holland and Gretchen Deuzler took their time getting out, locking up and letting themselves into the dark building.

I sat and pondered my options. I knew my chances of scaling National Allied quietly enough to spy on them through the murky skylights were slim. Metal is noisy. One slip or misstep and I'd be cooked. On the other hand . . .

But they saved me my decision. Just ten minutes after going in, they came out, Gretchen holding open the door for Brock, who carried a large pasteboard box in both hands. It didn't look heavy but it was big, and appeared to be sealed with packaging tape.

The Vigilant 4000 made my tail easy and safe. The moon was a waxing crescent and the night was dark around it. The fun couple headed back up State 78. At first, plenty of traffic for cover, then thinning as we dropped down into Borrego Valley.

But they didn't head to their love nest at La Casa del Zorro. Instead they headed off on Palm Canyon and turned into the Bighorn Motel. I pulled onto the Palm Canyon shoulder a hundred yards farther on, cut my lights, and parked facing the motel.

In the eerie green tincture of my night vision binoculars I watched the Suburban park in front of the last bungalow, nineteen, where Harris Broadman had received Dalton and me. Only four other cars in the lot. I noted that Broadman's silver Tahoe was parked outside the office, on the far side of the motel, where I'd seen it before. As was an aging white Corolla with a dented driver's door. I remembered the words of the young *caballero* I'd talked to out in Pala, where Natalie's Bimmer had been discovered and he had seen a woman in a dented white car examining the abandoned vehicle: *Sunglass big. Woman no big.*

Holland and Deuzler got out of the Suburban, green-limned figures in the unlit lot. Holland opened the rear lift gate, handed his companion the key, leaned in, and backed out with the big box in his arms.

Gretchen shut the door with the fob and the two of them walked to the bungalow.

Where, outside to hold the door open, stood Harris Broadman, spectral in white.

And beside him: Natalie Strait.

She was dressed in desert camouflage and combat boots, her black-green hair alive in the desert breeze.

Brock Holland carried the box in, followed by Gretchen.

Broadman followed Natalie back inside.

Then he came back out and looked around the lot as if he'd left something behind. Stared out in my direction while my heart thumped a steady rhythm.

Finally went in.

I'd found my missing person. And no matter what had happened to her, or whoever she had become, she was about to be mine.

THIRTY-FOUR

In the darkness I hunkered down in a nearby stand of yuccas to watch unseen. Really observing for the first time, I saw that bungalow nineteen was different from the other units. It was slightly larger. The front door was arched and there was a grated security window built in. It stood farther apart from its third-row neighbors. It was the sole seventh unit on the three legs of the Bighorn horseshoe. Added on?

Waiting there, watching. So much like Fallujah. Not only the hot, dry desert but this nervy lead-up to engagement. In Iraq it was the long waiting for dawn—the insurgents rarely fought at night—when you couldn't sleep and couldn't think and couldn't do much more than stare up at whatever happened to be above you, listening for the waking sounds of a war that would soon come reaching out to take you. Wondering why you had come here. Why your father and forefathers had obligated you to this bloody fight with peoples in strange lands thousands of miles away. When in fact your father and his father hadn't. It was you. Wanting to hit back. Wanting to show them what you could do and why you were not to be fucked with. Wanting to get it over with so you could say you did it. I didn't know my war was a bad war when I signed up. I was twenty-two when the towers fell. I didn't see falsehood on the sellers' faces when they pitched that war to me on TV. I wasn't cynical enough. Only later.

The breeze moved through the yuccas, their knifelike spines moving in unison. The sliver of moon threw its insignificant light.

I tried to shake off my hauntings from Iraq, but cheerful thoughts found no traction in the desert night. Instead, my brain down-hilled to last year's beating by armed "security guards" wearing helmets. They'd used a little drone to spot me. They seemed like an army. Later, I'd gotten some revenge, though not enough. Now, staring out at the faintly lit unit, I touched the .45 tucked into the small of my back.

I circled deeper into the desert for a view of the back side. The curtains were drawn but there was movement inside, shadows on the move. Purposeful. Approaching in the soft sand of a wash, I found the bank and took a knee behind it. Brought up the night vision binoculars again. Saw the neat little patio behind the casita, a low wall. Potted flowers and a small fountain turned off for the night. A shimmer of water in the tray. Saw the parabolic mic mounted to the roof tile, with a security camera next to it, their indicators blipping red in the dark. Felt the ugly surprise at being seen and heard. The light still showed from inside but no movement.

I moved back around to the front, squatted again, and brought up the glasses. There was a low wall as in the rear, and a small porch. Potted cacti and bougainvillea, decorative boulders. A yellow bug light on the wall. The front door was darkly finished wood, with a small window protected by an elegant wrought iron grate.

Nothing moving inside.

With my boots I cleared a small circle of sand and settled down cross-legged. The sand had trapped the heat a few inches down. I sat still with the binoculars around my neck, silently chiding myself for having blundered into the well-monitored back side of the unit. Would they be watching the camera feed this late at night? Would they have the microphone speakers turned up? How sensitive was that mic, really, with the constant desert breeze? Much more to the point, what were they *doing*?

Life is waiting. I wait therefore I am: a private eye, making an hourly wage not yet collected from a California assemblyman who had recently been indicted for campaign financial misdeeds. While running for reelection and blaming his wife. A woman who, two weeks ago, had been plucked from her life as a committed partner, a good mother, a successful seller of luxury cars, and a capable manager of political campaigns, only to be transformed into . . . what? Who are you now, Natalie Strait?

Breeze cooling, my Rolling Thunder Security windbreaker earned its keep.

Nothing is slower than time.

Or louder than silence.

Every few minutes I lifted the binoculars to the same scene. Lights still on. No movement, no change. As if four people had frozen in place at the sight or sound of me watching them from the desert.

An hour became midnight then early morning.

I saw the front door crack open but when I brought up the field glasses I realized I was seeing things. Hopeful, untrue things.

I allowed myself to think of Tola Strait, so thoroughly imploded by the deaths of Kirby and Charity, and her employees up in the Palomar Mountains. Tola, shivering in the spring cool of my bedroom, wrapped in a blanket, her face a tragic mask in the firelight. As she spilled out good childhood memories of her older brother. Only the good ones, of course, empowered by his death.

"I apologize for putting you into the middle of all that," she'd said.

"I asked for it."

"All you did was say yes to a few bucks," she said. "And to a fool playing with people's lives."

"It was the fool who drew me, not the bucks."

"I owe you."

"Nothing."

Through her tear-and-makeup-streaked mask she'd given me a blank stare.

"This is my lowest valley," she said. "My bottom. I can do better. I'm going to do better with everything I touch in life. In the future. I promise."

I smelled her tears and the musky sweet scent of dope in her hair.

———

In the first faint light of morning, no more than a blurring of the darkness in the black Borrego sky, I gave up my pretense of secrecy and walked to the front door of bungalow nineteen.

Looked through the grated window at the sofa and chairs covered in bird-of-paradise upholstery, the small desk and coffee table, the wall-mounted TV. It looked like the motel room it professed to be. Except for the large telescope mounted on a tripod before the big picture window.

I pushed the doorbell button, heard the faint chime. Waited, then rang again. And once more.

Door locked, of course.

I picked the lock in less than a minute and stepped in, closing the door with my back.

Heart thumping, eyes clear, adrenaline high: *Go.*

See, don't think. Long steps, all angles, no frontals. Room to room.

I drew the .45 and cleared the place swiftly: two bedrooms, two baths, closets and cabinets.

No one there and no evidence that anyone had been

there recently. The kitchen and bathroom sinks were clean and dry, the refrigerator empty, beds neatly made. Two TV remotes on the coffee table squared side by side over the satellite guide.

The kitchen suddenly sprang with motion—fast and airborne. I swung my pistol toward a big white cat sliding across the countertop, surprised as I was, trying to reverse course on smooth tile and knocking over a phone that slid off the counter and clattered to the floor. I picked it up and set it back in its cradle. No messages on the recorder. The cat disappeared under the couch.

Standing in the hallway, gun down and still amped by the cat, I asked myself if four people could have possibly left while I was out there watching. Gone out the front when I'd staked out the back? But from the rear I'd still been able to see the Suburban, and it hadn't moved. And out front I'd planted myself at a distance and angle that gave me a view of most of the desert behind the little building—good enough to see them picking their way through the cactus-mined desert, headed for . . . where? If they had managed any of those feats on my watch, it was time for me to consider a new career.

Which left two options: an attic or a basement.

I looked up to see an attic hatch neatly framed in the old plaster ceiling, exactly where you'd expect to find it in a building this size and shape. They could easily have climbed through and pulled the ladder up behind them. Which could partially account for the motion I saw through the curtains. Which meant they could be up there right now.

However, I also saw that the colorful kilim hall runner at my feet lay askew. As if recently disturbed.

Dragging it aside with my boot, I saw the dark cut lines through the pavers, neatly done but still visible. In the shape of a trapdoor, large enough for people. No handles or recessed pulls. No easy way in. So, likewise, they could be just feet below me in a basement or crawl space, waiting for me to pass. I toed the runner back into place.

Then retreated outside and through the desert darkness to my truck. Continued my watch. Puzzled and off-balance.

═══

The darkness surrendered to gray, and the calls of desert songbirds joined the morning. Across the parking lot from bungalow nineteen the office light was on but none of the other units were stirring yet. There were only two cars besides Holland's Suburban, Cassy Weisberg's Beetle, and Broadman's silver Chevy Tahoe.

A few minutes later, Brock Holland and Gretchen Deuzler came from the front door of bungalow nineteen, quickly got into the white Suburban and drove toward town. I didn't even have to duck and hide.

I got my Vigilant 4000 up and running. Noted that Holland and Deuzler were headed west, toward San Diego.

I waited another hour, then drove into the Bighorn lot and parked up near the office, one space over from Broadman's silver Tahoe and Cassy Weisberg's sun-blanched blue Beetle.

Cassy buzzed me into the office, welcomed me with a distant smile.

"Hello, Cass, is Harris around today?"

"Who wants to know?"

"The PI, Roland Ford."

"I was only kidding you, Mr. Ford."

"You're a good kidder, then."

"Mr. Broadman is sleeping, no doubt. He doesn't usually get up until after noon."

"Would you tell him I'm here?"

"I'm not supposed to wake him."

I tried to look disappointed and I was probably sleep-deprived enough to be convincing.

She pressed something on the counter I couldn't see. "Mr. Broadman, Roland Ford is here to see you. The PI."

The soft buzz of static, like the sound of a phone being picked up but not answered.

"Probably sleeping, like I said."

"May I see him?"

"I don't see how."

"Can I just go knock?"

"That's rude, Mr. Ford. I can't allow that."

My first impulse was to embrace rudeness. Natalie Strait was alive and kicking, and last seen a couple of hundred feet from where I now stood. Maybe, if I was face-to-face with Broadman, I'd be face-to-face with Natalie, too. My second thought was that Cassy Weisberg, employed by a kidnapper, and undergoing chemotherapy for cancer, might suffer for my rudeness more than me.

"Roland, what do you want?" asked Harris Broadman through the speaker.

"I have a question about Natalie Strait," I said.

"I know nothing about her."

Did he know it was me watching them last night? If not, I could still be just a harmless pest to him. If so, he would try to derail me.

I stalled and threw out something that Dalton had told me just recently.

"Dalton said he used to brag about her when you were in Fallujah," I said. "That you three talked on Skype once, and you told Dalton he'd better take good care of her when he got home or you would."

"And what's the matter with that?"

"I'm trying to figure out if Natalie might have looked you up recently," I said. "As a friend of her husband."

"She did not. She did not."

"No communication from her at all?"

"I've told you. None. Be gone, Ford. You're trespassing on my property and my patience."

"It's my job, but thank you, Sergeant. I apologize for getting you up so early with long-shot questions."

"You know I will always help."

I thanked Cassy and told her to have a great day.

Stopped in front of bungalow six. The blinds were open.

Broadman looked back at me from the far side of the living room. He was sitting on the same '50s turquoise sofa as when we'd first talked here and he'd told me about the IED that Dalton Strait had not quite saved him from. Same molten face. Same white clothes, white ball cap, and aviator sunglasses. Same sprigs of downy white hair.

He pointed the remote at me and the blinds shut tight.

THIRTY-FIVE

The Chaos Committee's "gift" to California, promised days earlier, was opened by Gail Winfield, the police chief of tiny Hopedale, in the western Sierra Nevada, at 8:35 a.m. on Wednesday, May 27th.

I'd been home from the Bighorn less than an hour when Lark called.

"It killed her instantly," he said. "They're using better materials and less of them. The box that Chief Winfield opened could have been a coffee table book. It weighed about the same. It arrived UPS the day before, from an insecure drop box in Hemet. Another bogus sender and return address. Fires just set in Stockton and Grass Valley. And another officer wounded in Sacramento, shot with a rifle."

Hemet is forty-three miles from Fallbrook, where the first Chaos Committee bomb was mailed. And seventy-seven miles from Ramona, where the second bomb originated. The third bomb's origin, which killed Congressman Clark Nisson in Encinitas, was of course still unknown.

"Three of four bombs posted from my backyard," I said to Special Agent Lark. "I hope you don't come after me."

"We might. Have you looked at all the surveillance video?"

"Nothing," I said.

"I'm counting on you, Roland. This one's for Joan. Remember? What's new on Natalie Strait?"

"Nothing since the blouse and the letter from Justine," I lied.

"The cops think Dalton wrote it and mailed himself the evidence as a smoke screen," said Lark. "They think it's possible that he had her bagged as cover for his campaign crimes."

"Is that why you haven't opened an official FBI investigation?"

"That's part of it. Hazzard says Dalton wasn't where he said he was the morning she vanished."

"He's got an embarrassing alibi for that morning," I said.

"I didn't think you *could* embarrass that guy," said Lark. "Every time I see him he's talking about his wife handling all the finances. How he never touched the money. I mean, you can stick up for him because of Fallujah, but . . ."

"But?"

"But if I learn anything I'll share it with you," Lark

said. "We're letting Hazzard run with it. For us feds, it's all Chaos Committee now. They're operating in my backyard, too, Roland. They're fomenting revolution, making me look bad. It's triage and priorities right now. So get on that security video, will you? Jackie O mailed that first bomb from Fallbrook. Find her again. Use that twenty-ten vision of yours for something more than beating me at the range."

"Glad it pissed you off."

"Everything pisses me off."

I ended the call. Checked the Vigilant 4000 to find Brock Holland's white Suburban en route from Borrego Valley to San Diego.

Perfect. Two fewer people to deal with.

Burt stepped into my office. "Ready when you are."

———

The Bighorn Motel parking lot was down to two vehicles: Cassy Weisberg's Beetle and a wind-blasted station wagon circa 1975 with rust patches the size of dinner plates.

Better than I'd planned for: No Harris Broadman. No Brock Holland or Gretchen Deuzler. Just me and the motel from which Natalie Strait had apparently disappeared less than twelve hours earlier.

Once again I waited just off Palm Canyon Drive. My lucky spot. Watched Burt's perfect red Eldorado convertible sail into the lot and park outside the office. White leather and a red-and-chrome dash. Burt got out and looked around, dressed for golf—green pants, yellow shirt, black PGA vest and visor. Wiped a folded white hankie over a spot on the driver's door and palmed it back into a rear pocket.

The truck thermometer read 92 degrees. I gave Burt a moment to engage Cassy, then locked up and trudged out into the desert again to approach bungalow nineteen out of view from the office.

Someone had locked the door since I'd last picked it open. And turned off the interior lights. Interesting. The cleaning people? I doubted it.

I picked the lock again and stepped in. The AC was off and the room was warm. Curtains drawn as they were last night. The big white cat was on the couch, green-eyed and dreamy.

I toured the place once more, gun at the small of my back under a loose shirt. The cat followed me, nosing the wall edges, tail up.

I parted the curtains over the picture window. Burt's car was now parked outside of unit two. From the back seat he pulled a small rolling suitcase and set it on the asphalt. Then shouldered his precious clubs—woods, irons, and putter all cloaked in red-and-white covers embossed with his initials. He didn't let them touch the ground. He rarely uses the cavernous Eldorado trunk because he has to jump to close the lid. I tease him about the BS but never about his height. He locked up, grabbed his suitcase handle, and bumped his way to his room.

In the hallway I looked directly up at the attic access panel. All I needed for that was the ladder in the closet. One of my detective friends with the SDPD taught me to look up. At a crime scene, he said, always look up.

I fetched and climbed the ladder, slid aside the attic lid and looked in. Hit the handy light switch. Small and not much to see: beams and rafters with roll-in insulation in between, the air conditioner exchange unit, ducts and electrical and copper water lines to and from the heater below. Two un-sprung rat traps, freshly baited. Not enough room to stand.

I made sure the cover was as before, put the ladder back, and studied the floor hatch. No handles or grip. A switch, I thought, or a button.

Nothing obvious on the walls, but I found a promising candidate in the bathroom just across the hall—an everyday light switch hiding behind a hung hand towel.

Flipped it and watched the hallway floor hatch rise, pavers and all, to form a neat square opening just big enough for human traffic. The hinges were stout and the motor was quiet. A nylon strap nailed to the underside. A light went on. Metal steps and metal railings.

Down I went. Four-by-four uprights rose on either side of me, bound by flat steel T-straps. Two-by-four framing, with heavy sandbag walls down low, and lighter plywood sheets up higher. A tunnel designed for the treacherous desert soil. The ceiling was just high enough that I didn't have to duck. A line of overhead lightbulbs ran straight down its center, every bulb working. The reinforcement lumber still looked fresh, the nail heads glimmered, and the T-straps were shiny black.

Recently built or well preserved by the desert dry?

By my difficult reckoning, the tunnel ran along one side of the pool and toward the first wing of rooms. The light was good but it was difficult to get a sense of direction underground. I moved slowly and made a soft left turn.

Then on to the first row of the Bighorn Motel horseshoe, aimed roughly at Broadman's unit six. Where I saw a trapdoor very much like the one through which I'd just descended. I looked up at the ladder tucked under the hatch and the dangling pull-rope, feeling a vertiginous dread—Alice falling down the rabbit hole.

The tunnel continued another fifty feet past what I guessed was the office, then began to lead me away from the motel. But this was not the same tunnel I'd started off in. The walls became solid rock—not reinforced by beams, sandbags, or plywood. It took another gentle turn and, if my sense of direction was right, headed into the hills behind the Bighorn, to the east. The hills that I'd seen the first time I came to the Bighorn—scarred by old mine tailings and scaffolding and pits, and, apparently, undercut by tunnels. The hills with the homes built into the boulders.

A hundred feet more to another turn, then a hundred feet more.

Bringing me to another ladder and another trapdoor.

I'm not claustrophobic but my gut was tight and a pool of panic simmered.

I climbed up and muscled open the hatch. Heard the grind of the hinge and felt the weight on the strap as I lowered the cover to the floor.

Pulled myself up and out and into a large, faintly lit room.

No windows and almost no light. Found a switch and the room flickered to life.

It was large, with brick walls and a low ceiling of recessed fluorescent lights. Bunker-like. Stone silent. One wall fitted with heavy shackles for arms and ankles. Bookshelves on three sides. Desks and tables with newspapers and magazines piling up. Stacks of books. Lamps for reading. Fast-food litter, drink cans. Rugs on a polished concrete floor. A closed door with a poster of a Guy Fawkes demonstrator on it.

A torture chamber? A library? Study hall? Museum?

The far wall arrested my attention. It was hung with masks from around the world, crowded together cheek to cheek: African, Greek and Roman, European, Native American, Asian, Pacific Islands, Australian. Many I couldn't place. Both ancient and modern. Washington and Lincoln. Reagan and Nixon. Obama and Trump. Superheroes. The world in masks. Grotesque. Amusing. Unnerving.

And down low, within easy reach:

A Hannya theater mask.

A madly grimacing Iroquois.

A WWI splatter mask.

Standing in the cool silence, I couldn't take my eyes off them.

═══

I let Burt into bungalow nineteen through the back patio door, out of Cassy Weisberg's view from the Bighorn Motel office.

A few minutes later we stood in the bunker, before the wall of masks.

"Hair and makeup for The Chaos Committee," he said.

"Check the Iroquois," I said. It had the same insane grin and crazed eyes, the same stumpy wooden teeth, and a head of bristling black hair that looked much like the horsehairs found in Natalie Strait's blue SUV.

"Broadman, Holland, and Deuzler make three of five committee members," said Burt.

"Leaving two ninjas from the TV takeover," I said. "One female and one male. Possibly Jackie O. For a committee of five—minimum."

"Let's see what Mr. Fawkes is guarding," said Burt.

I couldn't get the lock open. I learned my lock picking on residential American models and this one was German, industrial and expensive.

"One more round, champ," Burt said.

I finally got the tension wrench and pick working together and the last pin moved into place. I pushed open the door.

An apartment, spacious and apparently lived in. Bars on the windows and just the one door leading in and out. Brick walls and beam ceilings, a hardwood floor. A good-sized fireplace, black with the years, in the corner of the living room. A stack of firewood left over from winter.

Dishes in the sink, food in the refrigerator, bread, jam, and peanut butter on the counter.

A bath towel hung from the bathroom door hook. A blue dress dried on a hanger hooked to the shower. A shower cap on the nozzle inside. A brush on the vanity counter, matted with dark hair.

"She was still here this morning, when I saw Broadman," I said. "After I left, he got her out of hiding and they hit the road."

"Which means they made you last night," said Burt. "Maybe that's a good thing. They could have jumped you but they didn't."

I checked the Vigilant 4000. Saw that Brock Holland's Suburban had been stationary for the last fifty-seven minutes at the same GPS coordinates in Ramona, a little over an hour away from Borrego Springs.

Ramona, where Natalie Galland had grown up and met earnest Dalton Strait through his bad-boy older brother, Kirby. Where the second Chaos Committee bomb had been mailed to San Diego County Administration Center.

Burt looked at me.

"I have to tell Lark what we found," I said. "But I'm not done with Natalie. It's better we retrieve her than our overworked and sometimes reckless bureau."

"Certainly."

"Time kills, Burt. Natalie Strait is a valuable captive and these people will exploit her any way they can."

"Sounds to me like she was dressed for combat last night," Burt said. "Stockholm syndrome? Or maybe another psychotic break? More than enough has happened to her in the last two weeks to bring one on. But don't forget that they expect a ransom. What kind, I don't know."

"Is Holland still in Ramona?"

I checked the Vigilant and nodded.

=====

An hour later, Brock Holland's Ramona GPS coordinates led us to a dirt shoulder of Pine Street, from which we stared through a chain-link fence to the empty lot beyond.

No Suburban.

No Harris Broadman, Brock Holland, Gretchen Deuzler, or Natalie Strait.

Just weeds going brown and ground squirrels leading their squirrely lives. Trash flapped against the windward side of the fence, from which hung a collection of campaign posters.

Dalton Strait

Assembly

Straight for California

Something flashed red in the empty lot.

I used my binoculars to find the Vigilant 4000 blinking from atop a boulder in the afternoon sun. Passed them to Burt just as the Suburban came up fast behind us, someone spraying three-round bursts that sent us scrambling under the truck and returning fire from the ground. Dirt and gravel kicked up in my face, rattled off my sunglasses. Bullets twanged above. I heard the lead punching through the truck body and the windows as I squeezed off rounds at the driver. Burt fired away beside me. The Suburban's windshield blossomed and the vehicle swerved suddenly onto two tires—hovered a perilous second—then righted itself and roared back onto the street and away.

"We can run them down but we can't match the firepower," said Burt.

"I hate calling cops," I said.

"Me too."

I called 911.

THIRTY-SIX

That night, the Irregulars, Tola Strait, and I watched a San Diego News special titled "Chaos in California" on the big TV in the palapa. My phone sat on the table for updates from Proetto. Silence. The white Suburban had so far vanished into the highways of Southern California, Proetto speculating that The Chaos Committee might have many sympathizers and safe havens.

Burt and I had been lucky. I had a bandaged shrapnel cut on one cheek and Burt's right knuckles were wrapped in gauze.

Here at Rancho de los Robles, Wednesday is known as Catfish Wednesday. Which means that Grandpa Dick deep-fries his favorite dish and all participants bring something at least vaguely Southern to complement the fried fish.

We all try to be thankful and contrite on Catfish

Wednesdays, no matter what strife, rancor, or disappointment might be piling up inside us or in the world around us. We agree to let the day be more than the sum of its problems.

And try we did: ice-cold prosecco or lemonade at cocktail hour; social Ping-Pong with evenly matched teams; an upbeat "I-Ching" consult for each of us from Odile; much sympathy for and genuine interest in Tola, her business, and her bereaved family; improved guitar from Frank on his native Salvadoran folk songs; reduced squabbling between Grandpa Dick and Grandma Liz; Burt garrulously refilling drinks and offering bacon-wrapped devil dogs from Fallbrook's Oink and Moo restaurant; even the mongrel Triunfo napped under the picnic table rather than chasing and crunching the Ping-Pong balls.

For a while I felt the blessing of surviving machine-gun fire, the goodness of our world and the people in it, the comfort of kindness and respect, the hope that comes from belief that the next day can be better and the day after that better still. Why not? In Tola's occasional looks I felt the optimism of love, how it takes you over and makes you want to be better. I remembered her tearful words after the slaughter on Palomar, the way she blamed it all on herself. *This is my lowest valley. My bottom. I'm going to do better with everything I touch in life.*

But as I turned on the gigantic-screen TV to watch "Chaos in California" I felt cold dread wash over me, knowing that the show would flood our little campfire of human decency like an icy river.

Cohosting "Chaos in California" were familiar San Diego News anchors Loren Clement and Amber Hunt.

Over a video backdrop of burning cars jamming a street in San Bernardino, Clement led off:

"Never in history has California experienced the willful taking of life and destruction of property of the last two weeks. This unprecedented violence is being inspired by the self-proclaimed Chaos Committee, a group of masked terrorists as mysterious as it is deadly . . .

"But first, the facts," he said.

Clement's affable mug was replaced by a street brawl in Oakland, over which Clement narrated offscreen:

"CC-claimed victims" were three—a small-town police chief, one U.S. congressman, and his aide—all killed by mail bombs. But murders "directed or inspired" by the CC were thirteen across the state, and included six sworn officers, four of whom were shot in the back from long distances.

"CC-inspired destruction of property" statewide was estimated at $675 million and consisted mostly of arson-set fires of government buildings, schools, and places of worship. Scores of retail businesses had been set on fire, hundreds of cars had been torched, thousands of windows smashed. Emergency rooms across the state were experiencing record numbers of gunshot injuries and violently broken bones.

"Over half of California's public schools have experienced shutdowns of three or more days," said Amber Hunt, whose usually pleasant face now appeared tense and determined.

"Most hard hit are high school students, teenagers who have grown up with classroom killings and active-shooter drills and who seem almost unanimously to have *expected* this terrible violence. And then, there are elementary school children who have little understanding at all of what is happening in their world. Let's let some of these terrified people speak for themselves . . ."

Faithful ministers, firm rabbis, beseeching imams.

Sobbing children, fierce mothers, stoic dads.

"I don't know how much more of this we can stand," said Liz. "As a people."

"It will end when they kill The Chaos Committee," said Dick. "And America can get back to baseball."

"This is no time for jock humor, dear."

"But then what comes next?" asked Odile.

"Civil war," said Frank.

Triunfo perked up at his master's words, then clunked his head back down to the flagstone.

Tola gave me an absent look. Checked her phone under the table and away from me. Took my hand.

Loren Clement:

"Who are and what is The Chaos Committee? We're going to replay the *Local Live!* takeover video again. But rather than try to speculate on the philosophy of this deadly band—perhaps much larger in numbers than a mere band, according to the FBI—we'll let them explain their beliefs in their own words."

I watched the studio invasion commence anew—the grotesque masks, the clumsy violence, the pistols held to the heads of two terrified reporters—and wondered again that it hadn't ended in blood. I tried to tell who was behind each mask. It looked like Broadman was the Iroquois and Holland the WWI splatter mask. Gretchen very possibly the female Hannya. Leaving the two ninjas. The voice of the Iroquois came as before, digitally augmented, Vaderesque.

"Allow us to introduce ourselves. We are representatives of The Chaos Committee . . . We wanted to give you a chance to meet us. Face-to-mask . . ."

I half listened to the doomsday voice coming from behind the grinning Iroquois tribal mask. The other half of my attention roamed the underground tunnels and The Chaos Committee "headquarters." I expected Lark had raided the Bighorn and its warrens by now. I hoped they would treat Cassy Weisberg with care. I doubted that Broadman, Holland, and Deuzler would be found anywhere near Borrego Springs. All the while I wondered, too, if Natalie—after being stolen by these people, body, heart, and mind—had finally fallen in with them. And like everyone else, I wondered where the next bomb would explode.

I watched the screen as anchorman Dwayne Swift fainted and his ninja attacker tried to drag him back up into his seat.

Looked out across the pond as I listened to the Iroquois mask, so pompous and proud of his stupid ideas.

"My brothers and sisters in arms. As proof of our power and the power of our ideas, witness the Encinitas office of Representative Clark Nisson. Good night!"

Again the masks advanced on the cameras and again the picture went dark.

"Why have these calls to anarchy taken hold in the most prosperous nation on earth?" asked Amber Hunt. "To answer this, we'll talk to experts—all of whom agree that a 'perfect storm' of economics, politics, religion, and race has been brewing in our country for years. Later in the show, we'll talk to American voters and see just how this sudden jump in American terror will influence their decisions in November."

November seemed far away.

THIRTY-SEVEN

Tola lay against me, damp and big pupiled, her hair dark on the pillow and her eyes pale green in the minor light.

She rose on one elbow, checked her phone, then put it back under the pillow. "Things," she whispered.

"What things?"

"Don't worry."

"Why would I worry on a night like this?"

"You're my rock. And my roll. I wish you were mine."

I stroked her hair and listened to her breathing. Through the window I could see the same waxing crescent of moon that had led me to Natalie Strait the night prior in the dark, wind-rattled desert. Natalie in camouflage, part of the gang. The tunnels. The wall of masks. Where did they make the bombs? Who was mailing them? Where was Jackie O?

Even making love to Tola Strait couldn't prevent the riptides of the last weeks from pulling me back out to sea with them. Dread and darkness, treading through the undertow.

While she slept I went to the kitchen, got a roll of duct tape from a drawer and tore off two short strips.

Outside I stood for a moment beside my bullet-riddled F-150, which stood alone in the chill spring air, as beloved a vehicle as I've ever owned. I felt her pain. The bullet holes were dull silver against the black paint. The divots were mild, due to the velocity of the 5.56mm rounds from the M4. The bullet-resistant glass—$50 per square foot—and the angle of attack had left the windshield intact and without holes. It had only been a few months since I'd had six bullet wounds operated on by the body shop. A long story. Today's miracle was no damage under the hood other than a punctured radiator hose, and two ruined tires. I'd limped my baby to the nearest tire store in Ramona, Burt riding shotgun, literally. An hour later we were on our way.

Standing beside my truck I touched the driver's door, mumbled thanks and a short promise of vengeance. Thought I should name the truck after all we'd been through. My first idea was Vivian and I liked it. Sprightly and unusual. Of or related to life.

I pasted the tape over the rear left taillight of Tola's Jeep. All night I'd sensed her departure, but I had no idea to where or why.

When I got back into bed she was awake.

"Wanna hear the story of Kirby and the baby gorilla?" she asked.

How do you say no to that?

"He was fifteen and some of his older friends were animal breeders and dealers. You know, exotic stuff for the pet trade, mostly from Mexico and Central America. Well, Kirby loved creatures of any kind, so he'd clean cages and run errands for these jaspers, get to hang with the animals and make a little pocket money. So, the dealers take a baby western lowland gorilla in payment for something. No brains, no headaches for the dealers, right? She'd been delivered by cesarean section and weighed less than five pounds. Name of Tumaini, which is Swahili for hope. Of course she stopped drinking her formula around strangers, so they sold her to Kirby for a hundred dollars and he snuck her into his room."

Tola kissed me lightly on the lips, checked her phone again.

"That gorilla was cute as a bug, Roland, had this soulful little face and beautiful eyes and this straight-up black hair like she was surprised or something. She looked so old! Little white diapers. Kirby cleaned out a bottom dresser drawer and made a bed for her. The first day he showed her to me she was clinging to him like Kirby was her mom. Animals always loved him. She started drinking from the bottle again. He bought her a big plush gorilla that cost him a fortune but Tumaini really liked it.

"This was when Mom was off and wandering and before Kirby's fight that ruined Dad. So, Dad being distracted by Mom's adventures and gone all the time running Better Burger, everything was cool for a week. He couldn't figure why Kirb spent so much time in his room. The truancy calls from the school got Dad riled enough to raid the bedroom and find the gorilla. Dad laid waste to Kirby and raided his exotic-animal friends. Charged them a grand for his trouble and the gorilla's room and board. Gave them some Better Burger discount coupons. Gave Tumaini to the San Diego Zoo and made a publicity stunt out of it. So Dad."

Feeling her breath on my chest, I said, "Amber Hunt covered it for San Diego News. Your dad got permission to use Tumaini's image for advertising and named a veggie burger after her."

"The Gorilla Gobble. It never took off. Ahead of its time."

Tola's warm breath turned liquid on my skin and I felt her hard-fought sobs.

"It's good to remember," she said. "Even when you want to forget."

No more truthful words than those, I thought.

Family stories.

I told her about my sister, who was still traveling the world as a professional surfer. Janine is one of the few female big-wave riders and to watch her compete at Mavericks or Cloudbreak puts my heart in my throat until she comes striding up the beach with her board under one arm and that dazed smile on her face.

I went on and on about my brother, Jack—a bright and troubled man—who travels with Janine as an assistant, trainer, companion, and fellow surfer after his grueling years as a SEAL.

Tola recounted brother Dalton's run for high school junior class president, his defeat and his bitter protest of rigged ballot counting. He'd made such a big issue of it with a local paper that the principal had duly questioned the election committee students and found that one of them had in fact counted her own vote for Dalton's opponent twice because Dalton had passed over her in favor of Natalie Galland of Ramona. One vote being enough to change the outcome. She'd had no idea it was that close. Dalton had happily taken office. And, not long after, taken his baseball bat to older brother Kirby, staking his claim to Natalie once and for all.

Then the stories tailed into silence and I listened to the heartbeat of my home and the woman in my bed. Moon and a breeze through the window screen. Thought nothing about anything. Amazing grace.

We made strong love and in the afterglow Tola's phone buzzed. She listened and hung up.

"I don't need you on this," she said.

"I'll help."

"I don't need it."

She carried her overnight back into the bathroom and emerged shortly in a trim black business suit, a tastefully low-cut black blouse, low-heeled leather boots, the elegant chartreuse satin duster I'd seen that night in Sacramento draped over one shoulder. Hair in a ponytail, tight and out of her way.

We walked to her Jeep in heavy silence.

"Sure you don't need me?" I asked.

"I got this one."

She kissed me hard, then tossed the duster onto the front seat, climbed in, and rolled down the window.

"Roland, I love you like a twister loves a trailer. But don't follow me and don't wait up."

"I'll leave a light on for you."

Down the drive. I waited a moment, then got into sweet, battle-scarred Vivian and followed.

THIRTY-EIGHT

Tola's red Jeep was easy enough to track with the blacked-out taillight. South down the interstate. I didn't really care if she saw me or not. I was bent to do what I could for her. The PI Roland—knight-errant, by love inspired, the tools of his trade within easy reach. Steering down Interstate 15 south in the service of his queen.

To the 8 East and into the mountains of Cleveland National Forest, down the long grade past Virgil Strait's rocky stronghold and on into Imperial Valley. Wind and blowing sand and big rigs bound for Arizona. Off at Bonds Corner, then into Buena Vista.

She parked on the U.S. side, on a potholed boulevard in the restaurant and bar district. Turned off her lights and called me.

"I knew you'd pull this," she said.

"You didn't fight it very hard."

"I made a specific request."

"I don't work for you," I said. "What is this?"

"Calderon told New Generation about my appointment at the Buena Vista Credit Union. Providing an opportunity on Palomar in my absence and the skeleton crew at the grow. My own trusting stupidity failed to foresee and prevent what happened. His unhappy notary is an acquaintance of mine."

"They should have taken us out at the credit union," I said. "Or the Hotel Casa Grande. Easy target, easy money."

"Kirby meant nothing to them except a warning to me," she said. "New Generation wants everything I've worked for. My money, my plants, my retail, my savings and loan. My mail-order start-up and my California regulator you told me not to trust and by the way you were right. That craggy sonofabitch I trusted is FBI. The cleanest way for New Generation to get all that is to get *me* on their payroll. I've turned down some awfully lucrative advances. Leading to what happened. But I'm coming to the table tonight at the Casa Grande at their invitation. We're going to clear it all up."

"It can't all be cleared up tonight, Tola."

"Some of it, then," she said.

A flat tone to her voice. I wondered what part she was hoping to clear up and what she'd let slide.

"I accept your offer of help tonight, Roland. Be a calming influence. If things don't go well, we've got a way out, east of town. Ride with us or you might never get back across."

Virgil Strait picked us up in an old Econoline commercial van, once white, few windows but lots of rust. Plenty of Bondo above the taillights but a capable growl at idle.

Virgil peered at me through faint interior lamplight, a *take it or leave it* expression on his tortoise face. A passenger beside him, more riders in the bench seats behind. "Make room," he said.

The slam of the door, then grumbles, grunts, and names. I was placed in the middle bench seat between Tola and one of her Strait Shooters from the Nectar Barn, Gar. Behind me sat Marcus from the Palomar grow, flanked by two other large, stone-faced braves, Erik and Eli. Up front in the passenger seat sat Archie Strait—father of Tola, Kirby, and Dalton—the once proud patriarch seriously injured in contest with his eldest son. The face of a hundred billboards. Dressed in a yoked black cowboy jacket over a white shirt, and his signature red bandana in place. Groomed and alert looking but motionless as a manikin, just as when I'd met him in Virgil's eyrie.

I noted the others' business-meeting attire: suits or sports coats. The van smelled of hair product and nerves.

"You should have told me about the dress code," I said.

"You just shut up and do what Tola tells you to," said Virgil.

"Sir, yes sir."

"Dumb jarhead," he said.

"Dumb Okie," I said.

"Men," said Tola. "Please, let's bow our heads in prayer. This is our practice, Roland. We welcome your participation but it's not required."

I looked at the floor carpet, worn down to metal between my feet. And listened to Tola's low smooth voice in prayer over the idling engine.

"God in heaven we ask your blessing upon us. We believe in you but we don't claim to know who you are or what you want. We know that you might not like us very much. Which makes us humble before you, heads bowed in hope that you will protect us, but fearful that you might choose not to. We deserve nothing. But we desire the best of your earth and want your permission to take it. In return we will be kind to the poor, and brave against the wicked. And we will honor your name, God, our silent and invisible partner, forever. Amen."

An easy crossing south at the border. The young U.S. agent studied Virgil and his famous passenger without a trace of recognition, focused on Virgil's passport, looked up, said nothing, and waved us through.

The Mexican border guard did likewise, but gave Archie a smile as the crossarm lifted. "Welcome to Mexico," he said.

Virgil handed him what looked like an eight-by-ten picture of his son, the same image that had graced the highway billboards for all the years.

"Here," said Virgil. "He wants you to have this. From back when he could still sign his name."

═══

The Hotel Casa Grande stood on Avenida Revolución, a building with one hundred and fifty years of history. Missions and ranchos, wealth and squalor, Indians and Anglos, revolution and reform. Pancho Villa slept here. No mention of General Pershing. The plastered adobe was two stories, built around the interior courtyard where Tola and I had eaten. All of it carefully maintained and charmingly lit.

Virgil parked the heavy-laden van opposite the hotel and a block away, aimed back in the direction from which we had come. The engine dieseled and died.

"Tola does the negotiating," he said. "We're here to keep things well mannered. If anything less than good manners prevails, get back to the van fast. If you can't, the desert north of here is passable. Just stick to the riverbed and dodge the rattlesnakes. It's five hundred yards back to the U.S.A. No wall yet, no troops anymore. They'll want our phones, so leave them here—they can't take what we don't have."

"They'll take the whole damned van," said someone in the dark.

"The van is secure," said Virgil.

I followed his crooked finger pointing through the windshield and saw the men approaching, three more of Tola's Strait Shooters from the Julian Nectar Barn.

"It's going to go smoothly," said Tola, her voice taut. "It's going to go exactly how I want it to."

"Vamos con Dios," said a voice from behind me.

Tola and I led the way, her boots sharp on the old cobbles, her flowing duster buttoned not quite high enough to hide her plunging neckline. Behind us came the rest, Marcus pushing Archie Strait in his wheelchair, his head braced but bouncing sharply on the bumpy street, his white shirt bright under the streetlamp. His hands were folded on his lap and his face set in a serene expression.

"I can't get free from seeing Kirby," she said. "Hanging there in the cottonwoods. All white like the tree trunks. I can separate personal from business, Roland. I've always done that. But what about Kirbs? He can't do anything at all now. They took it all away from him, right down to his right to breathe. From Charity, too. And from three more of my people. I'm having trouble shaking that from my brain."

"Shake it now, Tola," I said. "Vengeance later."

"That's what Dad said."

"I didn't know he could talk."

"He tightens a finger once for yes and twice for no. It works. It just takes time for complex ideas."

There seemed to be no end to Strait family surprises.

We were shown into the courtyard restaurant by a solemn gentleman in a black suit. Columned archways ran along all four sides, framing the tiled floor and the heavy wooden chairs and tables. Above and beyond them guest rooms, curtained for privacy, some lit and others not. In the courtyard wrought iron sconces with electric candles threw light on the profusion of potted plants that had surrounded Tola and me on what now seemed to be a very distant evening, never to be repeated.

Six New Generation gangsters took their seats at a spacious table for twelve, their *jefe* at one head. Virgil took the other head as his five confederates claimed alternating chairs amid the *narcotraficantes*. The illegals favored urban fashions and street bling, high-end watches, big rings, gold bracelets. Tola's wannabe legals wore conservative western attire—some in cowboy boots and hats, their weapons purposely ill concealed. Tattoos for all. I stood at the wall with a nervy beat to my pulse, Archie beside me, Tola with her back to us mid-table.

The men stood and introduced themselves gravely, handshakes and fist bumps and an air of guarded conviviality: Leo was the jefe, then Matteo, Domingo, Israel, El Poco, and El Suerte—The Small and The Lucky.

Then the northerners: Virgil, who introduced his granddaughter, his son behind her, then Marcus, Gar, Erik, and Eli.

When the introductions were finished and the players had sat, a waiter pulled back Leo's chair and El Jefe stood.

"My English *no bueno*," he said. "But for to honor you, *bonita Nordica*, I try. We are having too much blood in your country. The United States is the customer we all need. She is the not-ending source of dollars for us. *La plaza última*. Can we share? Yes, but only if we share together. Not as *guerreros* but as friends. As businessmen. We all know this. Sinaloa knows. New Generation knows, Tijuana knows. *La Familia* knows. All of the politicians in Mexico and *los Estados Unidos* know this. *You* know. Many of your businesses are legal but they no can operate. So, only on native land. And the natives know. Billions of dollars grow from *los Estados Unidos*, like plants. The dollars are reaching up to offer themselves. So, Tola, why do we compete? Why do we not join our people—right here, tonight—a pledge of business and honor? Your brother, he is no more. But maybe we honor him, and those of New Generation, with peace. Peace and cooperation. We have many lawyers. So do you. Too many lawyers. They make the details. But only if we agree, tonight."

Leo looked down at Tola, then at each of the seated *norteños*. He turned and nodded at Archie, then sat.

In the awkward silence that followed, an army of waiters marched in, bearing a magnum of wine, pitchers of beer, and trays of liquor bottles crowded tightly as high-rises. They were stoic and formal and served the Mexicans first.

When the last of the waiters exited through the columns of the arcade, Tola stood and raised a beer stein.

"To the future," she said.

"*El futuro!*" a few voices rang out, none of them from her own people. It was then that I thought I knew why this strange convention had been called, and what was going to happen.

"And to Kirby Strait," she added. "One more victim of New Generation greed and stupidity."

Another silence, this one more loaded.

"Your slaughter on Palomar has done more than break

my heart," she said. "It's made terrible trouble for us at home. The local police are investigating. The San Diego sheriffs. The Bureau of Cannabis Control. The FBI, the DEA, and the Department of Homeland Security. Our sympathetic representatives and state assembly can't help us with headlines like the ones that you have created. You have brought all this wrath upon my people in order to what? To bully me into a partnership? If any one of you in this room thinks that I'm weak and foolish enough to give in to your violence, let him raise his hand and be counted right now."

Their eyes were hard upon Tola, and their faces set in contempt, but not a hand went up.

"Good," she said. "You're right, Leo. We can't bring back Kirby or his woman, or the three fine people I lost on Palomar that day. We can only honor them. With grand words and fading memories of who they were and what they paid."

Tola upped her stein and took what looked to me, from behind, like a measured swallow.

"With respect, Miss Tola," said El Poco, standing and opening his hands in the air. He was a huge man with a Zapata mustache and soulful eyes. "Your brother and his *amiga* were not supposed to die that day. They were collaterals."

"Which makes his dying even worse," said Tola. "More wasteful and inept. They shot up his body long after he'd died, Poco. Is there such a thing as collateral mutilation?"

"I will discipline the guilty," he said.

The silence was Tola's to break or keep. "I forgive you all. I forgive you, to a man."

El Jefe stood and raised his glass of wine. "To our friendship and new business relation!"

Tola set down her beer stein. "I said nothing about friendship or business."

"But . . ."

"I simply forgave you before saying hello to you from Kirby."

Beneath the chartreuse satin Tola's shoulders rolled, and the back of the duster loosened and an orange flash blew Leo off his feet and back into his chair. The Honcho. She turned and shot El Poco in his face as he sat, swung the coach gun down-table to cut down half-risen Matteo. Virgil pistol-shot Israel, seated next to him, point-blank; Eli swept a small knife through El Suerte's throat; Gar shot drop-jawed Domingo with a small machine pistol; and Marcus swung his pistol left and right through the gun smoke, futilely searching for a living target.

I pushed Archie fast for the courtyard exit, watching in astonishment as he curled a finger around the side of his wheelchair arm, launching a smoke bomb from the back frame. It rose as high as the second-story guest rooms, then fell back into the restaurant in a billowing cloud.

Barreling toward the lobby I was aware of the waitstaff and the maître d' peering at us from behind the archway columns, and the guests proned out on the floor, and the cooks pressed to the kitchen door windows, and the lights in the guest room windows going out as the smoke hung. I muscled Archie through the lobby and down the colonnade toward the Econoline.

Virgil drove briskly toward the border, most of us chattering nervously and wiping off blood. Tola sat speechless beside me, pale as a ghost, her head lolling as I cleaned off her face with my shirtsleeve.

We got the same Mexican border guard, who was once again pleased to see the celebrity Archie Strait in the passenger seat, smartly groomed and pleasant faced.

"I give my wife the picture," he said.

"Splendid, Pedro," said Virgil. "Now open that gate and we'll be on our way."

The U.S. agent waved us through and Virgil stomped on it.

THIRTY-NINE

Tola dreamed and trembled. Terrified words and anguished yowls.

At dawn the Marine Corps artillery started up on Camp Pendleton, just a few miles from where I live. Thunder on thunder. Practice makes perfect. Tola was tightly balled under the covers, only a slice of her face and a flood of red hair visible.

"Sound of freedom," I said.

"Maybe I should join up. Do they accept killers?"

"They create them."

"I'd be ahead of the curve."

Downstairs I made coffee and breakfast, brought them up. She stood in my robe, showered, her hair up in a towel, looking out to the pond as the artillery thumped and the window glass shook.

We sat on the hefty old trunk at the foot of my bed, plates on our knees and coffee cups on the floor.

"My soul is gone," she said.

"It'll come back when it trusts you again."

"Will you trust me again?"

"You killed three men last night, Tola. You can say they deserved it and you might be right. Varying gods would weigh in with varying opinions. The one you prayed to in the van? The one you said may possibly not like you? My guess is that that god would approve."

She gave me a long look, her face specter white with dark hollows. Her eyes flat green pools.

"Get me out of here," she said. "Anywhere."

———

I drove Justine's red Boxster convertible. Put the top down and a CD from her wallet into the player.

I couldn't clearly define my emotions as I tore through the curving back-country roads toward I-5: the slaughters on Palomar and in the hotel just hours ago; memories of Justine flooding me as I sat inches away from Tola, hearing the old music.

We stood on a bluff at Fort Rosecrans National Cemetery, facing the grave of Private First Class Ernest Avalos, 1985–2004.

In our hearts forever

"Why here?" asked Tola.

"Perspective." I told her about Avalos in Fallujah.

"Here but for the grace of God are you?" she asked.

"Certainly."

"Do you feel responsible?"

"Just that I got the luck that day and he didn't."

"A good guy?"

"A good man. Humble and kind-natured."

"I didn't think marines could be that."

I smiled.

Tola took my arm and we watched a burial taking place two hills over, the headstones fanning away from us in diminishing perspective, perfectly uniform, an undulating river of stones, over a hundred thousand in all. One hundred thousand. The gulls wheeled over Point Loma.

"I feel that I have sinned," she said. "And I feel that if I was asked to do last night again, I would. I know I would."

"Do something good for someone living," I said. "You'll feel better about yourself."

"Feeling better about myself doesn't seem like an appropriate motivation. On the backs of three dead men."

I thought of my Five. The Five I'd never told anyone about until I confessed to Harris Broadman and Dalton Strait that day in bungalow nineteen. What good could come of opening those wounds to Tola?

But I did.

When I was finished her head hit my shoulder and I felt the strength of her grip on my arm. Felt the strength it takes to keep going, to fight fear with hope, to bear heartbreak on the slender shoulders of joy.

"Take me to a church," she said. "One with a lenient god and rituals I don't understand."

Which landed us at St. Peter the Apostle Catholic Parish back in Fallbrook.

Tola wanted to talk to the priest, so I waited outside. A buzz in my pocket and Lark on the phone:

"We shot it out with Weld and Deuzler an hour ago at his home in Valley Center," he said. "Weld's dead but Gretchen Deuzler is going to be okay. Weld took a bullet from you or Burt when they flipped your tracker in Ramona. No sign of Broadman and the rest of The Chaos Committee. No sign of Natalie Strait, either. There's almost five hundred feet of tunnel under and out of the Bighorn. Some new, some part of the old mine. The masks, the torture wall, the anarchist library—never seen anything like it."

I asked Lark if the National Allied Building in San Ysidro had panned out.

"Pan out? It's bomb-making central behind the import storefront. Small room, no windows. Explosives, fuses, timers, wires, blasting caps, Semtex—you name it. Shipping boxes and envelopes from every delivery service in the country. Lists of prospective targets and their addresses. Guess who made the list?"

"Special Agent Mike Lark. You owe me a solid," I said.

"Name it."

"We'll see."

"Where's Dalton?" he asked.

"Moving between his home, his campaign headquarters, and his apartment in Sacramento."

"And maybe McKenzie Doyle in Newport Beach?"

"Maybe," I said. "He's due in court again next week. He's being sued for slandering Ammna Safar as blood related to known terrorists."

A beat of silence.

"Broadman abducted Natalie out of vengeance," said Lark. "I fear for her state of body and mind. Broadman's Chaos Committee might be shot up, but I think he's more dangerous now, not less. Dalton is personal."

"I agree."

"Let's hope he's got enough sense to stay away from packages that arrive by mail."

"He's fearless," I said. "Choosing off The Chaos Committee in the media, when he knows they've got his wife."

"What did he call them in that last tweet?" Lark asked.

"Impotent morons."

"Proetto and Hazzard have backed off on him," said Lark. "They don't think he was involved in her abduction. In spite of his shaky timeline. Doyle offered herself as his alibi."

"That was never the right call."

"And you be careful, too, Roland. You're the pesky PI who put the feds onto Broadman. You came out of Fallujah in one piece and he didn't. Broadman might enjoy blowing you to bits."

I saw Tola and the priest walking slowly side by side in the parish garden. A pool and a waterfall and statues of the saints. A riot of springtime colors, the priest's hands behind his back, Tola's head bowed in thought.

"I thought of that favor you can do me," I said.

A grunt from Lark.

"Tola took Crag Face's bait, right?"

"That's right."

"Are you also going to bring her up on schedule-one drug charges?"

"We might."

I watched Tola and the priest ambling past the roses and groomed palms.

"Can you help her out?" I asked.

"I cannot. Did you ask her about the six cartel men gunned down in Mexican Buena Vista last night?" he asked.

"I didn't have to. I was there."

"Fuck," said Lark. "Talk to me."

When I was done, another long Lark silence.

"Roland, the drug charges are the DEA's but I can make it my business if I really want to."

"I gave you The Chaos Committee, Mike. Now I'm trying to help a friend."

"A *murderer*," he said. "It's wrong and you know it and you're covering her murdering ass. I understand—I understand *why*, but *why* doesn't matter. *What* matters. Why only counts for kids and dogs."

Lark punched off.

Tola and the priest were approaching and I heard their voices on the breeze but not their words.

Tola introduced us and the father thanked me for bringing Tola to the parish. He sized me up, then said I had done a brave thing in protecting San Diego from a terrible attack a few months ago. Or was it a year by now? He had a grave expression and I wondered what Tola had confessed.

"Please come visit us any time you'd like," he said. "Both of you. You are always welcome in the house of God."

We walked the beach in Oceanside. Got lunch. Watched the surfers from the pier, fed some quarters into the mounted telescopes and got good views north and south. Took a siesta in a shady patch of grass under rotund Canary Island palms. Some of Tola's turmoil ebbed out of her as she slept, her head heavy on my chest.

My phone rang and Dalton's name and number appeared.

"Natalie just called!" he boomed. "She's okay, Roland! She's okay! I can pick her up but she's not sure where or when. She'll call. They don't want money and I can bring a second. You. It's going to happen somewhere remote. In daylight, so they can see that we're playing fair. This phone isn't leaving my hand!"

"It's a trap, Dalton," I said. "They're shot up and desperate."

"Maybe, Roland, but I'm going. I feel good about this. What you do is up to you."

FORTY

We were sitting in my downtown office when Broadman's call came through. It was 6:10 p.m., an hour and forty minutes before sunset. Dalton had been talking nonstop, sipping bourbon from the bottle. I did not. My senses were resting for whatever was coming in the next hours. My old boxing scar was itching like a bug bite. My heart felt heavy and my soul felt old.

Broadman had dispensed with the voice changer he'd used before. I could see his mangled face and hear his low, even voice clearly through Dalton's phone speaker.

"Dalton, come to the visitor's center at Anza-Borrego Desert State Park. Use Montezuma Valley Road, in from the southwest. Follow the signs to the center. I need the make, color, and year of the car you'll be using, and of course the plates. Make sure your phone is charged, on, and your GPS active. Natalie is waiting, but I'm not sure how forward she's looking to seeing you. Time has passed. People change."

"If you've hurt her, sir, I'll kill you."

Broadman chuckled softly, then listened as Dalton gave his SUV description and license plate.

"I'm assuming you're somewhere near home right now, with your good friend Roland. Hello, Roland. You have one hour to get here."

He hung up and Dalton strode to the door.

"Stay cool, Dalton," I said. "Broadman is going to run us around at least a little, make sure we're alone."

I attached my remaining Vigilant 4000 to the trailer hitch of Dalton's black X5, set my riot gun on the front seat, worked my paddle-holstered .45 into its warm lair at the small of my back, put a cold water in the cup holder.

I drove while Dalton looked wide-eyed out the windows, talking about Natalie. And the war. And the election. And his sons. And the Straits when he was a kid and thought his father and Virgil were almost gods, brave and wise, how much they knew and all the ways they had to get people to do what they wanted. Even Kirby was a hero in Dalton's memory, the big brother who'd introduced Dalton to the love of his life, then gallantly surrendered his interest, the big brother who'd been cursed by God when he lost his temper and knocked their father into the barbecue pit out at grandpa's place that night.

"I'd give up my other leg to get him back alive," said Dalton. "As much as we fought and sometimes hated each other. There's something in blood that you can't deny. I'm glad Tola did what she did."

I took the back roads to Highway 76, past Lake Henshaw to Highway 79, north to Montezuma Valley Road. The sun hid high in the trees. The yellow center line wound through the mountains then straightened as we descended toward the desert. I kept an eye on the rearview mirror.

The visitor center entrance was closed, as I knew it would be. A breezy 92 degrees. Three cars in the parking lot. Employees? After-hours tourists? I pulled into the turnaround, knowing that this is where a rifle ambush would take place if Broadman's goal was simply to kill us. The high rock walls of the building were perfect battlements, overlooking our lumbering target of a vehicle. Perfect light and clarity. But I thought Broadman and what was left of his Chaos Committee wanted more than that. Something less merciful than death.

Dalton's phone on speaker:

"Park on the shoulder and wait ten minutes. Then drive Palm Canyon into Christmas Circle and take the first right onto Borrego Springs Road. Park outside the Bighorn Motel. You won't be able to get into the lot. Ten minutes, friends."

I looked for motion in the visitor center cars, but saw none. Scanned the near sky for a drone but saw and heard nothing. Best bet was Broadman or his people were in some middle distance with their spotting scopes or binoculars trained on us, looking for our backup. We got out and hunkered in the shade of the SUV, Dalton with his bad leg out straight in the sand and his good one tucked up close for balance. We faced the sparse horizontal sprawl of Borrego Springs in the near distance.

"It's been over two weeks since I've seen her," he said. "The longest time apart since we got married. And that was a long time ago. I can still see her that day, though. And I sense that she's somewhere close."

I felt the hot breeze on my face, and the sweat dripping from the paddle holster against my back. Felt that pre-combat slowdown, time putting on its brakes.

"Is it enough for you to get her back?" I asked.

"What do you mean?"

"Broadman and his Chaos Committee are responsible for three bombing deaths," I said. "Including a congressman and a chief of police. They've incited the shooting of six cops and mayhem across the state."

"What are you saying?"

"We have obligations beyond Natalie, Dalton. What if she's not as willing to come back with you as you think she is?"

"How could she not be?"

I hung that question on the breeze. "Like Broadman says, time has passed. People change."

"You don't think Natalie's changed, do you?"

For probably the hundredth time in the last two weeks I wondered if Dalton Strait was as childlike and oblivious to reality as he often seemed.

"Dalton," I said. "I told you what I saw. How Natalie was dressed and how she behaved with her captors. Are you going to have my back if Natalie doesn't *want* to come back to you?"

"Then why did she call? Not to lure me into a trap, like you said. She'd never do that."

"That's exactly why she called, if she's fallen in with them. You've got to factor in her state of mind, Dalton—the bipolar, the abduction, the indictments, the campaign pressure."

Dalton thought a moment. Reached into his coat pocket and pulled out his M9 combat sidearm. The hammer caught on his pocket liner and he almost dropped the gun.

"There's three Chaos fuckers left," he said. "If you go by the TV station raid. We can take them."

"Three at least," I said.

Dalton turned to me, frowning. "If you could shoot phone video of me fighting them, it would help me in November. Better than any ad I could afford. Can do?"

"I might be a little busy for that," I said. "Put the gun away until you need it."

"Fine. Okay. We just have to make sure Natalie is safe, Roland. She's all that matters to me."

Dalton worried the gun back into his pocket. I checked my watch.

"Back to the Bighorn," I said.

———

I parked off the road across from the motel. Yellow crime scene tape rippled across the entrance. More crime scene tape across the office and several of the bungalow doors—notably six and nineteen. A San Diego Sheriff cruiser parked outside the office. Another in front of bungalow eight. No other cars. A coyote trotted across the lot, tail bushy and low.

I got the binoculars from under the seat, glassed the hills behind the motel. Old tailings from the mines glittered blue and yellow in the lowering sun, the windows of the rock homes peering out from low ground like snipers. Atop a distant boulder I saw the sudden flash of sunlight on glass, then movement. A woman?

Dalton's phone:

"Our federal government ruined the Bighorn, thanks to you, Roland. I take great umbrage at that. Dalton? Natalie is dying to see you. Retrace your way to Christmas Circle and continue north on Borrego Springs Drive until you come to San Ysidro Drive. Go right. It's a dirt road. Park in the shade of the *Serpent*. You can't miss her. She's thirty feet high, three hundred and fifty feet long, with the head of a dragon and the tail of a rattlesnake. Get out of your cute little BMW and stand still with your hands up. Any different, we'll cut you to ribbons."

"Please be careful, Dalton," said Natalie. "Please do exactly what we say. Everything depends on you."

We, I thought. But Dalton didn't skip a beat.

"I love you, Nats."

"I always hated it when you called me that."

"I didn't know. There's so much I need to learn."

"I never spent much on myself," said Natalie. "Target and JCPenney for me. Why did you tell everyone that I'm crazy and spent all the campaign money?"

"I needed an out. I'll set the record straight after you plead guilty in court. Don't worry!"

"I worry a lot, Dalton. Come and get me. It's time we see each other face-to-face."

I headed into the traffic circle, merged behind a gleaming silver-and-black motor home that went back toward town. Four bikes on the back, two of them small and pink—a late spring fling for Mom, Dad, and the girls. I continued north.

The sun hung fat and orange in the west. I made the right onto San Ysidro and saw the enormous iron head of the *Serpent* glaring down from the cloudless blue. I thought of Odile's vision of Natalie Strait coming to harm in the desert. Slowly picked my way across the sand flat and parked in the shade of it. Shut off the engine.

An openmouthed dragon towered above us. Red-rusted tendrils dripping from its jaws, sabers of bared teeth, iron spikes flaring back over its eyes in a crown of rage. Big enough to eat the little-pink-bicycle family and their shiny motor home in one bite. One of many Ricardo Breceda sculptures scattered throughout the Borrego desert.

"Wow," said Dalton.

No cars. No people.

I got out, went to the front of the vehicle and raised my hands as instructed. Dalton did the same. I could see down the length of the *Serpent* all the way to the rattlesnake tail, roughly a football field away, its long body looping up from the sand in diminishing arches, scaled and spiked, a serpent in a sea of sand.

From under the last rising coil Broadman's silver Tahoe emerged toward us. Followed by a black Yukon.

"Game on," said Dalton.

"Steady," I said.

"My middle name."

FORTY-ONE

The Tahoe came slowly toward us and parked next to the first coil of the *Serpent*, just a hundred feet away. The Yukon swept wide across the flat to our left and parked lengthwise, its left flank facing us. Two men I didn't recognize braced long guns on the hood, aimed our way. The driver's window and the window behind it both rolled down and gun barrels glinted in the sun.

Jackie O climbed out of Broadman's silver Tahoe, her sunglasses just like those in Lark's video, and a machine pistol in her hands. Unmistakably Jackie O. So unique yet so ordinary. The face that had launched a thousand futile searches.

Natalie Strait dropped to the sand in her desert fatigues and combat boots, landing lightly and throwing her big dark hair back with a shake of her head.

"Jesus," whispered Dalton.

It was as jarring a change as I'd ever seen in a person in such a short time.

Behind her followed Cassy Weisberg with a little machine gun of her own. A wide-brimmed straw gardening hat with a chin strap. A little piece of my heart fell away when I realized she'd been part of The Chaos Committee all along.

Then Broadman, dressed in white, a white ball cap shading his face, a large black backpack over one shoulder. He had a smartphone in one hand and a pistol in the other.

"Keep those hands up," he called out. "Otherwise, you can probably guess what."

He dropped his phone into his pants pocket, slung the black backpack off, and handed it to Cassy.

They came toward us slowly—Broadman, Natalie, Cassy, and Jackie O—stopping forty feet from where we stood. Then Cassy continued. Her pale face was shaded by the hat. She dangled the backpack from one hand and kept the machine pistol tucked tight to her side, pointed at us. Stumbled once, slightly. Handed Dalton the pack.

"Put it on," she said.

"If you put it on, he'll blow you up," I said.

Dalton gave me a look of disdain as he worked on the pack and rolled his shoulders.

"Okay, Sarge. I'm all strapped in, so let her go."

"Not up to me, PFC Strait. It's up to Natalie. She knows her own mind now, and has the strength to speak it. Chaos has set her free."

In the shimmering distant mirage I saw two vehicles moving slowly across the desert toward us. Tiny things with puffs of dust settling behind them. My confederates, answering the call of the Vigilant, I hoped.

"What do you want from me?" asked Dalton.

"I want what Natalie wants, Dalton. I've been a fan of hers since you showed me those pictures in Fallujah and called her a schizoid sexpot. Step closer to us. Halfway but no more."

Dalton stopped halfway.

"Tell him what you want, Natalie," said Broadman.

"First I want you to apologize for belittling me and cheating on me and blaming me and trying to send me to prison for something that was your idea."

"I'd drop to one knee," he said. "But . . ."

Instead, he sat heavily on his good leg well clear of a patch of cholla cactus, and extended the other leg in front of him. Looking up at her he clasped and pumped his hands as if in emphatic prayer.

"I, Dalton Strait, do apologize to you, Natalie, my one and only true love from the beginning, for all the terrible, cowardly, dishonest, and genuinely shitty things I've done. I owe you everything that is good in my life. I have squandered much. Please forgive me. I will never let you down again. Give me a second chance."

I watched the emotions play across Natalie's face, from contempt to anger to doubt.

"Tell her about the whore in Germany and the lobbyist in Newport Beach," said Broadman.

"They meant nothing."

"You chose nothing over me?"

"And tell her about the IRA you cashed out for

Terrell's college but spent on golf junkets for you and your buddies," Broadman added.

I saw a bitter ripple of surprise pass over her. A change in her breathing. Then some deep inner retreat.

"So much betrayal, Dalton," she said, her voice distant. "I just really don't know what to do with you."

Broadman pointed his phone at Strait. "Let me tell you what Natalie did when she saw you in the press conference in her own home, suggesting that she was responsible for the misspent campaign money. She became ill in her apartment—the one in the hills behind the Bighorn. She cursed and vomited and tried to slash her wrist with the small pink razor I allowed her. Unsuccessfully. That was her low point. The point at which all of the past stopped and the future started. After that, your wife began to see you for who you really are. And to see me for who I really am."

"Who's that?" asked Dalton.

"A simple man trying to save a nation from itself."

"You blow up innocent people and get nuts to shoot cops. Get all the angry losers to burn cars in the streets. You're not saving anybody from anything."

"I'm not finished with my mission, Private. Of course there's work to do. Much to rebuild. My compound, my factory, my organization."

"Come on, Natalie," said Dalton, bending his bad knee with one hand and pushing off with the other for the long task of standing up. "Sarge has lost it. Let's get out of here."

"You owe him an apology, too," she said.

"For what? For trying to save his life while half of Fallujah was shooting at me?"

The distant desert cars had come closer. I recognized the dull body of the old pickup truck I keep in the barn for occasions like this. The other vehicle I'd never seen: a shining metallic green-on-white '57 Chevy convertible, top off, with enormous white-sidewall tires and a gleaming chrome roll cage overhead.

Broadman turned to look, then back at me. "Tell them to stop or I'll kill both of you *and* them."

I dialed Burt and a moment later saw the vehicles come to a stop, overtaken by advancing clouds of dust.

Dalton finally staggered upright and got his balance. The backpack was still snugly in place. I wondered how powerful a charge Broadman had created.

"I'll give you one last chance to beg my forgiveness, Dalton," said Broadman. "I was hoping you'd do that the day you visited me in bungalow nineteen. When you saw what your cowardice had done to me. That's why I wanted to see you. But you refused to even remember that day in Fallujah."

"I remember how hard I tried to get you out, the flames and the heat and the harness that I couldn't cut through. Then the bullets snapping past. Christ, Sarge— I was *terrified* . . . Made some bad decisions . . ."

"You didn't try to get me out. You didn't get me into the road. I got myself there. You were behind the K-rails the whole time. I know from Axel and Donald. Others who saw it. *They* were the ones who helped. You were hiding the whole time. Crying and peeing your pants."

Dalton held both arms out, palms up and fingers spread as he limped toward his wife and his sergeant. He stopped twenty feet from them, no more.

"I've been trying to make up for that day ever since! Can't you see that? Natalie? Sarge?"

Broadman offered Natalie his phone. Whispered in her ear. She looked up into his ruined face for a moment before taking it.

Then stepped slowly toward Dalton, the eager, rough-cut boy she'd fallen in love with twenty-five years, two sons, and a war ago. She stopped ten feet short of him. I'm not sure what I saw on her face. Hope. Surrender. Resolve.

I stood in the shade of the dragon's head. I was three seconds from my pistol and ninety feet away from four gunmen in a black Yukon.

Natalie studied her husband with a doubtful squint then turned back to Broadman.

"I can't do this, Harris."

"You can and you will, Natalie. You are free and brave."

Dalton took a step toward her, swinging his plastic limb in clumsy determination and unslinging the pack from his back. Another patch of cholla stopped him.

"Natalie!" Broadman called out in his calm clear voice. "Everything we talked about. Everything you are and everything we need to do."

She turned to him again. Then back to Dalton, trying to pick his way through the cactus as the needled balls broke off and clung to his legs.

She looked down at the phone in her hand again, as if surprised to find it there.

Now entangled in the cactus patch, Dalton swept frantically with his bad leg, then tried to windmill the bomb at Broadman. But the heavy pack caught the cholla on its way up, blooped into the air, and landed between him and Natalie.

Natalie froze in confusion.

Jackie O and Cassy ran.

Broadman lifted a second phone and worked it with his thumb.

"Run, Natalie!" he yelled.

Dalton lurched from the cactus patch and dove onto the pack.

I backed against the *Serpent*'s neck, drew my gun and shot Broadman in the chest. I didn't hear the .45 go off. Only the sharp explosion that lifted Dalton off the ground in a bloody shrug and sent a cloud of red and white sand into the air.

Bullets banged wildly off the *Serpent* as the Yukon tore off into the desert toward Cassy and Jackie O. I rose to one knee, led the vehicle, and shot fast. Dalton lay heaped and shredded, Natalie on her knees beside him, screaming, her hands on his back as the flesh and blood and sand rained down. *"You're okay, Dalton. You're okay. Honey, you're okay!"*

I approached low in a shooter's stance and found white-clad Broadman dead in the sand, heart-shot, one leg buckled under the other, the phone still in his hand.

In the middle distance I saw the black Yukon sliding to a stop near Cassy and Jackie O, as my old pickup truck and the Mad Max '57 Chevy sped across the desert to engage them.

Natalie bent over Dalton, head on his back, sobbing.

I listened to the wind and the diminishing whine of the engines and the tremendous pounding of my heart. Stood there for a long while, gun dangling in one hand as my old pickup and the crazy-looking '57 Chevy pinned down the black Yukon in a cross fire. Heard the *pop-pop* of battle I knew too well, watched Burt and Tola take cover behind my old truck, heard the twang of bullets through metal. Watched as Virgil Strait and three of his confederates fired down from a roll-caged platform on the crudely armored, huge-tired green-and-white convertible. Saw Cassy and Jackie O go down near the Yukon, followed by two Chaos Committee gunmen, the bullets passing through them to kick up sand as they fell. The two remaining soldiers ran haphazardly away, one of them limping, as Virgil and his men ran them down in the Chevy and killed them in an extravagant fusillade.

After which the Mad Max war wagon and the old pickup truck tore up the desert in victorious circles around the Yukon and the dead, dust rose into the darkening sky.

The sun lowered into purple mountains, painting the vast white desert and the tiny vehicles upon it a luminous gold.

While through the golden glow, the man-made *Serpent* looked down at the carnage with his starved and violent grimace.

I helped Natalie stand.

FORTY-TWO

Another Wednesday with the Irregulars: Dick's deep-fried catfish and group-effort appetizers cooled and complemented by a pitcher of Grandma Liz's greyhounds made with fresh-squeezed grapefruit juice and a touch of blood orange liqueur.

At cocktail hour we played Ping-Pong and commiserated over the Padres' un-great spring. Most agreed that Phil Rivers, our beloved Chargers QB, should—at thirty-eight—take his spring training more gingerly. To live near San Diego is to love our sports teams, even when they betray us for money and move away.

"We should have built the stadium," said Liz.

"Absolute waste of taxpayer money," said Dick. "The city would have to buy up the empty seats for games again, just to keep the Chargers in town."

"What's more important than that?" asked Liz.

"The homeless, dear. Those less fortunate than us. They're everywhere you look downtown."

"I know you, Dick Ford, and you don't care one bit about the homeless or the poor."

"Absolutely true, which should tell you exactly how bad an investment I think a stadium would be."

"You're a hateful miser," said his wife. "That's why I live as far away from you as I can."

A tart reference to their longtime living arrangements here at Rancho de los Robles—Dick in casita one and Liz as far down the breezeway as you can get, in casita six.

Odile, the gentle psychic, cleared her throat. "God must love the common man because he made so many of them."

"And dogs, too," said Francisco, running his hand down Triunfo's sleek black head.

"Dogs are superior to us, psychically," said Odile. "They have purer minds."

"That's because they're animals," said Dick. "No real minds at all. They've got it easy."

"I disagree," said Odile.

"We suffer greatly," said Dick. "Because we know the end. We know there *is* an end. They don't."

Odile considered Dick as she sipped the greyhound. She has a beautiful complexion and an innocent's gaze, which belie her empathy for the darkness in us.

"But the fact that life ends allows us grace," she said. "For example, I sense there's been a change in my clients over the last week. Since The Chaos Committee was stopped. Since our chances of death seem less now. I receive strength and optimism from my clients. Hope and determination. Their auras have much more energy than before. Even the timbres of their voices express positive force."

"I've noticed that, too," said Burt. "On the links."

"People are just flat-out exhausted," said Dick.

"But their drives are carrying better," said Burt, offering Dick his weird smile.

"And relieved," said Liz. "It's only been a week but I'm already having trouble believing it really happened. Two weeks of chaos in the state. Or whatever they're calling it."

And they were right. The curse of The Chaos Committee was beginning to lift. Their leader and seven of his followers had been killed; one remained hospitalized and two suspects had been arrested. The investigation would continue.

The cop shootings abated as abruptly as they'd begun, leaving six officers dead and seven wounded across the state. Followed by civilian vigils in support of law enforcement, all of which drew large crowds and no violence.

After the Borrego shootout, the street assaults and car burnings tapered off quickly, too, which cut down the number of citizens trying to fight their way into emergency rooms and urgent care clinics. Schools and houses of worship reopened; the post office and private carriers resumed daily deliveries; the freeway traffic got back to its former congestion. The governor appeared ubiquitously. Federal and state declarations of emergency ended. The damage to property was now estimated at over $500 million.

In pattern with our times, the violence incited by The Chaos Committee and their deadly bombs was replaced by public and media fascination over The Chaos Committee members themselves: Who were these people, what motivated them, how did they come together, could this happen again?

That night on my poor man's jumbotron we watched a San Diego Channel 8 special, "Anger, Anarchy, and Chaos," about the perpetrators. Sponsored by Ford Motor Company and the redesigned Explorer. It ran complete with pictures and video:

Harris Broadman, forty-two, motel owner and organizer, wounded in Iraq and awarded a Purple Heart. Born and raised in Kenton, Ohio, an athletic boy who became an aloof young man, earning a degree in European history and briefly publishing an anarchist blog after returning from Iraq with burns over thirty percent of his body. Showed him at two, smiling with his arm around an Australian Shepherd. And at thirty-eight, lying in a hospital bed after his seventeenth surgery.

Brock Holland, thirty-one, a Miami native who had done prison time for computer fraud and assaulting a police officer. He'd worked security for two cruise lines, casinos in Las Vegas and Temecula, and various San Diego area hotels. The Channel 8 anchor reported that Holland had "developed a friendship" with Assemblyman Dalton Strait's wife, Natalie, later kidnapping her for use by The Chaos Committee.

Holland photos showed a serious boy, a defiant teen, and a seductively handsome and confident young man.

"Vile," said Liz.

Holland's Chaos Committee "partner," said the news, was Denton-Texas-born Gretchen Deuzler, thirty-one, daughter of a mining engineer and a college math professor. Channel 8 said that Gretchen had learned the basics of blasting from her father, who used to take her along in fieldwork, and had excelled at physics under Mom. She wrote a popular blog after being raped at a college party. She was believed to be the lead bomb maker. In the pictures she was cute as a girl and sternly pretty as a woman. She was expected to make a full recovery and would face a list of charges that could get her the death penalty.

"They seem to be living normal lives, then something goes wrong," said Liz. "The IED for Broadman. Weld's attack on the policeman. The woman's rape."

"Are those reasons for terror, or excuses?" asked her husband.

"People act according to how they are treated," said Liz.

"And some, their light becomes dimmed," said Odile.

"While the rest of us battle it out with our dark friends inside," said Burt.

It was the first time I'd heard Burt Short confess to any kind of inner struggle. Years ago he'd offered to kill a man to protect my life, and he had done so. But never hinted at the cost to himself. To his soul, or a dark friend inside.

Cassy Weisberg was twenty-six when she died in the Borrego shootout. She'd come to Los Angeles after high school in Athol, Massachusetts. Worked for Marriott and Hilton as a desk receptionist, then a series of boutique hotels in and around Palm Springs. Then the Bighorn Motel, hired by Harris Broadman. She was described by high school acquaintances as a shy and solitary girl. Her mother hadn't heard from her in eight years and she had developed no friendships that reporters could discover. She was believed to have mailed the Encinitas bombs. She was being treated for uterine cancer at the time of her death. Her high school yearbook pictured the same wan girl who had fooled me into believing she was nothing more than an ailing desk clerk in a small desert motel.

Jackie O was Roxana Rajavi, thirty, an American-born daughter of Iranian refugees living legally in Seattle. She was a good student and a devout Muslim and, like Cassy Weisberg, socially withdrawn. She had moved to Ramona five years ago and met Harris Broadman through the Internet shortly thereafter. She had mailed the first two Chaos Committee bombs and likely the bomb that had killed the police chief in Hopedale, California. She was believed to be communicating with possible sponsors of terror in Tehran, but investigators had found no concrete evidence that Iranian treasure or know-how had benefited The Chaos Committee. She was believed to be a part of the *Local Live!* studio takeover.

"The last two girls seem so young and lost," said Liz.

"Old enough to hate," said Dick.

"And to fall under the spells of evil men," said Odile.

"Girls cast spells of their own," said Dick.

I looked at the brief video and photographs of Roxana

Rajavi, seeing the same woman I'd watched in Lark's post office video so many times. In better focus, and when not mailing a box of death to an innocent person, she looked pleasant and composed.

The other four committee members killed in Borrego—the gunmen in the black Yukon—were:

Daniel Dawes, a fifty-one-year-old school custodian living in Warner Springs, thirty miles from the Bighorn Motel. Bachelor, loner, and a U.S. Army veteran of Operation Iraqi Freedom. He was believed to be one of the ninja gunmen in the *Local Live!* takeover.

Lamont Anthony, forty-nine, the sole black Chaos Committee member discovered so far, was a Portland, Oregon, native who'd gotten a philosophy degree from Oregon State and worked his entire adult life for the United States Postal Service. He was believed to have been the driver during the kidnapping of Natalie Strait.

James Diggory, twenty-five, born in L.A., a community college student with an interest in martial arts and Norwegian black metal music. He had no criminal record, no friends that could be located, and no social network presence.

Trent Hodge was a thirty-three-year-old Tennessean who had joined the French Foreign Legion at eighteen because the marines rejected him for excessive tattoos. He'd fought in Syria and Yemen for six years. Had a tattoo that read *L'Enfant Terrible* above his right eyebrow.

"Quite the collection," said Grandpa Dick.

"They actually seem kind of normal, except for the French Foreign Legion boy," said Liz.

"I sense great histories of abuse and pain in their faces," said Odile.

"A United Nations of misfits," said Dick.

"Led by a man who lost his face in a war," said Burt.

"Do you sympathize with him?" asked Dick.

"I sympathize with all men and no causes."

FORTY-THREE

When I picked her up the next morning, Tola looked as professional as I'd ever seen her, stepping from her tiled portico into the good June sun. Leaning on my truck I watched her walk toward me, her smile and sunglasses on, and a cinnamon-colored business suit that showed off her fair skin and red hair, which was up and held loosely in place by a faux ivory Nectar Barn cannabis-leaf barrette.

"Thanks for drumming up the media," she said. "Hope they all show."

"I still think that was a bad call."

"You can't use celebrity. I can."

A beautiful and complex woman. I pictured her in the courtyard of the Hotel Casa Grande, pleading her case before taking her bloody, triple-barreled vengeance. I'd never forget what happened there. Did it lessen her?

Clearly. But the part of me that was drawn to Tola argued that those men had it coming and, therefore, what she'd done was justice. Frontier style, appropriate to its time and place. So was I lessened, too? I *was* there. On her account. For now I was going to let my demons wrestle it out.

We came into San Diego on an inland route, sweeping through the edge of Balboa Park, under the Cabrillo Bridge, spilling into downtown on Eleventh Avenue, then Ash to Front to F to Union to the federal jail.

"Abel said this'll take an hour or two and I'll be on my way."

"Nothing federal takes an hour or two."

"Thanks, Daniel Downer," said Tola.

"Call me when you're ready and I'll pick you up."

"Sure you don't want to stay?"

"I'll stay until we hit the cameras," I said. "Abel can take over from there. I'm kind of sick of me."

"In the news, you mean?"

"Yes, ma'am."

"They say that Abel tries his cases in the media," she said. "All that hair and bluster."

"If you ever get to trial, it's going to be a circus, Tola."

"I love the circus. And I love you, Roland. Really a lot. I'm sorry I'm just a murderous lowlife, but I try to be a good person."

"You acted according to your nature."

A courtroom silence. She stared straight ahead. The bump of tires on the downtown streets.

"I'll call you as soon as I get myself free," she said.

I pulled into the parking structure, found a ten-minute space. Gave her a hand down.

In a big bright rectangle beyond the dark structure I could see the crowd of reporters and camera operators, all their mics and baffles, booms, lights, and logos. Some of the people I recognized. Along with Abel Cruzon, Mike Lark and two of Lark's agents, and two uniformed marshals. And two hard-hatted, orange-vested workers puzzling over the concrete near the curb as pigeons bobbed around. All of this tableau in a panoramic sun-shot theater toward which I escorted Tola, her hand firm on my upper arm.

"I'll take what I deserve," she said. "What the law says I deserve. That's okay. It's my responsibility as a citizen."

I had the thought that if Tola had been arrested for a premeditated triple murder in Buena Vista, Mexico, in-stead of attempted bribery of a federal officer in San Di-ego, she would quite possibly never see the outside of a prison again.

"You've got the best lawyer in the city," I said. "You'll surrender and post bail today, plea down later, and prob-ably do a few months of federal time."

"Attempted bribery of a federal agent can carry five years," she said, squeezing my arm. "But I can run the Nectar Barns from the slammer. I could see you every other day. That's the policy. I've looked into it. The rules say, when you come see me, we can shake hands, embrace lightly, and kiss briefly upon arrival and departure. Visi-tors' behavior is considered to be the responsibility of the inmate. So if you go all mating dance on me, I'm the one they dock. You'll need to show some self-control."

We walked toward the knot of people gathered in the sunlight.

Then Tola stopped and turned to me. Her eyes searched my face and I felt the pain in them.

"I really don't expect to see much of you in or out of prison, Roland. You're better than me. But I'm harder. You can take the Straits out of East County . . . and we'll be fine wherever we land. What's left of the Straits, anyway."

"You and Virgil will carry the flame," I said.

"We absolutely will."

Lark turned to us as Abel Cruzon raised a hand and started our way. Currents of movement through the reporters, the marshals hemming them in. The hard hats still looking down at their projects. Tola let go of my arm and the pigeons fluttered up as she walked into the sunlight.

FORTY-FOUR

Natalie and her two sons arrived on time for the morning appointment in my Main Avenue office.

She'd lost some weight as a captive of The Chaos Committee—compared to the robust BMW pitchwoman whom half the county had seen on TV—and there was a dark calm about her.

She came in on the arm of the older son, Lee, who seated her brusquely and bypassed my hand to hug and clap me on the back. He was in his NROTC uniform, hair cut high and tight in the marine manner.

"Thanks for everything you've done," he said.

Younger Terrell, who'd made the admiring and insightful film about his mother, gave me a polite handshake, then sat down on the other side of his mother.

Natalie pulled a white envelope from her purse and set it on my desk.

"I think I figured this up right," she said. "Based on your contract and counting the days on the calendar. I put in some extra."

"Thank you," I said. In fact, Dalton had paid me nothing, so whatever the envelope contained was a plus.

"No," she said. "Thank *you*, Mr. Ford. If you hadn't found the Borrego compound you wouldn't have found me. And if you hadn't found me right *then*, I don't know what kind of woman you would have discovered later. I'm not sure I could have found my way back."

"You did a great job, Mom," said Lee. He gave her, then me, his father's eager, open-faced smile.

"Yes," said Terrell. "Thank you for everything, Mr. Ford."

Lee sat forward, set his hands on his knees. I thought of Dalton sitting right there not long ago, getting ready to toss his prosthesis at me.

"Mr. Ford," said Lee, "I'm going to cut to the chase here. "Mom and us wanted to thank you and to pay up. But we have a larger mission. I'm going to run for Dad's assembly seat in November and we'd like to have you in some TV ads with Mom. Everybody knows what The Chaos Committee did to her. And how you came to the rescue. You can't find a Republican in the county who won't vote for me in Dad's honor. And plenty of Dems, too, what with the terror scandal around Ms. Safar. The money is pouring in. The media is all over me. I'm a write-in because of the filing deadlines, but I've got a shot at it."

My surprise was swift but short-lived. Of course Dalton's son would try to turn his father's death into an opportunity. Pure Strait.

"I'll be creating the TV ads," said Terrell. "But you'll have editorial freedom to say what you want."

"You've only got a hundred and thirty-some days," I said.

"Not a problem," said Lee.

"How old are you?"

"Twenty. But you only have to be eighteen for the California Assembly. So, I feel that destiny has handed me a Big Mac, and I'd be a fool to hand it back."

Terrell closed his eyes and slowly shook his head.

Their mother smiled. Almost the same smile she'd always had. Almost the same sweet spirit behind the same sweet face. But less light now. Reduced wattage. Purposefully withheld or frightened out of her? Temporary or permanent? Impossible to tell.

"We'd like to shoot a spot this evening," said Lee. "Right, Terrell?"

"Ideally," his brother said. "Some establishing scenes at Dad's grave out at Rosecrans. We'd like you to be standing there, looking down with the markers all around you while you talk in voice-over. Remembering Dad's character and courage. All like that. You can write that part."

"No, but thank you."

"Why not?" asked Lee.

"I have my privacy to protect and a business to run."

A puzzled stare from Lee. "Fine, Mr. Ford. But don't forget that Dalton Strait is a true American hero."

"Mr. Ford is a hero, too," said Natalie. "I wouldn't be here if not for him."

"Then how about a heroic campaign contribution?" Lee asked. "I really hope to continue Dad's work, and improve on his record. I want to get student debt under control. I think I can get things done across the aisle."

I picked up the envelope that Natalie had set on my desk. Stood and handed it to Lee.

"Good luck," I said.

"Thanks again for everything you did. You'll remember this day when they swear me in."

An awkward silence.

Natalie was the last to leave. She stopped in the doorway and turned around. I heard the boys clomping down the old wooden stairs.

"I owe my life to you," she said.

"Mainly to Dalton."

She looked out at me from within her substantial hauntings.

"Why did you go to the San Diego FBI?" I asked.

"To talk about the finances. Early on they tried to turn me against Dalton."

"And Asclepia headquarters?"

A soft flinch. "McKenzie Doyle. I saw one of her texts to Dalton. Wanted to have a look at her. Why?"

"Just filling in the details," I said. "I like your boys, especially Terrell. He showed me *A Day in a Life* and it lit a fire under me to locate you. I saw how much you are loved and needed."

"He's another one of my heroes. Terrell."

"Hold on to the good memories you have of Dalton," I said. "They're your friends. They can help you find your way."

"You've had experience at that."

"We all will."

She gave me a long stare and a short smile. So many storms. I heard Lee's voice booming from down in the foyer. Reminded me of Dalton when he'd finally learned that Natalie was still alive.

"I won't be going back to the dealership," she said. "Or running Lee's campaign. It's time to fix some of the things that got this family into our financial mess in the first place. I can take full-time work when I'm ready. We'll be okay. Dalton had a small life insurance policy he'd kept secret, and there's some veterans money for his death and disability. I pled down to one count from the feds, in return for telling the truth about what happened. I'm really looking forward to better days. For all of us."

Lee, shouting up again.

"You'll get some better days, Natalie."

"Goodbye, Roland."

After dinner with the Irregulars that night I excused myself for a walk around the pond. Triunfo led the way. The sun hung low in the west, over a layer of dark clouds gliding in from the Pacific.

I found my usual boulder and the dog scratched his way up beside me. We watched the sun go down and I waited for the flash of green, which I have never seen but some people say exists. Something to do with gasses and refracted sunlight, though perhaps only an optical illusion. No flash of green on this June night.

I sat awhile and let the last of the light dissolve around me. Felt the cool creeping up from the earth. Let the good thoughts in. Turned the bad ones back. Finally got rid of thoughts altogether.

After being knocked out in that fight and carried to my stool, I sat there and watched myself, but from above, disembodied, and I understood that there are two of us, one who does and one who watches. Understood that I had been beaten but would fight again.

Sitting on that rock in the dark I watched my thoughtless self for a while, then got up and walked home.

Later I drove to a ballroom dance club downtown where you can always find a willing partner. Saturdays are Latin Madness there, so I was all of that, late into the night.

T. JEFFERSON PARKER

"T. Jefferson Parker is the poet
of American crime fiction."

—C. J. Box